CURE OR DIE

JENNIFER L HART

ELEMENTS UNLEASHED MEDIA

CURE OR DIE

A Damaged Goods Mystery
Hart, Jennifer L./Cure or Die

1.Mystery—Fiction. 2. Women Sleuths—Fiction 3.Property
Management—Fiction 4. Miami—Fiction 5.Contemporary
Romance—Fiction 6.BBW—Fiction 7.Alpha Male—Fiction
8.Eviction Specialists—Fiction 9. Murder Mystery—Fiction
10. Mystery Romance—Fiction Title.

Cure or Die
Book 3 in the Damaged Goods Mystery Series

Certified Process Server Jackie Parker could do a case study
in bizarre human behavior. Like the time the Damaged
Goods property management team found a man fermenting
his own fecal matter to get high. Or the angry downstairs
tenant who threatened to spit on her. And that was just one
building in the Miami art district.

Returning to the scene of the crime a year later at the
request of the landlord, Jackie believes she's ready for

anything. Since Logan, A.K.A. the Dark Prince, left the team, she and Luke have gone through an amicable divorce and maybe just this one time she can manage to not land face first in something foul. But what they find in the vacated apartment is far worse than on their earlier visit and Jackie's situation is about to get a whole lot messier.

Cue Logan.

Don't miss the epic finale to the Damaged Goods trilogy. It's a laugh a minute and what one reader described as "more addictive than krokodil"!

CURE OR DIE

"We got this, Ace. Stay in the truck." Luke squeezed my hand once before popping his own door and heading into the condemned building.

"Stay in the truck, meh, meh meh," I grumbled, sick to death of that phrase.

The third man of our three-person eviction team, laughed. His chuckle, both raspy and rude, grated on my last nerve. "That's mature. People are gonna think you guys are still married."

"Well, those people can suck it." It had been one of the most painless dissolutions of marriage in history. We had no children and our divorce was amicable, with the added bonus of no lawyers to gum up the works of our property management business, Damaged Goods.

I flipped down the visor and narrowed my eyes on the man in the back seat in the mirror. "Not that it's any of your business. Are you going in with him or not?"

My companion shrugged. "I don't get what he sees in you."

"Yes, well, I don't get what Celeste sees in you, so we're even on that score." My mother's love life had sunk to an all-time low and the situation was even more awkward because the man she was shtupping rode shotgun for us. Well, he would ride shotgun if he ever got his ass in gear and actually backed Luke up.

I turned in my seat. "Dude, I have a Taser and I'm not afraid to use it."

"Keep your panties on," John Garrison finally popped the door and hefted his bulk out onto the street.

I grimaced as his colossal backside disappeared into the same doorway Luke had gone through. Big John was a hill-billy pain in the kiester, but I had to face facts, we needed a three-man team—or in our case, two men and one woman —to operate effectively in property management. Tenants lied, tenants got angry and threw things and if there was one thing John Garrison was good for, it was being a big target.

I never thought I'd miss working with my brother-in-law, A.K.A the Dark Prince.

There was a rubber band on my wrist and I snapped it, the same way I did every time I thought about Logan Parker. I'd read in some magazine that negative reinforcement helped break bad habits. So far the only results of my efforts were a red wrist and a short temper.

Removing my cell phone from the car charger, I checked for texts. Three from Celeste of the *we need to talk* variety. I deleted those. True, my mother and I were on better terms than we had been before the holidays but I wasn't ready to throw the door open wide on my life for her just yet. There was an offer to meet up for lunch from Marcy Regan at our favorite tapas bar. I wrote back, *Sounds good.* Then thought about it and added, *As long as I don't get covered in anything gross beforehand.*

The phone dinged a minute later, a reply from Marcy. *You have such a fun job.*

I blew out a sigh. Fun. Right, sitting in the truck while the guys did all the work totally rocked the career casbah. Of course, it could be worse like that time I'd been thrown in a kiddie pool full of baby oil. My hair had been greasy for weeks afterward. But sitting in the truck gave my mind too much time to wander down paths better left unexplored. Like last Christmas, the last time I'd seen Logan. When he vowed he wouldn't wait around for me anymore.

"Ow," I said as the rubber band stung me again. Snapping it was almost involuntary by this point. "Seriously, though who buys a house and doesn't live in it? Ow, frigging Dark Prince. Ow."

Training my gaze on the building, I forced myself to refocus on the task at hand. One reason I'd agreed to wait in the car was that the downstairs tenant had once spat on me and I wasn't eager for another close encounter with The Expectorater. He was a difficult tenant, one better handled by some big hulking muscle like Luke and the mouth breather in my mother's life.

Luke appeared through the doorway and waved me forward. Cautiously, I popped the door to the truck, clipboard in hand.

"Did you find out why he isn't paying his rent?" I asked, keeping a wary eye on the door.

Luke nodded, his expression grim. "Don't worry, John's got him around back looking at the stain."

I frowned. "What stain?"

"There's a brownish-red stain on the ceiling of his gallery. He claims it ruined one of his paintings and he wants the landlord to comp his rent until the problem is solved." Luke raised an eyebrow as if asking if that was an actual possibility.

3

Tenants sometimes got confused about what the landlord was or was not responsible for. While the tenant would have been well within his rights to call a plumber and send the property owner the bill, a stain was not a legal reason to withhold rent.

I shook my head. "The painting should be covered by his renter's insurance."

"I asked him about that. They're denying the claim, saying that the artist is unknown and there's no way to appraise the value. Couldn't you just work your magic here so everybody wins?" Luke looked hopeful.

I frowned at the door to the art gallery. "Really? You're asking me to do him a favor? Did you forget that he spit on me? Not to mention the name-calling. I believe 'lazy slut' were his precise words."

Luke did a palms-up gesture. "Would you rather go talk to the mad spitter? If he does it again, you can threaten him with assault and battery."

I blew out a sigh. "No, for some odd reason, our client wants to keep him as a tenant. Personally. I don't see the appeal but it's not my call. Any idea of what's causing the stain? It would go better with the property owner if we knew the source."

Luke shrugged. "Probably rust from one of the pipes leading from the upstairs loft. The building is from the sixties, lots of stuff that was grandfathered in and is no longer up to code."

I grimaced. "As long as that's all it is." The former tenant from the upstairs loft had a bizarre habit of huffing fumes from his own excrement. Even after a thorough scrubbing—done by the kind of people who clean up crime scenes after the police are through investigating—no one had rented the space. Go figure.

"Come on, let's check it out." Luke turned the corner

toward the outer set of stairs leading up to the loft apartment. "Maybe I can fix it. If we save the client the plumber's fee, he might be more willing to compensate the tenant."

I didn't say anything, just followed him up the stairs, trying to ignore the growing sense of apprehension gnawing at my insides. I did not have fond memories of this place and investigating mysterious stains wasn't exactly what I'd had in mind for a relaxing day.

Because the apartment was currently vacant and we'd been supplied with sets of keys for the entire building, we were able to go right in. Luke unlocked the door and pushed it open. The space smelled a hell of a lot better than the last time we'd been there, fresh paint and new carpet instead of human waste. I tried the light switch near the door but nothing happened. "Utilities are still in service, right?"

Luke grabbed a flashlight off his belt. "They were for the gallery. And the building's serviced as a whole."

He shone the flashlight upward. "No overhead lights. The switch is probably connected to an outlet."

"Still, better safe than sorry." I squinted and made a note on my clipboard to have an electrician come to run an inspection. Older buildings could be tricky and the last thing our tenant needed was an electrical fire to burn the place to the ground. I focused all my attention on my auditory senses, listening for the telltale hum of strained wiring.

Luke must have been doing the same thing because he put a hand on my arm and asked, "Did you hear that?"

"What?" I murmured even as the sound of a soft groan filtered to me. "What the hell?"

"Someone's in here." Luke's grip on me tightened. "Go outside and call the police. Report a B&E."

I was out on the landing when I realized he hadn't followed me. "Luke!"

5

"What's going on up there?" John called from the bottom of the steps.

I had my cell out, ready to dial 911, but waiting for Luke to report back with more detail. "Get up here, we think there's someone in the loft."

"Jackie!" Luke's hoarse voice called out from inside the apartment. "Tell them we need an ambulance."

"What's wrong?" I shouted. He didn't respond. "Is it the former tenant?" Sometimes drug users who have been evicted return to their old residences because the surroundings are familiar. I wasn't sure if the same could be said for poop sniffers, but it was a working theory.

"No. Tell them to hurry." Luke's tone sounded strangled.

"Is the place clear?" I dialed the number and charged back into the unit, night vision wrecked from the bright Florida sunshine. I tripped and went down on one knee, dropping the phone to catch myself even as the official greeting clipped through the speaker of my cell.

"911, what's the nature of the emergency?" The woman had a Latina accent, but her tone was brusque and to the point.

I dove for the phone and lifted it to my ear. Without preamble, I gave the operator my name and our current address along with the information about a possible B&E.

"The police are on their way." she informed me when I'd brought her up to speed.

"My partner says we need an ambulance." There was a light on toward the back of the house, I could see the glow spilling out into the hall from the open bedroom door and I headed toward it. Big John was still back there, working his bulk up the stairs.

"Can you describe the nature of the injury?" 911 lady asked me.

"I'm working on it," I gasped and rounded the corner from the bedroom and into the bathroom.

The phone dropped from my nerveless fingers at the sight.

Red everywhere, contrasting grotesquely with the white linoleum. Water tinted by the woman bleeding in the tub. Luke kneeling beside her, heedless of the mess on the floor. "Is she dead?"

Luke shook his head, and I could see he'd whipped off his shirt and stuffed it against the woman's side. "Not yet. Where's that ambulance?"

It took me a minute to respond, I was so stunned at the sight before me. Her lips were blue, her skin had a deathly gray-green cast. Long dark hair spilled over the edge of the white tub along with buckets of dislodged water. We'd found the source of the gallery stain.

I picked up the phone again and did my damndest to describe the scene to the operator, ending on the words, "Possible suicide."

But Luke was shaking his head. "No, someone else did this to her."

911 lady was squawking something at me and I held the phone away, frowning at him. "How do you know?"

"There's ice in the tub." His eyes met mine. "And the wound looks like someone deliberately cut her up."

I blinked at him and repeated the words, mostly because I couldn't believe
what he was saying. "Cut her up?"

Luke turned back to the woman in the tub. "Someone carved out her kidneys."

"WHO HAS KEYS TO THIS BUILDING?" The detective, a portly woman with a face like a bulldog asked me.

Despite the ever-present Miami heat, I stood with my arms wrapped around myself. My insides had flash frozen the instant I'd thought the words organ harvesting. I must have related the information to the 911 operator, but I had no memory of it. Or of the police and the paramedics storming into the apartment and ordering Luke and I to wait outside. The image of the victim strapped to a gurney and being loaded into the ambulance would haunt me until the day I died.

Luke had wrapped an arm around my shoulders, the first physical contact we'd had in weeks. Though I knew I had to get used to not leaning on him the way I once had, I was too shaken to pull away. We'd stood together while the ambulance drove off and the police swarmed the building.

"Mrs. Parker?" The bulldog prodded.

"Sorry, I'm a little shaken." I refocused on her. "What did you ask?"

"I need a list of everyone who has keys to that apartment."

"I'll have to check with the landlord, but I'm pretty sure he's the only one besides us." A thought occurred to me. "Although we haven't changed the locks since the former tenant was evicted so it's possible he has a set."

She scribbled something down in her notebook. "And you work for the owner?"

I nodded absently, my gaze straying up the stairs to the apartment. Big John was up at the top of the stairs, securing the place behind the police. "Who would do something like that?"

I hadn't realized I'd spoken aloud until bulldog answered me. "Don't worry, we'll catch whoever did this to her."

I forced a smile that I didn't feel. "I just hope she's going to be all right. Whoever she is."

"She's lucky your team stopped in today. Any longer and you would have found her corpse."

I blanched. If not for the mad spitter complaining about the stain, we wouldn't have been there and no one would have found the girl until it was too late. Bulldog tucked her notebook away and straightened her blue jacket. "I have your card, I'll contact you if we have any further questions."

From my own experience with law enforcement, I knew she would be true to her word and that was my official warning to not take any unexpected trips. I didn't take it personally. She was doing her job, treating everyone like a suspect until they could be cleared of such a heinous crime.

Luke patted my arm once then moved off towards a police vehicle. I scanned the area and spied the downstairs tenant several yards away, being questioned by a uniformed officer.

Big John descended the stairs, his expression carefully neutral. He was a crusty old SOB, but I had a feeling even he was shaken by the gruesome discovery.

"Can you distract the downstairs tenant for a few minutes?" I asked him. So far the mad spitter hadn't spotted me and I wanted to keep it that way.

He narrowed his piggy eyes at me. "Why?"

"I want to look at the stain."

He blanched. "Is this some sicko fetish of yours?"

I made a disgusted noise. "Yes, John, bloodstains get me hot."

"Well that ain't right," he began, puffing up his chest. "Ain't no porkin' way, Jackie."

This was getting me nowhere fast and I didn't want to add that I was maybe kinda sorta sneaking in to investigate a crime scene. I knew better than to bait him, the man just didn't pick up on sarcasm at all. Probably why we couldn't communicate since ninety-nine point nine percent of what came out of my mouth fell under that subheading. "I was kidding, John. Please, I just want a look."

"Fine," he grumbled like a bear with indigestion. "But make it quick."

I nodded and slipped through the back door to the art gallery. The door led to what looked like a combination office and prep area where a bunch of paintings were sheathed in heavy plastic. I sniffed delicately. The place certainly smelled better than it had the last time I'd been there. Ignoring the stacks of canvas propped up against a workbench and the battered desk strewn with papers, I picked my way carefully through the room and out into the long corridor that led to the main display area. I moved back and to the left until I stood beneath the bedroom and bathroom of the upstairs loft.

I spied the stain right away. The blindingly white gallery walls telegraphed it well, like some horror movie backdrop. The ruined canvas had been what looked like a picture in a Rorschach test, all black and white abstract splotches, except for one corner that was stained with brownish-red that oozed down the wall from the ceiling above. Taking a step closer, I studied the pattern of the stain. Up close to the ceiling, the color was darker, as though it were still wet, but down the wall, it paled out as though it had been given time to dry. I pulled a tissue from the back pocket of my jeans and pressed it against the canvas. Sure enough, it came away clean.

The blood was dry on the canvas. I was no forensics expert, but I doubted that the victim would still have been alive in that tub given the amount of time it took for blood to dry. And the mad spitter's complaint about the stain had come in a few days before.

"She wasn't the first one in the tub," I mumbled to myself.

"What makes you think that?" A male voice asked from behind me.

I spun around, plastering a dimwitted smile on my face. It slid off as I saw that the man who had spoken carried himself like a police officer, though he wasn't in uniform and didn't offer a shield. He was older than me by almost two decades though he wore the years well. He had thick dark hair shot through with gray and there were laugh lines around his eyes and mouth, indicating that he knew how to smile, even though he wasn't doing it now.

"I, I—" I stammered and then cleared my throat, wondering what it was about that man that I found so disconcerting. Was it just because I'd been sneaking around behind the cops' backs and he'd busted me? Usually, my fibs came to my rescue a hell of a lot faster than this.

He took a step closer to me, bright blue eyes curious. "What made you think the woman in the tub wasn't the first?"

I showed him the tissue. "The blood on the canvas had time to dry. Both of her kidneys were removed. I'm not sure how long somebody can live that way sans dialysis, but I doubt she would still be alive if that was her blood."

He nodded, his expression thoughtful. "Who are you?"

"I work for the property owner. I was just ass—" Gulp, swallow, breathe, spit it out, Jackie. "—assessing the extent of the damage." There, that sounded plausible.

"You should go." He said, that voice making it clear it wasn't a suggestion.

Chucking my thumb at the door idiotically, I burbled, "I was just leaving."

He watched me back up, his gaze focused as though warning me not to try anything. I'd almost made it through the door when it was yanked open behind me.

"You!" The mad spitter accused, his voice laced with outrage.

"Gotta go," I dashed for the Big Black Truck before he could collect enough saliva to hock one at me.

John was already inside and had the engine going and the AC cranked.

"What happened?" I asked him. "You were supposed to keep the tenant occupied."

"It's hot out there," John complained. "Besides, you ought not to be messing around with no bloodstains. Your mama wouldn't like that."

I stared at him incredulously. "You're supposed to have my back, John whether or not it's hot. That tenant has threatened me in the past. For all we know he could have been the one who carved that lady up like a Christmas goose!"

"People really don't eat goose no more, do they?" John asked.

Not bothering to answer, I stared back at the gallery, wondering what the hell it was about that detective that made all the little hairs on my arm stand on end. Before I could put too much thought into it Luke popped the driver's side door, effectively diffusing me with the pale and drawn look on his face. He slid behind the wheel and shut the door but made no move to put the truck in gear.

"Luke?" I asked wanting to reach for him but knowing I shouldn't.

"She didn't make it," he said. "Had a heart attack on the way to the hospital and was declared dead on arrival. The police were notified over the radio. This just became a homicide investigation."

Oh, God. "I'm sorry," I said, because I was. "Luke, you did everything you could for her."

He met my gaze in the rearview mirror. "What did you find inside?"

So he had noticed me going into the gallery. "The bloodstain is old, well some of it is. The part that defaced the painting was dried."

He let that soak in for a minute. "What do you think that means?"

I swallowed, not wanting to voice my suspicions.

"Jackie?" He prompted.

He wasn't going to let this one go. I knew Luke well enough to know that. "I think she wasn't the first person to be harvested in that bathtub."

2

An hour later, Luke pulled up in front of our little bungalow. "See you in the morning, John?"

After the morning we'd had, we'd all decided to call it quits for the day.

"Sounds good." John oozed out of the truck, waddled to his own vehicle and sped off.

"He's in a hurry to go shag my mother." I grimaced as the words escaped before I thought better of them. "Kill me now."

"Give him a break, he makes Celeste happy." Luke cast me one of those looks he'd been giving me lately. It said, *I used to grab you and kiss the hell out of you in moments like this but now I don't know what to do.*

I knew exactly where he was coming from. It was so weird, our relationship had always been very physical, and not just sexually. We'd hugged and kissed, held hands as a matter of course and I'd had to stop myself from reaching for him out of habit more than once. Since Luke had been deployed for the majority of our marriage, we'd fallen into a pattern of soaking up affection whenever we were near each other, a habit we now had to make an effort to disrupt.

Luke looked away first.

"I'm glad she's happy," I murmured. Mostly I was glad that someone was happy these days. "I just wished I didn't have the mental slideshow of the two of them naked as an accompaniment."

Luke chuckled but the amusement didn't reach his gaze and the smile faded fast. "I keep thinking," he cleared his throat.

"What?" I prompted. "What are you thinking?"

He blew out a breath. "That maybe if Logan had been with us, we could have saved her."

"Oh Luke," I breathed, not knowing what else to say. It was true that my soon-to-be ex-brother-in-law had medical training, he'd been a Navy corpsman. But would his having been with us made any difference? "I'm not sure there was much more that could have been done for her. We don't know how long she'd been like that. She was under the care of the real professionals when she died."

Luke stared out the window and I wasn't sure if he heard me. "I'm going to ask him to come back."

I blinked, not sure I'd heard him correctly. "Say what now?"

He looked at me then, a muscle jumping in his jaw. "John told me he's looking to retire from property management. It's a young man's game and he's been feeling the strain of it. Both his sons have found other work. And you and I both know we're more effective with Logan as our third man. Can you honestly tell me you don't have questions you think he could answer?"

No, I couldn't. Logan had skill neither Luke nor I possessed. He would know exactly how long a person could survive in a bathtub without her kidneys. He would have known what to do to give her the best chance for survival.

My throat had gone completely dry and I licked my lips, squeezing my hands into fists to keep from snapping the ever-loving gobstoppers out of my rubber band. "Have you spoken to Logan? About coming back?"

Luke shook his head, keeping his eyes on my face. "I wanted to feel you out about the possibility first."

I couldn't hold his gaze and turned to look out the window. How did I feel about the possibility of Logan rejoining Damaged Goods? Might as well ask me the square root of 6,789 for all the answer I had ready. I sorted through my emotions in a quick shuffle, but the only word that came to mind was queasy. "He might not be interested in working with us again. Things were…dicey over Christmas. He was the one who walked away, remember?"

"I figure it's worth asking him at least. He can always say no." We climbed from the truck and Luke extracted keys from his pocket. Inside I could hear the clicking of dog nails as Sasquatch did her happy dance of greeting. "You coming in?"

I shook my head. "I'm meeting Marcy for lunch and then I promised Rebecca I'd babysit the twins this afternoon." All healthy life-affirming stuff to help take my mind off the unintentional organ donor.

Luke stared down at floorboards. "In that case, I'll see if I can get some work done around here." Luke had spent every spare minute restoring our bungalow. It was odd, the more completed the house, the hollower I felt. Like it was the end of an era.

"Put Sasquatch in the back yard, I'll walk her when I get back." So civilized. You do this, I'll take care of that. We were still a good team, married or not.

He looked up at me. "Are you coming tonight?"

I'd half turned away and paused, raising an eyebrow. "What's tonight?"

He tugged on his ear and didn't meet my eye. "Ursula's 90th."

Ursula was his grandmother on his father's side and a cranky old biddy. Shoot, I'd forgotten all about it, he'd mentioned it the week before. "I don't know if that's a good idea."

"I was gonna tell Mom and Dad after." Luke turned away, a muscle jumping in his jaw. "About the divorce."

I felt bad, and not just because I couldn't offer him physical comfort anymore. Luke had had a rough time adjusting to life post-military and he'd made some monumentally bad choices. He blamed himself for our marriage tanking and no matter how many times I told him that it wasn't exclusively his fault, the message wasn't soaking in. "I'll come with you. We'll tell them together. It'll probably go over better if they see us together not in some big dramatic cold war standoff."

He looked at me then, his expression relieved, but it soured quickly. "I guess I need to get used to doing the tough stuff without you."

Though I'd drawn a line in the sand about touching, I reached for his arm and squeezed lightly. "No need for that, I'll always be here for you. Now, go let that animal out before she shreds the sheetrock in the bathroom again." Both of our pets had separation anxiety, though Abu was much worse than Sasquatch. He actually went to monkey daycare at Marcy's sister's place. Gertie was something of a shut-in and enjoyed Abu's company. Plus when he was there, I didn't have to worry about monkey poo on my rug or smeared over my new Venetian plaster treatment. Total win-win.

"Yes, Ma'am." Luke gave me a smile and went into the house while I headed to Bessie Mae, my old jalopy car. She wasn't the prettiest girl at the dance but she gave great gas mileage and was easy to park, pretty much my requirements for a car.

I drove downtown to the restaurant and parked in the dubious shade of two intertwining palms at the far edge of the lot. The afternoon was heating up fast so I secured a booth inside and ordered a mango smoothie. I had nothing against the occasional cocktail at lunch, but not when I would be in charge of Rebecca's twins all afternoon.

Rebecca Murphy was the daughter of the man who used to own the bungalow next door. She was a single mom and the caretaker for her elderly father, I'd been her go-to babysitter whenever she needed a hand.

"Speak of the devil," I said when my phone lit up with her photo. I slid the talk icon over. "I was just thinking about you. Are we still on for this afternoon?"

"I hope so," Rebecca always sounded overworked and flustered, which considering the circumstances, made sense. "Unfortunately a pipe burst and my dining room carpet is saturated. Any way you can watch the girls at your place?"

"Luke's working there this afternoon. It'll be like a demilitarized zone." I'd been living in the unfinished bungalow for years now, but the sawhorses, exposed plumbing and sheetrock dust wasn't exactly kid-friendly.

"Ugh. I really need to get dad to the doctors'. He's not doing well."

"Sorry to hear it." A thought occurred and I made the offer before I thought it through. "Hey, what about your dad's old place?"

"You mean Logan's?"

Snap went the rubber band. The server dropping off my smoothie glanced at me, then pivoted on his heel and sped off to check on the non-crazy section. "Yeah. I can take them to the park so they don't destroy the place and the beds are there if they need a nap."

"I love how optimistic you are, Jackie. Thanks so much."

I hung up just as Marcy sashayed through the front door.

I hopped up and we hugged and squealed a little, our standard greeting.

"It's been too long," Marcy said as she set her bag down in the seat opposite me. "I was starting to think you were avoiding me."

I shifted, the seat that had been comfortable a minute ago had gone lumpy and I wasn't able to meet her gaze. I was a shitty friend.

"Jackie?"

Marcy had been dating Logan a few months ago. I'd never told her about our convoluted history, probably because I'd been doing my best to pretend that it had never happened. At the time, I'd been committed to Luke and figured it was all in the past. But now….

"Luke and I are divorced." That was only the second time I'd said the words out loud and it wasn't any easier.

"Divorced?" Marcy's big blue eyes got even bigger. "Oh, wow Jackie. I'm so sorry. Was it Logan?"

I choked a little on my smoothie. "What?"

My friend rolled her eyes. "I'm not an idiot, you know. I saw the way he looked at you. To be honest, I think that's what made him so attractive to me. I want a guy who'll look at me like that. Of course, it took a while for me to figure out that he *only* has eyes for you."

I sat back against the booth, stunned. "You asked me if he was gay."

She blushed, her pale skin turning as red as my strawberry garnish. "Yeah well, when a hot guy isn't attracted to you it's easier to pretend he's gay than to admit he's just not into you. I know he's not gay, he's just…neutered."

I made a strangled sound. "He's definitely *not* neutered."

There was a gleam in her eye. "Do you know that firsthand?"

I was beginning to regret the lack of rum in my drink. "Um....?"

"Spill it," Marcy demanded. "I want to know everything."

"It was before Luke," I told her, the words pouring out like water from a fountain. "Way before. And I didn't know they were brothers until after Luke proposed."

She whistled low. "Does Luke know?"

"Yeah, but I didn't know that he knew, and neither did Logan, not until recently. That's why he was such a jerk to me all that time, because I made him keep our history from Luke."

But Marcy was shaking her head. "That's not why at all. You picked Luke over him. He wanted you for himself but you chose his brother. Girl, your life is like a telenovela."

"People in telenovelas don't roll around in human excrement," I said dryly.

She waved it off as though it was of no consequence. "That only happened once."

"It was enough." I gestured the waiter over. Time to change the subject. Did I have to snap the rubber band when Marcy was the one who brought Logan up?

I decided to cut my wrist a break and we placed our orders. The second the server turned his back, Marcy pounced like a ravening lioness on a crippled wildebeest. "So you never answered my question. Is Logan the reason you and Luke split up?"

I stared down at the table, remembering the way he looked at me the last time I'd seen him.

"Admit that you're scared." Logan wrapped his forefinger beneath my chin. *"That you're using Luke's feelings as a convenient excuse to keep from doing what you're too afraid to do.*

Because you aren't really worried that we won't work out, Jackie. You're terrified that we will."

"He told me a truth I didn't want to face," I said to Marcy, trying to forget the way Logan's blue gaze had seared me down to my marrow. "He always tells me the truth, even when I don't want to hear it." Hell, who was I kidding, *especially* when I didn't want to hear it.

She nodded sagely. "Sounds like you miss him."

"At times I do." Like when I was awake. Squaring my shoulders, I reminded myself why Logan and I weren't going to happen. "Luke's already hurting enough and I think if Logan and I ever did try a relationship it would be more than he could take. So no, Logan isn't the reason."

Marcy studied me a moment. "I think that you're just scared."

I shifted under her scrutiny. "Can we talk about something else? Are you seeing anybody?"

Good friend that she was Marcy took the conversational bit between her teeth and ran with it. "Oh my God, you would not believe the creep I went out with last week. I went to the ladies room and caught him going through my purse. I had Rhonda run a background check on him, and he's been charged with fifteen counts of identity fraud. Can you freaking believe that?"

The mood lightened and we laughed through our lunch together, just like we had in the good old days. I managed to put the divorce and the Dark Prince out of my mind for a blissful snap-free meal and all the way out to the parking lot.

"This was fun, we need to get together more often." I gave my friend a quick hug, glad at least that this part of my life was back to normal.

She nodded, obviously distracted. "Don't jump down my throat, but I have to say this."

I braced myself and then nodded. "Go ahead."

"Jackie, do yourself a favor and make a decision for your sake, not Luke's. I like him, he's a great guy but his happiness isn't your responsibility."

"I know that."

"Do you?"

Marcy only had the cliff notes version of events, not the whole story. There was a reason I'd married Luke, a reason I owed him my loyalty even if we weren't destined to live happily ever after.

She put her hands on my shoulders and shook me a little. "Just promise me you'll think about it, okay?"

"Sure," I said lightly.

She rolled her eyes. "Yeah, right. I'll see you later."

I made my way over to Bessie Mae and rolled down the windows, letting the small vehicle air out. Sweat popped out on my forehead. I really needed to get the air conditioning recharged. While I waited I checked my phone. There was a text from a number I didn't recognize and I swiped it closed without reading it. Probably just more spam from my blood-sucking service provider. How could those people sleep at night?

The thought of sleepless nights led my mind back to the woman who'd been found in the vacant apartment. That image was going to give me nightmares for sure. I'd debated bringing it up with Marcy, but had ultimately decided against an open discourse. For one thing, I didn't want to come across like I was gossiping about something so tragic, for another Marcy was a single woman living alone and there was enough to worry about aside from a roving band of organ pirates.

But were they random though? Or had the woman been an acquaintance of theirs, someone they knew, maybe someone who had betrayed them? And how had they gotten inside? My mind was whirling with too many thoughts. I needed answers and there was one person I knew who might give them to me.

"No," Sargent Enrique Vasquez barked when he picked up the phone. "Whatever it is Jackie, no."

"What kind of way is that to answer the phone?" I asked.

"A proactive one," he grumbled.

"No how's it going, Jackie? Whatchya been up to?"

"There are no less than five open homicide cases on my desk, all of them requiring my attention. I don't have time for bullshit."

Down to brass tacks then. "I was on site this morning when they found that woman in the bathtub." Though Miami was a hotbed of criminal activity, an illegal organ harvest was unique enough that Vasquez must have heard about it.

He sighed. "You were the one who called it in then?"

"Yeah."

"I'm sorry about that. It's not something anyone should see. Was Luke with you?"

"He's blaming himself that he didn't do more for her."

"I don't have specifics, this is Detective Bates's case, but there's not a hell of a lot anyone could have done to keep her from dying of shock."

Bates must be the woman who looked like a bulldog. "I'll be sure to let him know, it might be comforting. There's uh, something else. I didn't get a chance to tell the other detective since I was dodging the mad spitter."

Vazquez's tone sharpened. "What other detective?"

"The guy? About five-eleven, craggy face, bright blue eyes, in his late forties or early fifties, if I'm any judge. He snuck up on me when I was examining the bloodstained painting in the gallery."

"Did you see a badge? A uniform?"

"No, he was in a suit. That's why I thought he was a detective."

23

"Then how do you know he was a cop?"

I thought about it for a beat. "It was the way he stood, all stiff and at attention, like he was ready for anything. And then there were his eyes, he had that *don't lie to me because I'll know* look that you cops all have. Why, who is he?"

Vasquez muttered something in Spanish under his breath before switching back to English. "Detective Bates caught the case, there were no other detectives from this precinct at the scene this morning."

A chill swept over me. All of a sudden I felt very vulnerable in the empty parking lot, and I scrambled into my car, reaching to roll up the windows and locking the doors. "Then who was he?"

I could imagine Enrique Vasquez on the other end of the phone shaking his head. "I have no idea. But whoever he was, he shouldn't have been there."

"Maybe he was a patron of the art gallery?" I suggested. Even as the words left my mouth I knew it was a long shot.

Vasquez made a dismissive noise. "When most people see the parking lot full of flashing lights they'll rubberneck to see what's going on but won't approach. It's urban survival instinct to stay away from potentially harmful situations."

"So if he wasn't a patron and he wasn't a cop…?" I swallowed, not liking what that left.

"It's possible you met the organ pirate up close and personal," Vasquez said.

"I HOPE they weren't too much trouble," Rebecca Murphy said as she strapped her squirming twin terrors who I'd lovingly dubbed Thing 1 and Thing 2, into their stroller.

"Nah, they're good as gold," I grinned and handed Rebecca the final diaper bag. The woman always managed to load herself down like a pack mule crossing the Andes. She had mad mom skills though and I gave her serious props for busting her butt for her family. "The house gave them plenty of room to run. They should sleep well tonight."

"Bless you," Rebecca gave me a quick hug and then pushed the stroller out to the street where her car was parked. Then came the unbuckling from the stroller, re-buckling into the car seats, loading of gear, folding of the stroller before she could finally climb behind the wheel. I was exhausted just watching her.

She rolled down the window and I could hear some chipper kiddie tune playing from her stereo. "Hey, I've been meaning to ask, when's Logan coming back?"

My smile froze. "Um, I'm not sure. Why?"

"No reason." Rebecca blushed a little and my stomach knotted. Was there a woman alive that wasn't obsessed with my ex-brother-in-law?

I waved as she backed out of the driveway then turned back inside to clean up the house. They'd managed to get sticky fingerprints on all the windows in the Florida room and I wasn't about to leave it this way for Logan's return.

If he ever came home.

After three sharp rubber band snaps for good measure, I got the window cleaner out from where I'd stashed it above the stove and set to work. Logan had offered to bypass the real estate people and buy the house from the Murphys outright and the cash strapped mom had agreed. The house was a showplace, the perfect restored bungalow. I'd busted my butt calling in favors and maxing out our credit card to find the perfect Craftsman style furniture for it when it had been rented out over the holidays and it looked like a dream. An unfinished dream with no one to appreciate it.

With the west-facing windows once again sparkling in the late day sunshine, I wandered through the small space.

It's what I'd hoped my place would look like when it was finished, all neat and clean, well-thought-out and put together, a real home. With a pang, I remembered it wouldn't be my place forever, at least not the way I'd intended it, as my happily ever after home. Luke and I had agreed to finish the work and then sell, splitting the profits. I'd probably get an apartment somewhere, or maybe a condo. Someplace that allowed giant dogs and temperamental monkeys.

"Where the hell are you, Logan Parker?" I asked the empty house. "Are you ever coming back?"

Late at night, I worried that something bad had happened to the Dark Prince. He'd left everything behind, his third of Damaged Goods, his new home, his family. Just *poof*, gone without a backward glance. He'd done it before, gone walkabout and made zero contact with us, but this time was different. Another thing Luke blamed himself for, driving his brother away. That made me angry. Angry, I repeated to myself, not sad or hurt, I was flipping furious. Not bothering to snap my rubber band—why should I suffer when he made me this mad—I shut the front door with excessive force, locked it and headed into my own back yard.

Sasquatch greeted me with a thunderous *woof*. The massive dog still gave me pause. I'd seen her go feral beastie on an attacker and knew what she was capable of, but to her credit, that had been in my defense. To me and Luke, she was a giant snuggle puppy. And after the potential organ pirate run-in, I felt better having her nearby.

"Taking Sasquatch out," I called to Luke through the open screen.

He was up on a ladder in what would hopefully be a working half bathroom one of these days. "Okay, I'll just finish up here and then hit the shower. We need to be on the road by five."

I hesitated for a beat and he lowered his arms, dark brows forming a V over his nose. "Everything okay, Ace?"

"Sure," gifting him with a bright smile, I snagged the dog's leash off the hall tree, lassoed Sasquatch's massive head and let her drag me from the house.

Truth was, everything wasn't okay. Not just because Luke and I were living in purgatory or I had no idea where Logan was or if he'd actually come back to Damaged Goods. No, all that was just a distraction from the horrifying thought that the man who'd carved out a woman's kidneys and left her for us to find had stuck around to admire his handiwork had been not three feet away from me. I'd told him my name, the name of our company and from that, it wouldn't take him long to actually track me down, if he felt the urge. It might be completely innocent but it didn't feel that way to me. And I couldn't tell Luke about it. Well, I could, but then he'd want to ride to my rescue because that's what hero-types did. And that was the dead last place he should be.

Vasquez had offered to have patrol cars do random drive-bys of my neighborhood, but without any information on the man, that was about all he could do.

"I'm probably overreacting," I told Sasquatch as she dragged me down the street. After a block or so I could usually reign her in but she always took the lead, checking out the territory and for once I was cool with that. She could take on any creep who bothered me.

We schlepped our usual loop through the park and I took her into the house where she downed a massive amount of water before flopping on her dog bed and panting madly. Luke was in the shower so I waited in the living room, trying to mentally put together the perfect outfit to attend my ex grandmother-in-law's 9oth birthday celebration.

Luke came out but caught my arm as I tried to move past him into the only working bathroom. "Jackie, what's wrong?"

I sagged. "You know me so well."

His rueful smile said not well enough, but he remained quiet.

I blew out a sigh. "You remember I told you about the guy I thought was a cop that surprised me in the art gallery? Well, it turns out he wasn't a cop." I explained about my conversation with Vasquez and the conclusion the Sargent and I had come to.

Luke studied my face and then asked, "Will you let me help you?"

I actually sagged a little at his words. "Thank you." Not too long ago it would have been, *I'll handle this*, but the fact that he was actually asking for my permission was a good sign. If he hadn't asked, I might have refused regardless of how unsettled I felt about the whole thing. No way would I let the big strong dumbass take another bullet for me. He wasn't butting in or trying to take over, just asking if he could lend me a hand and that I could accept.

"You shouldn't be alone at all until the guy is apprehended. That means no more walks with Sasquatch and Abu unless someone is with you."

"Sasquatch is the best defensive weapon in my arsenal," I stooped down to pat her enormous head. She heaved a soul-deep sigh of contentment.

"But she can't call for help if someone grabs you," Luke pointed out. "I spoke to Logan this afternoon."

The transition seemed to come out of nowhere and I blinked up at him. "And?"

"And he's thinking about coming back." Luke was studying my face carefully.

I was even more careful to keep my expression neutral as I muttered, "You can't tell him about this."

"Jackie—"

"Damn it, Luke. I said no. Let him make the decision on

his own. You know if he thinks I'm in danger, he'll come back without thinking it through and eventually he'll resent me for it." Under my breath, I added, "And he already resents me enough."

Luke crouched down beside me. "Are we ever going to talk about this, Ace?"

"There's nothing to say," I lied. There was plenty to say, I just didn't have a clue how to say any of it.

Luke shook his head then rose. "Okay. You go get ready, I'll keep watch."

I breathed a little easier knowing I wasn't alone. Luke and I weren't a

couple but he still had my back.

It was also a relief that he hadn't worn that hurt look when I'd asked him not to tell Logan. I'd been afraid to even mention the Dark Prince's name in his presence, not wanting to provoke a fight. Jealousy was not rational. We both knew we couldn't live together forever, that eventually we'd both move on, but everything was still too raw and bringing my ancient history with Logan up wouldn't do either of us any good.

After my shower, I took an obscene amount of time on my hair. Using the flat iron was tedious, but I wanted to look my very best in case Logan did make a cameo at Ursula's party. I didn't want to see pity in his eyes when Luke and I made our official announcement. I wanted him to eat his black heart out.

Hair as manageable as I could make it, I padded into the closet. Unfortunately, I'd been eating my feelings too often of late and the zipper on the snazzy black and teal number wouldn't budge. "Damn you, Ben and Jerry, damn you to the darkest depths of the underworld."

Luke knocked on the door. "You almost ready?"

"Yeah," I gasped as I sucked in the blubber that was

obstructing the zipper's upward mobility. Sweat gathered as I hopped and shimmied, trying to squeeze everything into place. My carefully arranged hair was creeping back to pre-shower dishevelment. This was ridiculous. First thing in the morning I'd join a gym and go on a kale smoothie cleanse.

"Everything all right?" There was amusement in Luke's tone. He'd watched me struggle with this sort of thing often enough in the past and he probably had a pretty accurate mental picture of my latest kerfuffle.

"My zipper's stuck." Understatement of the year. The stupid thing had tangled itself in my bra hook and the metal bits were making sweet love back there. If Luke hadn't been waiting right outside the door I would have snagged a pair of pliers and maybe a vat of Crisco. When in doubt, use more lube.

But Luke held his freaking ground and he didn't show any signs of buggering off. "Do you, um, maybe need a hand?"

My hands fell to my sides in defeat. Barring an act of Congress, I'd have to live with the dress the way it was unless I accepted his help. Clearing my throat and brushing my hair out of my eyes, I squared my shoulders and marched over to unlock the door. "Please?"

He gave me a tight-lipped smile and did a little spinning motion with his finger. "I don't know why you don't just buy bigger clothes."

"Because I'm not a man," the words came out sounding tight because I was doing my best not to breathe. The bodice of the dress couldn't take the strain of a full inhale.

His fingers skimmed along my back. "No, you certainly aren't."

Involuntarily my eyes slid shut. It would be so easy to sway back into him, to turn my head and accept his kiss.

Sharing intimate moments with my ex-husband was the fastest way to screw up a good divorce. "Luke," I began.

There was a tug and the stubborn ass zipper finally gave over. "Got it." He stepped away, not meeting my eyes. "I'll go start the truck."

I stepped into my sandals and snagged my evening bag, relieved.

And only a little disappointed.

3

I 'd never intended to get married. Marriage seemed like something that other people did. People who were okay with commitment, who thought that they were up to the task of caring for another human being. I'd been taking care of Celeste for as long as I could remember, so why would I ever want to add another person to my stable of obligation? Or worse, become that sort of a burden for someone else to take on? I wanted fun, adventure but most of all, freedom.

Dating Luke had been fantastic. He was a sweet, funny guy who couldn't seem to keep his eyes, or his hands, off me. After a lifetime of bread and water, being with Luke was like a romantic smorgasbord and I couldn't get enough of him.

We spent every spare moment together, whenever I was off work and he was on leave. We never fought, there was nothing to fight about—it was as though we'd known each other forever and were instantly comfortable together. We shared a love of action movies and goofy comedies and within the first week, had a plethora of inside jokes that annoyed the hell out of all of our friends.

A few months into our relationship, Luke received his new orders. He'd be gone a year he said. By mutual agreement, we decided to wait to take our relationship to the next level. Meaning sex. Sure, there was a steady smoldering attraction between us but neither of us wanted to rush into a more physical relationship. We were having too much fun with the anticipation portion of events.

"I've made that mistake before." He'd told me one night when we were walking down at the beach.

"Maybe I just don't do it for you," I teased.

He pinched my not insubstantial backside and I yelped in astonished outrage, swatting him with the sandals I was carrying.

He caught my wrist and pulled me close until our bodies pressed together. "Believe me, that is *not* the problem."

"So there is a problem?" I asked the question lightly but he glanced away. "Luke?"

He was shaking his head. "Getting physical changes things and I don't want anything to change between us right now. Everything's just sort of… perfect. When I leave I want to remember you exactly how you are, at this moment."

It was undoubtedly the sweetest thing anyone had ever said to me. Up until he got down on one knee.

"What?" I stared down at him, shocked. "Luke, what the hell are you doing?"

"Trying to ask you to marry me. Now quit interrupting."

My jaw dropped. Passersby had stopped to watch what undoubtedly seemed like the most romantic proposal of all time. A sunset walk on the beach, a handsome man down on one knee, a totally shocked girl who was doing her level best not to upchuck as the fading sunlight was captured by the small diamond ring he offered.

"You just said," I whispered and had to swallow before continuing. "You didn't want anything to change."

"And it won't," he promised. "We'll be exactly like we are right now, we'll just be that way forever."

"Were you dropped on your head as a child?" I asked.

He laughed, though I could see apprehension creeping in around the tightening corners of his eyes. "So is that a no?"

I licked my lips, so tempted to say an immediate yes. Not because I wanted to get married. I didn't, but because saying yes would make him happy. In my mind's eye, I could see it, Luke slipping the ring on my finger, then lunging to his feet and whirling me around, laughing. He was the embodiment of pure joy and when I was with him, that sensation was contagious and addictive.

But marriage. That was a big deal, forever kind of thing. And as sweet and fun and terrific as Luke was, I seriously doubted I even had a forever worth giving.

"I—I don't know what to say." My apprehension must have been scrawled across my face like a hastily written note as I tried to communicate all my misgivings to him via telepathy. *I can't, this is nuts, it's too soon, you don't really know me. I haven't met your family, oh God, you'll expect to meet mine.*

Slowly the eagerness left Luke's expression and he visibly sobered. "I know you weren't expecting this. Do you want time to think about it?"

Time, yes, time was a good thing. Unable to speak I nodded like a bobblehead. Maybe if I were lucky the damn thing would fall right off.

"Okay, then I'll just hang on to this." He slipped the ring back in his pocket.

"You do that," Licking my lips, I paused, needing to say something but not knowing what would be appropriate.

The silence stretched out as he rose and grasped my hand, pulled me forward to start walking again. "Sorry, I didn't mean to freak you out."

"Luke," I didn't know how to translate my thoughts from crazy frantic images to normal human speech.

He squeezed my hand. "It's okay, Jackie. Really. It's just that I'm being deployed on Monday and I thought this would make it easier."

"Oh," I said, my heart sinking.

"Will you miss me?" He looked more vulnerable than I'd ever seen him.

"Like crazy," I admitted.

Luke escorted me to the bus stop and I remember staring at him through the foggy window. He still looked hopeful and I pressed my palm up against the glass in farewell and mouthed the word, "Bye."

Though I'd been hoping to talk to her, my mother was entertaining one of her plethora of male friends. I recognized the signs when I walked in. Clothes shed by the front door, empty booze bottles lying on the floor, not so discreet noises coming from the still open bedroom door.

Damn it, was this the same guy she'd had over the night before or another one? There had been twenty dollars missing from my purse that morning and I hadn't seen Celeste to confront her over the incident. For all I knew she'd taken the money herself. As I looked around the shabby trailer, taking in the threadbare carpet, the overflowing ashtray, the stained sofa where I slept because there was only one bedroom, my temper boiled over. How could I ever bring Luke—clean, smiling, perfect Luke—back to this pit?

In short, I couldn't. Not unless I wanted to die of shame.

On any other night, I would have ducked outside and sat on the steps to wait. Or maybe called Marcy up and gone to a movie. But the thought of that proposal was eating at me and I didn't like it. Not the proposal, but that I was considering it just because marrying Luke would mean I wouldn't have to come home to this anymore. "Celeste!" I barked. "I need to talk to you."

There was a thump, and a groan and finally the mutter of voices. A big, burly guy with hair on his knuckles but not on his head stumbled out of the bedroom. "Is that any way to talk to your mother?"

I ignored him and craned my neck to see Celeste sporting her silk kimono with the bright purple flowers and day-old makeup smears. She reeked of Jim Beam, stale cigarettes and something I didn't want to identify. "Jackie, as you can see, I've got a gentleman caller." She turned back to address the knuckle-dragger. "You'll have to excuse my daughter, she doesn't know the first thing about men."

Oy with the Blanche Dubois act. I knew better to rise to her bait when she was in this kind of confrontational mood. "Yeah, well we need to talk, so your gentleman caller can go kick rocks."

It happened in an instant, one minute I was squaring off with Celeste, the next the goon had shoved me up against the wall separating the living room from the kitchen. His breath was rank with decay and stale cigarettes and made me gag as he leaned in close to breathe, "Someone ought to teach you some manners."

He gave me a slow up and down that had my gorge rising. I knew that look, the one that announced he was thinking he should be the one to teach me the aforementioned lesson. Clothing wasn't required.

I was about to tell him where he could stick his pencil dick when I saw the expression on my mother's face. It wasn't worry for me, but a seething sort of envy. As if I were somehow *inviting* the Neanderthal she'd probably picked up at a truck stop to ogle me.

"Back off," I warned the knuckle dragger.

"Or what?" he sneered.

"Ed, let her go," Celeste was trying to pull the goon off me with no success. "Come' on, hon, don't be like this."

He shoved her, hard. She stumbled on her kitten heels and fell. Her head hit the counter with a sickening thud.

Ed's suffocating arm fell aside. We stood there, both frozen in place. For one terrifying instant I thought for sure she was dead. Then she groaned, rolling to her side.

"You bastard," I shrieked and launched myself on Ed's back, scratching and kicking him for all I was worth. "Get the hell out of here!"

He stumbled back under my assault and my back hit the same wall where he'd pinned me moments before. All the air went out of my lungs but I managed to rake my nails over his face before I hit the ground.

He howled, a hand-clapping over the scratches. "Stupid bitch."

He drew his leg back, his intent obvious. I curled into a ball covering my head with my arms. The kick landed hard in my gut. The delicious dinner I'd shared with Luke rose up and vomit spattered over his bare feet.

He made a disgusted sound and stumbled backward, giving me just enough room to reach for the coffee table drawer. I spat, still unable to suck air in properly and my hand shook as I aimed the revolver at him.

It wasn't loaded. I'd never bought bullets for it, wasn't sure why I'd even kept the thing. It had belonged to another of Celeste's "friends" and he'd left it in our custody when he turned himself in for his eighteen-month sentence for drug trafficking. We'd moved before he'd gotten released on parole and the handgun had come with us. As useless as a paperweight, but Ed didn't know that.

I aimed it at the maniac who'd been about to kick me to death. It took me a minute to suck in enough air to speak. "I work for the Sherriff's office, asshole. Leave or go to jail for assault, your choice."

"Crazy bitch," he spat and blood streamed down his face, but he picked up his pants and left. I stumbled to lock the door behind him, peering past the cheap shade and watching as his car reversed out of the parking lot.

The revolver fell from my nerveless fingers. I reached for it with shaking hands, then sat with it in my lap. Celeste groaned again, but I must have been in too shocked a state to consider that she might truly be hurt. All I knew in that instant was that she'd brought that bastard into our lives, let him into our home and had only interfered because she'd been jealous.

"I deserve better than you," I said to her unconscious form.

Eventually, I'd crawled to her side and checked for a pulse. I couldn't tell if she was concussed or just drunk but either way, she was in no shape to take the bus to the clinic to have herself looked at. So I called an ambulance and then went to brush my teeth and splash water on my face while I waited for them to arrive.

"She fell," I told the EMT flatly. "And I'm pretty sure she's drunk."

He studied me closely. "Were you with her when it happened?"

"No," I lied. "I was out with my fiancée. I just came in a little while ago."

"Do you want to ride with her to the hospital?"

I shook my pounding head. "I have a few calls to make so I'll stay here. I want to look into getting her placed in a program first."

The EMT had solid instincts, I could tell he knew I was lying, but his job was to get Celeste to the hospital so he didn't push any further. As soon as they left I reached for the phone and dialed Luke.

"Hello?" He sounded distracted.

"I changed my mind," I told him as I took one last look at the shabby trappings of my life. "Let's get married."

"WHO ARE YOU?" Granny Ursula snapped when I bent down to greet her. She knew perfectly well who I was, her snappish tone was par for the course.

"Jackie," I said, unfazed. "Happy Birthday, Ursula."

"Harumph," she said and then pivoted her wheelchair toward Luke. "I still say you can do better."

"I'll get you a drink." Marge was at my elbow, steering me away from the crabby old battleax. "You look a little pale. Don't mind Ursula, she's feistier than usual."

"I'm driving," I murmured, shaking off the uncomfortable prospects Granny Parker's words had evoked. "But I could do with some water. You look amazing by the way."

Marge beamed up at me. "Thanks for noticing. I had a seaweed wrap the other day. It's supposed to purge all of your toxins. Probably the most disgusting sensation ever, but I look great, so it might just be worth paying someone to coat me in slime. Speaking of which, how's business?"

"Busy, as usual." Probably not the best idea to bring up the organ harvester over dinner. It was, however, the perfect opportunity to ask if she'd heard from Logan, but a random relative came up and drew Marge's attention before I got the question out.

I moved back toward the bar and ordered a sparkling water with a lemon twist. It's less awkward to stand around by yourself in the middle of a crowd if you have a drink in your hand.

Luke and I had seats at the family table, but I didn't know if my seams could deal with the strain of sitting. Better blisters from standing around in heels all night than a full-scale blowout.

A pretty petite blonde who I didn't recognize stood on the other side of the potted palm. Her big blue eyes took in the crush of people and she looked about nervously. The Parkers had notoriously large gatherings with clients and all sorts of extended family so the fact that we hadn't met wasn't unusual. I gave her a warm smile and held out my free hand. "Jackie," I said.

"Corinne," she warmed right away and moved a little closer. "My fiancé got sucked into the crowd and abandoned me here."

The guy sounded like a jerk, but I kept my opinion to myself. "Are you a first-timer to the Parker gatherings?"

"Yes. How about you?"

"Nah, I'm an old hand at this. The trick is to excuse yourself periodically or you get passed from group to group like an hors-d'oeuvre tray. I once got stuck between a flock of menopausal women discussing hot flashes and some older gents griping about tax law. It took my husband an hour to rescue me. After that, we developed a hand signal and he offered to pull a fire alarm if I got caught up in the tide again."

"He sounds like a good guy," Corinne smiled.

I stared down into my water glass. "He's the best."

The crackle of a microphone interrupted us and we turned to face Gerald Parker, Luke and Logan's father, and Ursula's only son. "Thank you all for coming."

There was soft applause and Gerald pushed his glasses up on the bridge of his nose while he waited for the clapping to die down before continuing. "We're gathered here tonight to celebrate a very special birthday for the matriarch of our family. Mother, would you like to say a few words?"

He held the microphone down to Ursula. One withered claw wrapped around it and pulled it closer to her thin lips. "No."

Gerald blinked as she released the microphone back into his custody. A murmur of nervous laughter swept through the crowd.

"It's true what they say," I whispered to Corinne. "Only the good die young. Ursula will outlive us all."

"She scares me a little," Corinne admitted. "Oh, there's my guy. It was nice meeting you, Jackie."

"You too," I called to her back as it disappeared into the crush of people. I scanned the faces but didn't see anyone I recognized. Gerald had recovered though and was discussing Ursula's many accomplishments in detail. I tried to pay attention but my mind kept wandering to the conversation that would come after. The last thing I'd ever wanted was to hurt the Parker family. They'd accepted me as one of their own almost from day one, something I'd needed badly at the time. Well, everyone but Logan of course, but he had his own reasons to hold a grudge.

As if conjured from my thoughts, I spotted him up front, sitting between Luke and Ursula. Relief coursed through me followed by a wave of longing so strong I tottered on my heels. He was here, safe, not dead in a gutter somewhere. And I'd missed him. Despite my rubber band hematoma, I'd ached for his company.

He looked my way and those blue eyes flashed. A broad grin creased his face as he spotted me and I couldn't help but smile back, my heart pounding.

He was looking at me with such open affection, the last thing I'd expected after the way we'd parted. Though I'd promised Luke that I wouldn't pick up with his brother, though I'd told Logan it couldn't ever be, I needed to be near him again. Without realizing it, I took a step forward...

And watched as Corinne emerged from the crowd and Logan wrapped her in his embrace.

That look hadn't been for me. It had been for Corinne. Cute, shy, sweet little Corinne who had come here with her fiancé.

The room spun as the word echoed over and over in my head. *Fiancé.*

Logan was engaged.

A scream jolted me back to reality. For one horrifying moment, I thought it had come from me, but then more noise joined it, shouts and the crash of breaking glass. The microphone hit the floor with a tremendous thud and a high pitched whine.

"Dad!" That was Luke's voice, and I found him up and moving, the Dark Prince hot on his heels, racing toward where Gerald Parker had crumpled, clutching his chest.

4

I held Marge's hand tightly in mine, keeping my gaze fixed to peeling salmon paint on the far wall of the waiting room and doing my level best not to freak the hell out because my mother-in-law was close to losing it.

"I don't know what happened." It was the fifth time Marge had said that and we all knew what was coming next. I could feel her shaking her head beside me, back and forth like a pendulum. "One minute he was fine and the next...."

"Mom," Logan tried to break through to her. Though I wasn't looking, his voice came from directly across the room, where he sat with his flipping fiancé on an identical vinyl and chrome sofa. "We don't know anything yet. Let's wait and see what the doctors say, all right?"

Marge didn't answer, wasn't tracking anything going on around her. If I was to lay wages on it, I'd bet in her mind's eye she was reliving the moment Gerald had collapsed over and over.

"It just doesn't make any sense," she repeated.

I squeezed her hand but it was limp and cold in mine.

Gathering my courage, I looked over to Logan. I didn't

want to, but he probably had the best chance of discovering what was going on with Marge. He was seated on the far side of the room, his jaw freshly shaven, his back dinner jacket neatly pressed. Our gazes locked and I tilted my head just a little in his mother's direction.

He understood. I glanced away as he murmured something to Corinne and then rose and crossed the room. Logan crouched in front of his mother, taking her other hand in his and inspecting her closely. "She's in shock. Luke, see if you can get a blanket from one of the nurses."

Luke, who had been pacing the length of the room, jogged out the door, obviously eager to be doing something.

"What can I do?" Corinne had come up behind Logan and rested her hand on his shoulder.

You can go the hell away, I thought ungraciously and flinched when he put his hand over hers.

"Maybe see if you can get her a cup of coffee, lots of sugar. Or at least some water." Logan's tone was different than any I'd ever heard from him before, gentle and patient, not at all the standard snarl he used with me.

"Sure thing," Corinne said lightly. "I'll be back in a jiff."

"Who the hell says in a jiff anyway?" I asked when she'd left. I hadn't meant to, the words just came up automatically, like acid reflux for bitchy.

"You don't like her?" Logan asked.

Now was not the time or place to get into it with him. We weren't alone. Of course, Marge wasn't tracking very well, but still. "I don't know her."

He made a disbelieving noise and my temper flared.

"What, it's not like you could possibly know her all that well? It's been what, three months?"

Logan rose to his full imposing height. "I know enough."

I opened my mouth to say something pithy but Luke came back, carrying a blanket, which he draped around

Marge's shoulders, breaking me out of my confrontational mindset. Damn it, what had I been thinking, mixing it up with Logan when Gerald might be....

Shame scaled my face, and I looked away.

Logan took up the pacing and Luke wrapped an arm around his mother's shoulders, pulling her towards him. She didn't resist, just laid her head against him. They stayed that way until a man wearing green scrubs entered the room a few minutes later. "Mrs. Parker?"

For the first time since we'd arrived at the hospital, Marge showed signs of life. "Is he all right?"

The doctor nodded. "He's stable, for the moment. It was a massive coronary."

"A heart attack?" Luke whispered.

Marge squeezed my hand in a death grip. "But he's still alive?"

The doctor nodded. "For now. We're going to need to do surgery."

"What kind of surgery?" Logan rasped.

"Coronary Artery Bypass Grafting."

Out of the corner of my eye, I saw Logan sway on his feet. All the color had drained from his face. Without thinking, I got up and moved to stand in front of him and guide him into the chair before he fell flat on his face. Without prompting, he put his head between his knees and I rubbed his back.

"Can you repeat that in English?" Luke asked.

"Basically, we're going to connect a healthy artery or vein to the blocked coronary artery and create a new pathway to his heart. He's stable right now, but I recommend doing the surgery as soon as possible for his best chances at survival."

"Can we see him first?" Marge whispered.

"For a minute, one at a time. If you'll come with me."

Luke glanced at me and Logan as Marge shucked her

blanket and struggled to her feet. She was shaky as a newborn foal.

"Go with her," I urged Luke.

His chocolate gaze shifted to his brother's slumped form. "What about you, Logan?"

Logan didn't respond, so I offered, "He just needs a minute. He'll be right there."

"Keep an eye on him." Luke squeezed my shoulder and was gone before I could reply.

"Will do," I said, though I wasn't sure why. My hand made slow and steady circles across the planes of Logan's broad back. We sat there for a time, not saying anything.

"My dad's having open-heart surgery," Logan murmured several minutes later.

"Mmmhmmm," I hummed, keeping up the steady motion.

He turned his face toward me, though his eyes were still closed.

"Are you all right?" I asked him, pausing in the circular massage. "Do you need anything?"

"Keep doing that," he breathed. "It's helping."

"Okay," I closed my own eyes and shifted my weight closer to him and resumed my steady rhythm. Open-heart surgery—that was scary. Probably doubly so for Logan because he understood the logistics and probably had a better grasp on the risks as well. "You aren't sitting there imagining everything that can go wrong, are you?"

"It just hit me when he said that," he said. "Dad could've died. He could still die."

Talking about Gerald's possible demise wouldn't help him get his act together. "You looked like you were about to keel right over, like one of those fainting goats," I informed him.

I opened my eyes to see him staring up at me, his expression bemused. "Fainting goats?"

"Yeah, if you startle them they get all stiff and then *boom*, hit the ground. Don't you ever watch YouTube?"

"Must have missed that one," his lips twitched.

For a man, he had a beautiful mouth. His lips were sensuous and so expressive. From personal experience, I knew they were also velvety smooth, so soft and yet firm when they captured my own—

"What's going on?" a woman asked from the doorway.

Dragging my focus from Logan's lips, I turned to face Corinne, who stood just inside the waiting room and was cradling a steaming paper cup. Damn it, I'd forgotten all about her. Where had she gone to get coffee, Cuba?

Logan rose, turning his back on me. "My dad's in ICU, they're scheduling open heart surgery for him now. Come on, I want to talk to the doctor." He took the cup from her with one hand and put the other on her waist to guide her out of the room without looking my way.

I stayed where I was, too stunned to move. Logan had shut me out as though we hadn't been sharing one of our "moments". There had been countless times over the years when for one reason or another we'd looked into each other's eyes and then *zing*, the connection was forged. I couldn't recall if he had ever been the one to look away first. I was always the one who shut him down.

Things were different now, though. He was engaged. And how the hell come everyone else just accepted Corinne into the family like she hadn't just popped up on his radar out of the clear blue sky? Was I the only one who found the timing suspicious?

"Ace?"

I blinked, startled out of my latest obsessive trance to see Luke standing in the door to the waiting area.

"Hey," I pushed up off the chair and went to him. "Did you get a chance to see your dad?"

He nodded. "Mom's in with him now. I'm worried about her."

I took his hand in mine and gave it a firm squeeze. For the second time that day, I threw caution to the wind and made physical contact with the man who was no longer my husband, even as I mentally read myself the riot act. Stupid, selfish Jackie. Had I forgotten where I was, what had happened to poor Gerald, how Marge's world had been turned upside down? "Me too. You should see if she'll come home with us."

"She won't leave dad until he gets out of surgery." From the set of his jaw, I gathered Luke wasn't about to take off either. "You can take the truck if you want to head out."

"I'm not going anywhere." For one thing, Gerald had been part of my family for the better part of a decade. And though I hesitated to remind Luke, I was still freaked out about the organ pirate. Going home alone didn't seem like the smartest move I could make just then. "Wanna grab a coffee?"

He slumped onto the nearest seat. "I'm too wired. If I add caffeine to the mix I'll be climbing the walls."

"Work then? My laptop is in the truck. We can catch up on paperwork."

Luke shook his head. "I doubt I could focus. Maybe we can just…talk."

"Sure," I said lightly. "Anything you want to discuss?"

"Anything, I just need to think about something else other than Dad dying during surgery."

There was a topic I wanted to cover. Luke and Logan had been on the outs since our marriage dissolved. I knew they talked, but Luke had intentionally not spoken his brother's name to me until that morning. So what had changed? At the time I thought it had been because he wanted Logan's medical expertise backing us up. But now I wondered if his motives hadn't been a little less noble than I'd first believed.

It wouldn't be the first time I'd given Luke more credit than he deserved.

Unfortunately, this was neither the time nor the place for a full-scale inquisition, but I couldn't stop from probing gently. "Did you know?"

"Know what?" Luke didn't look in my direction, his gaze a million miles away.

"About Corinne."

He turned to me then, expression puzzled. "What about her?"

I blew out a sigh. "Come on Luke, level with me. Corinne is going around calling herself Logan's fiancée. I'm asking if this is such common knowledge, why didn't you tell me?"

I had to give him credit, he didn't try to bluster his way out of answering. Didn't claim that he thought I wouldn't care, or say he believed I knew already. Instead, he looked away, probably because he didn't want to witness the heartbreak in my expression as he said, "It wasn't my news to tell."

"Fair enough." More questions stacked up in my mind like cordwood. Was he living with her yet, was that why he hadn't been to his new house? Were they going to move into that cute little bungalow I'd gone into debt to furnish? Had they set the date? How long had they been engaged? Had he knocked her up?

I wrestled with those damn questions like a guy I'd once seen in the everglades wrestling gators. It wasn't pretty and there were times I was sure the idiot was going to have his head bitten off for his troubles, but in the end, man prevailed over nature.

Didn't make him any less an idiot.

"So, tell me about what you've been doing on the house," I said instead and then sat back and pretended to listen while Luke talked about all the items on his to-do list, my gaze never straying far from the waiting room door.

GERALD CAME through surgery as well as a man who had suffered a heart attack the day before could. At least, those were his cardiologist's words. That was the good news. The bad news was he was going to be in the hospital for the better part of a week and convincing Marge that her husband wasn't likely to die if she came home with us and took a shower required more effort than I had after spending all night on an uncomfortable vinyl loveseat.

In the end, it was Logan who convinced her to go with us. "Corinne and I will be right next door and any of us can drive you back to the hospital in a moment's notice. Dad will need you rested up, right?"

She'd patted his hand, smiled up at her older son. "You're right, of course, you're right."

It hadn't occurred to me until we stumbled through the door to our bungalow that we hadn't delivered the news we'd intended to share after the birthday party. Namely, that mine and Luke's circumstances had changed.

We exchanged a panicked glance when Marge shuffled toward the room she normally used when she and Gerald stayed with us. The room Luke and all his belongings currently occupied. "Um, Mom…?"

"Yes, dear?" She turned slowly, looking every one of her fifty-nine years.

I put my hand on his arm, stopping him before he could blurt out the truth. My mother-in-law had enough on her plate without hearing about our quicky divorce. I took in her frazzled hairdo, her wrinkled dress and inspiration struck. "Don't you want to shower before you lie down? I have some yoga pants and a t-shirt you can borrow to sleep in."

"Oh, that's a good idea." Marge smiled faintly, her expression telegraphing her obvious distraction.

"I just need to let Sasquatch out, then I'll put them on the bed for you when I get back in."

She waved me away. "Fine, dear. Take your time."

We waited until the master bathroom door closed and then flew into the third bedroom. There were t-shirts and shorts on the bed, the nightstand, the dresser, piled up on the floor. No way to tell if they were clean or dirty other than a sniff test and we didn't have time for that. It looked as if a clothing bomb had gone off.

"What the actual frick, Luke?" I stood on my tiptoes to yank a pair of his boxer shorts off the blade of the ceiling fan. "You've automatically regressed to single and living in your own filth already?"

"Abu got in here a few days ago and I haven't had a chance to clean up since." Luke stuffed a wad of clothes into his duffel bag.

"Sneak 'round the back and put all the laundry in Bessie Mae. I'll rewash everything." I made a disgusted noise as I found evidence of our wayward monkey in the form of a half-eaten banana stuck to the sheet. "You're just lucky you weren't sleeping on monkey turds."

We both froze and turned to face the chocolate brown duvet, which was the perfect color to hide any number of Abu related sins.

"I'll do the bedding too, just in case." I gathered up the sheets and comforter, heading for the laundry hamper in my room, all the while wondering where Luke would sleep now. It made the most sense for him to stay in the master bedroom with me, at least if we wanted to keep the ruse going until Gerald was on the mend. But could we both ignore the temptation of being in such close proximity to one another? Our divorce was going so well, having sex would both literally and figuratively screw everything up.

We'd both gone without for months on end before, of

course, we could resist the temptation for a few days. It probably wouldn't even be an issue. The man was worn out every night after the crazy hours we worked and the worry for his dad would be hanging over our heads. Ex-sex would be the last thing on his mind.

And if I was tempted, all I had to do was think of Logan and his fiancée snug as two bugs in a rug right next door. That would kill my desire in no time.

Loaded down with clean bedding, I made my way back to the third bedroom. Keeping my tone deliberately light, I said, "So I guess you're moving back in with me temporarily."

Luke took the sheets from me and began to remake the bed with precise military corners, the kind I could never manage. "I can just crash on the couch."

Picking up a pillow that didn't smell too much of monkey butt, I began stuffing it inside a matching pillowcase. "And then this whole mad scramble to hide the truth from her will have been for nothing. Come on, Luke, we're both adults. We can make this work for a few nights."

"All right," he spoke slowly as if he wasn't one hundred percent sure what he was agreeing to.

I made a face as I realized how that must have sounded as if I was cajoling him into bed with me. "Just for sleeping." I clarified.

"Right, for Mom's sake."

"Only temporary." We smiled at one another and I broke eye contact first.

"I'm going to go put on a pot of coffee and then call Gertie. Abu is going to be so pissed that he was the last monkey at KinderCare."

"John will be here in an hour. Didn't we have a job today?"

We had scheduled a walk-thru of a newly purchased property. "It's nothing that can't wait until you catch a nap."

"Aren't you tired?" Luke eyed me skeptically.

"Nah, I caught forty winks on that torture device the hospital calls a couch." I fibbed. Truth was, I was exhausted but between sharing a bed with Luke and thoughts of Logan's engagement, I doubted I could sleep.

Luke eyeballed me like he knew I was lying but he let it go. "Okay, well just don't go anywhere alone. I haven't forgotten about the creepy guy who may or may not be an organ pirate and you shouldn't either."

I held up two fingers. "Scout's honor."

After I was sure Luke and his mother were asleep, I slipped out the back door and pulled my phone from my pocket.

Marcy answered on the third ring. "What's up?"

"Do you have the number for that P.I. we met at the New Year's Eve party? I think her name was Daphne something." It was a rhetorical question. Marcy was the single most organized person on the face of the planet, she was like Google, only faster.

"Yeah, want me to text it to you?"

"That'd be great." I eyeballed the house next door. "I think I have a job for her."

5

L ogan knocked on the front door about an hour after I hung up with Daphne the P.I. I shifted guiltily from foot to foot, wondering if he somehow knew I was investigating the woman in his life and what he would say about it if he did.

"Hey," he forced a smile. His hair was wet from a recent shower and slicked back off his face so that his perfect cheekbones and intense blue eyes were on display.

"Couldn't sleep?" I held the door open wider and gestured for him to come in, trying to banish all thoughts of shower sex to the cesspit from whence they came.

He shook his head as he pushed past me into the house. "How's Mom?"

"Sleeping I think, or at least trying to." It was hard not to drink him in with my eyes.

Logan seated himself in the chair he always used when he stayed for dinner or we did paperwork late into the night. I'd been sitting there earlier when I pored over open case files. He glanced at them and then, with a smirk moved them aside. Arrogant ass.

"I was thinking we should call her doctor, see about getting her a prescription to help her sleep."

"I doubt she'll take anything, I know I wouldn't in her place. Want some coffee?" I headed toward the pot that had just finished perking, my second of the day.

"Sure." There was a pause and then, "Luke told me about what you guys found yesterday."

Coffee sloshed over my hand. "Ouch, damn it."

"Did you burn yourself?" the chair scraped as Logan got up to inspect the damage.

"It's not bad." I sidestepped over to the sink and turned on the faucet with my good hand. "Just the kitchen curse reminding me I shouldn't push my luck."

Logan moved closer and I could smell his intoxicating scent. I wondered what sort of soap he used. Fresh citrus maybe, and ozone with an underlying pop of freshly washed male skin. Whatever it was, I wanted to bury my face in his neck and inhale until my lungs burst. Too bad that smell didn't come in candle form, women worldwide would sell their firstborns to indulge in the Dark Prince's unique scent.

Mischief gleamed in his eyes as he reached for a clean dishtowel and my hand. "You're sure that's all it was?"

"What else would it be?" I tried to jerk away but he held firm. Strong fingers massaged my palm as he blotted the towel over stray water droplets and after a few moments, I forgot all about the burn.

He held the injury up to inspect. "Hmm, doesn't look too bad. Do you have any aloe?"

"No," I breathed.

"Burn cream?" One dark eyebrow jutted up and I shivered.

"Sorry," I whispered.

"You really should have a fully stocked first aid kit," he chastised.

"I'll keep that in mind."

A few months ago, Logan wouldn't have gotten this close, wouldn't have dared to look at me the way he was currently doing, with such clear heat. The water aerobics slideshow starring my ex-brother-in-law started up again. If I looked hard enough I could almost imagine the fantasies playing out behind those predatory eyes.

Somewhere down the hall, a door opened. I tugged my hand away more insistently this time and he let go, turning to see who it was.

Luke, who'd been tucking his shirt into his cargo pants, froze when he saw us. His gaze took in my face and his brother's. I waited for guilt to hit, the way it always had before when Logan and I shared a moment.

It wasn't there.

I almost sagged in relief. It was gone, totally and completely. Luke may not like my attraction to his brother, but I didn't have to hide it anymore and that was such a weight off my chest. I could have floated up to the ceiling, so filled with the weightlessness of sheer relief. So, this is what freedom felt like. I could get used to it.

"Logan," Luke's greeting to his brother was cool and calm. "Where's your fiancée?"

So much for free-floating. I hit the ground again with an almost audible plunk.

Logan didn't even have the decency to look guilty as he shrugged. "Sleeping next door. She volunteered to stay here with Mom when we head out."

My jaw dropped. He'd been smoldering at me while poor Corinne was dead to the world in his bed. God, he truly was evil incarnate. I could have cheerily smacked him, the thoughtless selfish, inconsiderate..., there weren't enough bad words in my vocabulary for him.

Manwhore would have to suffice.

And then the rest of his meaning sank in. "When we head out? So, you're back on board, just like that? And you're okay with this?" I directed the last part at Luke who shrugged unhelpfully.

"What's your damage?" Logan scowled. "I thought you'd be happy."

"Then you're delusional. I'm going to take a shower. The case files are on the table and Big John should be here soon."

Sick to death of the Parker brothers, I stormed into my bedroom, only refraining from slamming the door because Marge was in the house and I didn't want to wake her if she had managed to sleep.

My responding to Logan pissed me right the hell off. Why did I have to be attracted to such a faithless pig? Did I have zero sense? And him, what in the sweet chocolate ever after was his excuse?

If Logan thought we were going to continue flirting even after he committed to Corinne, he had another thing coming. Poor girl, someone ought to warn her about the Dark Prince and his wicked ways. Never mind that I'd hired a P.I to investigate her background. That was for the Parker family as a whole and had nothing to do with Logan.

Nothing at all.

I sat on the bed and put my head in my hands. There was only so much lying a girl could do to herself in the course of a day. And considering it wasn't even noon yet, I was well ahead of my quota. I was jealous, crazy freaking jealous. And the worst part, I didn't have the right to be. Logan had all but offered himself to me on a silver platter and I'd been too much of a coward to lift the lid and take him up on it. Could I really blame him for going out and finding a girl who had no problem claiming him publicly, instead of treating him like a dirty little secret?

Yes, yes I could. First, because he was too damn attractive

for his own good and used it to shameless advantage. And second, he had the morals of an alley cat. I'd known all along he'd be that kind of guy, the one with a sweet and loving woman at home and then a little something on the side.

But I'd be damned if that something was named Jackie Parker.

So what if he'd carried a torch for me for over a decade? The thing about torches, they went out eventually and usually at the most inconvenient times. Like, say, when you gave in and married them. That was the other problem with torches, they tended to burn people. That's why most people used lamps and flashlights instead.

Satisfied with my clever analogy, I sauntered into the shower.

JOHN SHOWED up just after noon with my mother in tow.

"How is poor Marge holding up?" Celeste asked as she dropped her purse on the table.

"About as well as can be expected under the circumstances." I looked Celeste over carefully. As much as I was loathed to admit it, the relationship with Big John was good for her. She'd toned her make up down and I hadn't seen her take a drink in months. Even the drama seemed to be scaled back several notches. He may be a classless pain in the butt, but he was steadily employed and treated my mother with respect. It was nice to see her taste in men had matured over the years.

"You'll hang here in case Marge wants to go back to the hospital?" I asked as I handed her the keys to Bessie Mae.

"Of course, Jackie. Don't worry, I'll take good care of her. And when you get a chance, I want to talk to you."

I paused at the door. "Now's not a good time...Mom."

Her lips parted, but the mom caught her off guard.

I lowered my voice. "Look, Marge doesn't know about me and Luke so please keep that under your hat for now."

"But—"

"Jackie!" Luke hollered from outside.

"I have to go." It was a relief to put a closed door between us.

Logan scowled at me as I approached the truck. "I told you, Corinne was going to look after Mom."

I offered him a bright smile. "Well, now she doesn't have to."

There was an awkward moment when both John and Logan headed for the passenger's side door. They looked at each other, then looked at me.

I exchanged a glance with Luke. "This could get ugly."

He stepped between the two men. "I need Jackie up front guys, to direct me."

Both men grunted in acknowledgment and I gave my ex a discreet thumbs-up. "Nice going."

"Next time just call shotgun and save us the trouble," he muttered

Our job was near the Lummus Park Historic District, an area that I loved for its famed Mediterranean Revival style architecture and rich history, something hard to come by in ever-changing Miami. Unfortunately, we wouldn't have time to take in the sights, not if what I suspected was true.

"The landlord is Fred Gains, we've worked with him before, and he bought the place in an auction last week. He wants us to inspect the house, document the items, assess any damages and inventory leftover belongings and tag them for auction."

"What's the catch?" Logan asked. Smart man

I turned around to face both him and John. "I looked up

the auction listing this morning and it said, and this is a direct quote, "Occupant status varied."

"Squatters," John translated. "We got porkin' squatters to deal with."

"At least a fifty percent chance of them," I agreed.

Squatters were about the hardest situation for a property owner. Without a contractual lease, the squatter had to prove residency, otherwise, we could file a motion for unlawful detainer with the courts, which would sue for any damages to the property as well as income lost had the place been open for legitimate renters. If the squatters could prove residency though, they then had to be treated as tenants. And some people made squatting into a professional occupation.

"We should talk to the neighbors first," Luke suggested. "See if we can find out if there are squatters in residence and how savvy they are so we know what we're up against."

It was a solid plan, but as we pulled up across the street from Mr. Gain's new house, the plan got flushed down the proverbial toilet.

"Sonofabitch," Logan grunted. "Is that who I think it is?"

Sure enough, the robust figure of Fred Gains was pounding on the door to his new house and swearing so loud they could probably hear him in the panhandle. "This is my house!"

Luke shook his head. "The man ought to know better."

"We got to get him out of here before they call the cops." John grumped. "Jackie, quick, flash him and get his attention."

Logan chuckled darkly. "Would get my attention."

Although I wasn't against using my boobs to get my way, that wasn't what the current situation required. "Shut up, you idiots. I'll get him."

I popped the door and called out, "Mr. Gains! You shouldn't be here."

"It's my house!" he raged.

"No argument here," I called back. "But you can't yell at them. They could sue you for harassment."

Mr. Gains made a disgusted noise. "I need them outta there."

"Just get back in your car and go back to your office," I spoke in my most soothing tones. "I promise, I'll call you as soon as they are out and we'll change the locks before we leave."

He didn't like it, I could tell, but he didn't have a leg to stand on.

"You know my team gets results," I added. "Let us do our job."

I about had him where I wanted him, in his car and away from here, when someone threw open an upstairs window and stuck a naked ass out at us. A neon blue ass.

"Is that what they mean when they talk about once in a blue moon?" Big John remarked as the rest of the team approached.

Mr. Gains lunged for the front door, but Luke caught him by the arm and hissed. "The tenant wants to get a rise out of you. If he's done this before he knows getting you worked up will strengthen his case to stay."

From the man's reddish-purple complexion, it was working. Either that or he was having an aneurism.

"I'm not budging one inch until those assholes are out of there."

"Phrasing," I coughed into my fist. Logan laughed, though he covered it quickly by clearing his throat.

"Well don't just stand there," Mr. Gains snapped at us. "Get them out!"

I looked over our crew. Big John was the most intimidating of us and the goal was to get the squatters to trust us. If we got them to let us in, we were more likely to get them to listen to us and find out exactly how much it would cost our property owner to entice them to leave.

"John, why don't you keep Mr. Gains company while we see what we can do here." Translation, our property owner is a hothead who'll only make things worse if he isn't monitored.

"I got my phone on," he grunted. "Shout if you need police backup."

I headed up the stairs, Luke and Logan flanking me on either side. "Logan, you carrying?" Luke asked in a low tone.

"No, you?" The Dark Prince asked his brother.

"Nonlethal only," Luke admitted.

"Well hopefully we won't even need that," I raised my fist and rapped on the front door.

"Go away!" A man shouted from inside the dwelling.

"Not until you talk to us!" I hollered back.

"I won't talk to that bastard!" The man shouted. I could only assume he meant Mr. Gains.

"He's all the way across the street. Look for yourself."

There was a pause and then the sound of footsteps. One of the shades was pulled aside and a long paint-stained nose bumped against the cracked single-pane window. It withdrew, leaving a reddish smear on the foggy glass.

"Who are you?" He called, once again behind the door.

"My name is Jackie," I did my best to sound as nonthreatening as possible.

The door cracked open and the absurdly long nose with a smeared drop of red paint on the end poked out across the chain. "What do you want, Jackie?"

I held my hands up so he could see I was unarmed. "Just to talk. What's your name?"

Mr. Red Nose Blue Ass took my assessment and then shifted his focus to the Parker brothers. "Marv."

"Well Marv, how long have you lived here?" Deliberately

squaring my shoulders and holding my hands where he could see them, I kept my posture open and receptive.

"A while," he answered noncommittally.

"Do you paint?" I asked, even though the answer was as plain as the nose...well, it was obvious.

"Art is my life," he grunted.

I leaned in a little closer so he could look down my blouse if he chose. With an artist, there was only about a fifty percent chance he would be interested in what I had to offer, but I'd been told the girls were remarkable enough that even a gay artist would want to capture their likeness.

He did look, and not with an artist's assessing eye either. Okay then. "I'd love to see some of your work. Could we come in?"

"Give me a minute." The door shut again.

"Drug user?" Luke asked.

Logan brushed past me and pressed his ear to the door. "I hope not. We should start bringing Sasquatch on these jobs, she could neutralize any canine threat. Plus most of the human ones."

"And she smells better than Big John," I added.

"I don't hear anything." Logan withdrew, resuming his place. "Jackie, keep him distracted so we can slip off and catalog what he's got going on."

It was a classic technique used by snoops worldwide and one of the reasons we operated best as a three-man team— one person could ask to use the bathroom and then poke around until he found something of use while the rest of the team kept the tenant distracted. In this case, what we needed was information that would help us get Marv's measure and force him to hurry on his way.

"Ssh, he's coming back," I cautioned when I heard the sound of footsteps approaching. Ready for anything.

Or so I thought.

6

M arv opened the door and stood back but I froze.

"Aren't you coming in?" Marv asked, his gaze focusing past us to where Big John stood with Mr. Gains. Lucky bugger.

"Ace?" Luke was a step down from me and couldn't see what Logan and I saw.

"Um...?" I said stupidly. "Aren't you going to put on pants?"

"I never wear pants when I create," he said, rather unnecessarily. He was covered from the neck down in paint of varying colors and not a stitch else. One arm was spattered purple and green while the other was streaked with bright orange. From neck to knees was coated in differing shades of yellow, golden up along his collarbone and fading to a pastel watery sunlight on his thighs. I couldn't seem to rip my gaze from the bright yellow banana and severely regretted displaying the girls. Had they contributed to its ongoing state of firmness? I shuddered in revulsion.

Logan nudged me and whispered. "The door's open. I'll

stay with you, but we need to get in there and give Luke a chance to look around."

He was right, I was stalling and we had a job to do.

Cautiously I took the first step across the threshold followed by the Parker brothers.

The hall was small and pokey—*don't think about pokey!*—and other than the occasional paint smudge, there wasn't too much out of place.

Then the hallway opened up into the living space. Carpet, walls and even the ceiling were coated with paint of every color of the rainbow. And it wasn't as if he'd just flicked a little here and there with a brush. No, Marv himself *was* the brush and he painted by pressing various bits of his anatomy against every available surface.

"You can't do this," I whispered, taking in the stains on the once beige carpeting. His backside was blue today but from the mess, it appeared the moon also came in red, orange and puce. I had no idea what sort of paint he was using or if even the best steam cleaner in the world could get the multihued butt prints out.

He misinterpreted my meaning. "I know it's edgy, but my house is my masterpiece."

"Only one problem, my man." Logan had recovered first. "It *isn't* your house. It's our client's house."

It was a common enough attitude among longtime renters. After spending some time living in a rental, the tenant often forgot that the property he inhabited wasn't his own.

"I have every right to be here," Marv shouted, obviously a bit techy over being contradicted. "I have a lease!"

I exchanged a glance with Luke. Our client had bought the property sight unseen and "as is." If Marv did have a legitimate lease, then Mr. Gains had taken on a tenant, not a squatter and the big paint smeared crazy that went with him.

"We need to see that," Logan said. "Your lease as well as any proof that you've been paying rent."

Marv grunted. "It's in the bedroom."

Oh no, no way was I following naked paint guy with a raging yellow boner into his bedroom. Having sensed my apprehension, Logan said, "We'll just wait here."

The second Marv exited the room, we scattered like roaches. Luke took the stairs two at a time to explore the upstairs, Logan headed into the small galley kitchen and I started opening closet doors. What we needed here was some sort of illegal activity to help force our case. While the naked body painting was highly disturbing, it wasn't against the law.

Of course depending on the stipulations of the lease, maybe Marv did have every right to let his freak flag fly all over this house. In that case, the best our client could hope for was suing the auction house for not disclosing that the property was contractually let and hoping to get back some of his investment that way.

"Anything?" Logan moved back into the room.

"Not so much as a crack spoon." I grumped as I shut the door to an ancient sideboard. It was actually a nice piece. In fact, there were several decent items in the space. The house had nice bones too, the doorframes were all made of dark hardwood. It just looked like crap, smeared as it was in dead skin cells and Technicolor. "This is awful, this house is too nice for this kind of treatment."

Logan nodded and moved toward a plastic-covered sofa. "The outside is misleading as hell. I doubt the lease is legit, the guy obviously has zero respect for the property. Look alive, he's coming back."

Sure enough, Marv was headed in our direction, banana, and nose proceeding him into the room.

I looked anywhere but at Marv but Logan had no such

compunction. "Doesn't that hurt? Having everything all, at the ready while you're just walking around like that?"

Marv handed him the papers with a shrug. "I'm used to suffering for my art."

Logan handed the papers to me even as he asked, "How many hours a day do you work?"

"Whenever I have the chance. Today it's been about eight hours."

All the color leached from Logan's face. "You're not serious. Do you take something?"

Marv shook his head. "Where did the other guy go?"

"Bathroom," I said quickly. "Logan, what's the matter?"

The Dark Prince looked distinctly uncomfortable as he stared Marv in the eye. "Man, I can't tell under all that paint, but I think you have priapism. You need to see a doctor. This could be serious."

Marv swayed on his feet, obviously shocked but then his chin went up. "No, I can't leave, I have to finish."

"Man, you could end up impotent," Logan warned. "Jackie, call an ambulance."

"Whoa!" The cry came from upstairs followed by a string of cussing.

"What's he doing?" Marv shrieked, heading for the stairs.

"Hold on a second," Logan said but Marv spun around and took a swing at him. The Dark Prince was lightning fast on his feet and had Marv subdued in a full nelson before I took two steps. It was the first time I'd ever seen him do that particular move. Usually, he pinned his attacker against a wall or down on the floor. The change was probably in consideration for the protruding parts.

"Luke?" I called. "Is everything okay?"

Luke charged down the stairs, white as a sheet. "He has a naked woman gagged and tied to the bed."

"She's my muse!" Marv struggled but Logan's grip held true.

"Is she there willingly?" I asked.

The Parker brothers just looked at me.

"What? I'm not saying sign me up for that, but it's a valid question. Different strokes for different folks, right?"

"She's unconscious." Luke shook his head. "I untied her, but she didn't budge. She's breathing though. I'd feel better if Logan took a look at her."

Logan shook his captive. "Did you do something to her? Give her drugs or something to keep her unconscious?"

"I don't have to tell you anything." Marv sneered.

"So we have him on possible kidnapping and I'm pretty sure this lease is fake," I told the Parker brothers.

"What makes you say that?" Luke asked.

"It's signed by Ronald McDonald." I held it up for his inspection. "So, Marv, are you listening? You have two choices. You can pay for the damages to the place and pack up your paint or we can have you arrested."

"Fuck you," Marv spat in my general direction.

"Not even in your paint-spattered dreams," I said sweetly. "So an ambulance or the police?"

The Dark Prince shifted. "He really does need to see a doctor about his erection. I wasn't B.S.ing. He could have severe damage or some underlying condition. And the woman might need medical attention too. Luke, can you take him so I can go assess her condition?"

"Sure." Luke trotted down a few more steps, probably intending to grip Marv in the same hold so Logan could slip-free. Without warning, Marv threw his head back, clobbering Logan where it counted. Logan made an *oof* sort of sound, and Marv wriggled like an eel. I moved forward to try to help contain him while Logan was incapacitated but he was slippery as a greased pig and with nothing to grab onto,

Logan lost his grip. Once freed, Marv took off and he was damn fast for a naked guy with an eight-hour boner.

"Damn it, make sure he's not going for a gun!" Logan gasped.

Luke had leaped down the last three stairs but I was still closer. I ran after Marv, shouting for him to stop. The closed backdoor slowed him down and then he had to turn the corner from the tiny back stoop onto the stairs. Without fully thinking about it I leaped and tackled Marv. The momentum took us both crashing through the railing and he landed face down on the concrete patio with my not so insubstantial form on top of him.

"Shit," Luke had followed as far as the steps. "Ace, are you all right?"

I couldn't move to see the Parker brothers but I could hear their approach. The impact had driven my diaphragm somewhere up into my nasal cavity but I managed a weak nod. Below me, Marv was making some sort of keening sound, similar to the slow air leak from a balloon.

"What about Marv. Is he all right?" Luke asked.

"If his erection didn't snap off, maybe," the Dark Prince intoned. "But I wouldn't bet on that."

Luke picked up the phone from where I'd dropped it and did his level best to answer the operator's urgent series of questions.

Not having the ability to draw a full breath is scary as hell. I flailed around like a turtle on her back until strong hands pulled me upright. Logan looked a little green around the gills, still suffering the after-effects from having been racked, but his hands on my shoulders were reassuring. "Try not to panic, it'll only make you pass out. You'll be able to draw a full breath in a minute."

My eyes bulged and I shook my head. He didn't understand, I was suffocating!

69

He gripped my face, holding me steady. "Jackie, listen, you're going to be all right."

And then I was. Air, beautiful fresh air filled my lungs, expanding my chest and I coughed, trying not to vomit.

It didn't work. I doubled over and all the coffee I'd ingested that morning came up. Logan turned me just in time, holding my hair out of the way, continuing to make soothing sounds.

"What in tarnation is going on back here?" I would have recognized the colloquialism anywhere, even if Big John hadn't come charging around the corner like a pissed off rhino. "You all right, princess?"

"She will be." Logan held the big man at bay. "Go to the truck and get the bottle of water from under the seat. She'll want to wash her mouth out."

John must have disappeared because I didn't hear him for a minute. "Did he just call me princess?" I whispered.

Logan tucked a stray curl behind my ear. "Maybe he'll adopt you when he marries your mom."

"You aren't funny," I wheezed.

"Who's joking?" Logan lifted my chin and studied my face. He touched a sore spot above my left eyebrow and I winced. "You feeling any better?"

I was, though I wanted nothing more to curl up and sleep for a week. "I'll live. How's Marv?"

We looked over just in time to see Luke roll the now zip-tied squatter onto his back, flagpole still at the ready.

"I think he passed out," Luke remarked. "That must have hurt like a sonofabitch."

I considered the woman still passed out upstairs. "He left her bound and gagged? Even if she was a willing participant, that's so freaking wrong." I drew my foot back, intending to whack Marv again, just for the hell of it.

There was a collective sound of breath being sucked in

from the peanut gallery. I glanced at my audience. Mr. Gains, Luke and Logan all covered their crotches in unison like a trio of do no evil monkeys.

"Bunch of babies," I lowered my foot without striking and shuffled off toward the truck. "Men can't take a joke."

IT TURNED out Marv's muse was a willing participant in his art and a heroin addict to boot. Logan spied the track marks when he examined her. She roused when the ambulance arrived, but was too out of it to make much sense.

"Get the locks changed," I advised Mr. Gains. "And don't let it sit empty too long. Marv might try to come back. If he can walk."

"Thanks, Jackie." Mr. Gains shook my hand and we piled back into the Big Black Truck and headed home.

Bessie Mae wasn't in the driveway when we arrived back at our house.

"Are you heading back to the hospital?" Logan asked his brother as we all climbed from the vehicle.

Luke slammed the door and rolled his shoulders. "I was thinking about it. Want to come with?"

The Dark Prince cast me a sideways look. "Are you going?"

I shook my head. "Can't. I have a mountain of paperwork and I need to pick up Abu." Nevermind return a call to my P.I. She'd texted me that I should call her as soon as I had a minute free to talk.

The three men exchanged glances like I wasn't even there.

"I'll stay and help you out with the paperwork, princess," John said at last.

"Um, it's okay." I shuddered. Alone time with Celeste's latest boy toy was not on my bucket list. True, John wasn't a total goober the way I'd first thought but I'd already had my fill of his crappy grammar for one day.

Another unreadable look passed between the men. "I'll go see him tonight." Logan finally decided.

John offered to drive Luke so that way he and my mom could head out and Luke could drive Bessie Mae back home.

I watched them clamber into John's SUV and then turned to face my doom.

"You really don't have to stay," I began but Logan held up a hand to stop me.

"Actually, I really do. Or have you forgotten there's an organ pirate out there somewhere who may or may not have his sights set on you?"

My jaw dropped and I sputtered in outrage. "I asked Luke not to tell you!"

"You guys aren't married anymore. So bros before hos, babe."

"I'm thinking very bad thoughts about you, Logan Parker."

Logan snorted. "Let me know how that works out for you."

I blew out a sigh, not sure which of the Parker brothers I was more annoyed with and pushed past him to stomp into the house.

Sasquatch jumped up to greet me, wagging and circling me like a doofy shark. "Aw, hey girl. You miss Abu, don't you? Don't worry, I'm going to go get him in a little bit. Yes, I am, oh yes I am." I spoke in that breathy voice I reserved exclusively for babies, animals, and idiots.

The creak of the loose floorboard reminded me that we weren't alone. Heat scalded my face when I glanced up to see Logan stare at me while I crooned like a lovesick moron to my puppy. He didn't say anything snide though, just watched with a blank expression on his face.

"What?" I asked in an irritable tone. He was the voyeur in this little scenario so why should I feel stupid?

He shook his head. "I've just never seen you like that is all."

"Like what?"

He shrugged and didn't respond.

Clearing my throat, I rose and made my way to the back-door like nothing had happened. Good girl that she was, Sasquatch ran outside, squatted, then beelined for the kitchen and the box of Milkbones I kept there. She took her treat to the carpet and I cast a sidelong glance at Logan, "I'm taking another shower."

He didn't respond, instead headed for the fridge, most likely to see if we had anything edible. Having trundled through the thing earlier, I wished him luck with that futile effort.

Twenty minutes later, the worst of the artist funk had slithered down the drain and I'd brushed my teeth until they squeaked with cleanliness. I stood swathed in only a towel and debated what to wear. After having the wind knocked out of me, the idea of putting on anything that constrained my midsection, like say, a bra or tight pants, sounded like the fifth circle of hell. Tossing on a loose-fitting tank dress I pulled my hair back into a clip and slid my feet into sandals. No makeup or jewelry, just clean and ready to get down to business.

The Dark Prince gave me a once over from the kitchen, where he was compiling a sandwich from God alone knew what. Men and sandwiches must be a Y chromosome thing. I shifted a little uncomfortably, wishing I'd rethought the bra thing as his gaze focused on my chest. "That doesn't look like work attire."

"It's paperwork attire. Meaning I don't have to talk to

tenants or landlords or appear in court and nobody's going to see me but you so I really don't give a damn."

He added pickles to his bread then took a huge bite. "I thought we were going out to pick up your monkey?"

"Like crazy Gertie is going to care what I'm wearing?" I shook my head. "Nope, not worth putting on a bra."

He shoved the sandwich aside and stalked around the counter. "What if you get stranded by the side of the road?"

I blew out a sigh. "Then I'll be better equipped to flash someone and get their attention."

"Jackie," he said, exasperated.

"Logan," I shot back in the exact same tone. "We've gotten into it before over my clothes. Remind me how that ended? With you calling me the whore of Babylon. Do you *really* want to repeat that argument? Because Luke isn't here to turn the hose on us so we might end up killing each other."

I saw his blush as he looked away.

The smart thing would have been to let it go. I'd forced the Dark Prince to back down. I shouldn't keep needling him. But when I opened my mouth, the question popped out. "Why the hell do you care what I'm wearing anyway?"

He stared at me for a minute, saying nothing, though his eyes were burning.

"Fine, don't tell me." I pushed past him to grab a bottle of water from the fridge, trying to ignore the churning in my stomach. I had tasks to accomplish, including tracking down the former tenant from the poopy apartment and find out what happened with his set of keys, retrieve my monkey and call my P.I. Logan Parker was not on my to-do list, damn him.

A hand landed on my shoulder and I heard him suck in a deep breath. "Because I'm having a hard enough time not touching you as it is and this goddamned dress looks like an invitation to sin. And baby, do I ever want to sin with you."

My jaw dropped and I turned to face him. "What. The. Hell?" Logan had never been so blunt with me before. Usually, he spoke in double entendres and cast me smoldering looks. Covertly, sometimes guiltily, other times with a simmering rage and passion, but this…?

He stalked me, prowling ever closer. "So is that what this is? An invitation?"

"You sound like a Neanderthal," I breathed. "Like I'm provoking you somehow."

"You always provoke me," he murmured, eyes turned to blue fire. "Come on, Jackie. Enough with the games. Do you want me?"

"I…?" Swallowing did nothing to help me speak. There was so much to say but nothing that made any sense to me so hope of translating it to something another human mind could understand was damn near impossible.

While I struggled, he pressed his advantage. "Your P.I. friend called while you were in the shower. Left a message saying she'd found something on Corinne. Tell me why you were looking for info on Corinne?"

Crap. Served me right for not texting her back. I licked suddenly dry lips. "I wanted to know who she was, for the family."

One sardonic eyebrow lifted. "For the family, huh?" He sounded as though he thought I was lying.

I scowled and shoved him. "Of course. Marge and Gerald have been good to me. Just because Luke and I are divorced doesn't mean I'm going to stop caring about them or looking out for them."

"For them?" He inched even closer. "Or for me?"

"I…," Again words failed me and I got a little lost in those neon blue eyes.

He backed me up against the nearest wall, heat radiating off him. "Just say it."

"Say what?"

"Admit that you're jealous."

"Jealous?" I made an overdone disbelieving sound.

"I want you," Logan pinned me with his stare. "And you want me. Admit it."

"Now?" I looked around but the only other living thing was Sasquatch and she was lying upside down with her big head hanging off the couch. No help from that quarter.

His gaze fell to my lips. "Why not?"

"Why not?" I repeated stupidly. "Because you're engaged, damn you."

"I'm not." He said it clearly with absolute conviction.

What? I narrowed my eyes at him. What kind of game was he playing?

"Have I ever lied to you?" he asked.

"Not to my knowledge," I admitted.

"Then trust me when I say I have no intention of marrying Corrine. Now, what else have you got?"

His eyes flashed with challenge and I felt my chin lifting in response. "Your…your Dad's in the hospital."

"So comfort me," he reached out and pressed both palms against the fridge, effectively trapping me.

"You're not looking for comfort," I whispered. "Unless that's what the kids are calling it these days."

One corner of his mouth twitched. "I've missed this. Sparring with you like this."

"Then why…?" I swallowed around the sudden lump in my throat. Too many questions. I had too many questions and didn't know which to ask first. I went with the one that mattered most, the one that had gutted me. "Why have you stayed away? Where have you been? And what's the deal with Corrine? Talk to me, Logan."

"I'm sick of talking. Talking never helps with you. You

just make me insane," he growled and then his lips were on mine.

It wasn't fair, I wasn't ready for him, hell I'd probably *never* be ready for him. But this time he'd taken me completely off guard. He knew it too, because he took full advantage, deepening the kiss. Blame the fatigue, the stress of the last thirty-six hours, or months of abstinence. All of them added up to make me weak and unable to shove him away or even recall why I should.

It had been too long since I'd been kissed with such a burning intensity and I noted every detail of it. He hadn't shaved that day and the scratch of his stubble abraded my chin even as the softness of his lips cushioned mine. The heat coming off of him was all-encompassing. Though our bodies didn't touch anywhere but our fused mouths, every cell I possessed was aware of him, was singing and dancing for his notice. I couldn't get enough of it, enough of him. His taste— of coffee and sin—his touch that was like a brand, scalding me much deeper than my skin and bones, marking me all the way to the place buried so deep inside me that only one person had ever left a mark.

Logan.

I couldn't resist his pull for another second. Wrapping myself around him, I gave in to desire completely.

He felt it too, felt my resolve crumble because he pulled back. If his expression had been smug or satisfied, I might have found the will to stop and put some distance between us but all I saw was the question in his eyes. And the fear. That I would shut him down or tell him to back off and pretend that this hadn't happened. One word slipped from his lips.

"Jackie," he breathed, the whisper full of reverence. He could have been seeking permission or verification from me, or reminding himself who I was and how long he'd wanted this.

Wanted me.

I didn't need reminding, I knew. "Shut up and kiss me, Logan."

He did.

7

"Gertie?" I called through her front door. Marcy's sister was a little odd at the best of times and I'd been prepared for several different scenarios. "It's Jackie Parker. I'm here to get my monkey."

"No, that only sounds a little dirty," Logan drawled.

"Hush up," I told him, fighting a smile.

"Make me," he pulled me against him and kissed me breathless, the way he'd been doing for the last hour. "I could get used to this," he murmured.

"Well don't," I said sourly, or as sourly as possible when I couldn't wipe the idiotic smile off my face. "This is happening much too fast."

He cupped my face in one hand. "By my reckoning, it's about a decade past due."

Kissing was as far as I was willing to take it until he coughed up some answers. As tempting as it was to strip off my easy access dress and engage in the horizontal mambo, there was too much unsaid between us, and the timing was off. I desperately wanted to ask about Corinne and where the freaking hell Logan had been for the last few months. How we would broach the subject with Luke, who wouldn't take this change in our relationship well.

But when he looked at me that way and my heart raced, I could almost believe answers were overrated.

I thought about how close we'd been to missing this and my eyes burned.

"What?" Logan asked. "What's wrong?"

"It's nothing—" I began, but he covered my mouth with his hand, careful not to upset me but I was effectively silenced.

He shook his head. "Don't lie to me, Jackie. This won't work if you lie to me."

I shoved him. "Well, it's nothing I want to get into on Gertie's front porch anyway. Jeez, let a girl finish her thought."

He conceded but there was a warning on his face. "I mean it, you can't lie to me. You're not the only one taking a terrible chance here."

I opened my mouth to tell him that I was risking my company, my living situation, my amicable divorce and the acceptance of the extended family I'd cherished as long as I'd known them, but the door opened and Gertie poked her head out. "Who are you?"

"Jackie Parker," I reminded her. "Marcy's friend."

Marcy's sister would never have been a great beauty, even if she had been "all there" mentally. She had a long neck that was more whooping crane than swan, a high forehead and a nose that could have given painter Marv a run for his money. Her eyes were small and she had a pinched mouth that never smiled. She'd answered the door wearing everything from Christmas Lights to Post-it notes, although blessedly, it was usually over her clothes.

Today though she looked truly bizarre. Her lank brown

hair stood on end, and she was sweating buckets through her tan blouse and gray skirt.

I stepped forward, concerned. "Are you feeling all right?"

She swayed on her bare feet, another alarming sign, Gertie never went barefoot.

Logan reached past me to steady her. Normally Gertie would have freaked out, but she was familiar with Logan since the Dark Prince had pseudo dated her sister a few months ago. She must have gotten used to him because she didn't go freak out when he made contact.

"Better call Marcy," Logan said. "Let her know what's going on."

"We don't even know what's up," I pointed out. "Or where my monkey is. Gertie, we're coming inside, okay?"

She didn't protest, an alarming feat. Marcy was the only person she ever allowed to enter her home. Marcy had once hired a cleaning lady to help her sister keep up with day to day chores, but that had lasted all of one visit before Gertie became so upset she threw a vase at the poor woman. Now Marcy stopped in whenever she could and cleaned Gertie's house.

The place wasn't in any great shape. Unopened mail piled on the floor of the entryway, presumably where the letter slot dumped them. I scooped the envelopes while Logan urged Gertie down the hall to her small and cluttered living room.

"It's dark in here." I reached for a light switch and nothing happened. "Damn, must have blown a bulb.

"Sit down." Logan urged Gertie. Once she was in place he took her pulse, then rose to face me. "Her heart rate is slow and her eyes are glassy. Do you think she'd let me examine her more closely? I don't want to risk freaking her out, but I think she's on something."

My brows went up. "You mean she's high?"

"Could be an overdose of an OTC."

But I was shaking my head. "Marcy doesn't keep anything like that around here, just Gertie's regular meds. Let me ask her, you go check the bathroom. And find Abu, I'm worried that I don't hear him."

Logan headed down the hall to the bathroom while I knelt in front of her.

"Gertie, it's Jackie Parker. Did you take something? Cold medicine maybe?"

Her eyelids drooped and her head lolled up against the couch. She mumbled something that I couldn't make out.

Screw it, I was calling Marcy.

My friend picked up on the first ring. "Jackie? Listen, can I call you back? I'm in the middle of something and—"

I didn't wait for her to finish. "I'm at Gertie's and something's wrong, Marcy. Logan thinks she might be on something. She's really out of it and her pulse is too slow. Do you want me to call an ambulance or try to take her to the hospital myself?"

Marcy's tone changed at once. "No, I'll call them. They'll probably have to sedate her to get her out of the house. Stay with her, I'll be there as soon as I can."

I'd just hung up when there was a screech and a crash and Abu bolted down the hall, proceeding a slew of colorful epithets. Spying me, the monkey scrambled over the coffee table and onto my face like a furry little alien. He was shaking and didn't smell too good, which made me choke and wheeze.

"He frigging bit me," Logan had a towel wrapped around his hand. "The little bastard bit me. Tell me he's had all of his shots."

I pulled the terrified monkey off so I could suck in air and obediently said, "He's had all his shots."

Logan narrowed his eyes. "You're lying."

"No really, he's had everything my vet recommends, though you might want to get a tetanus booster anyway. What did you do to him?"

"Me? Why do you assume I did anything?"

"Because he's never bitten anybody before."

Logan glared at me.

"What? I'm serious. He's thrown tantrums and made messes but he doesn't bite. Where was he?"

"Locked in the bathroom, covered in his own shit and half-crazed." Logan held up an empty prescription pill bottle. "Along with this."

I stood up and took the bottle from him. "This is a sleeping pill isn't it?"

"Yeah, and it's someone else's, someone named Rupert Dunn. Ring any bells?"

I shook my head. "You'd have to ask Marcy to be sure but Gertie's a shut-in, so she doesn't exactly have much of a social circle."

His gaze went to Gertie a moment and then refocused on me. "Do you think she tried to commit suicide?"

The thought was so shocking that I sat there, completely stunned for a minute. "I don't know."

He moved closer to me but paused when Abu screeched in warning. "Did you get through to Marcy?"

Despite the filth, I petted Abu, trying to calm him. "She's on her way. What should we do for her?"

"There was vomit in the bathroom, though no way to tell if it was her or Abu. If she sicked it all up, there's a good chance she'll be all right."

"Was there banana in it?" It was a stupid question to ask. Of course, that had never stopped me before.

Logan gave me a droll look. "I didn't examine it that closely."

Setting Abu aside with an admonishment that he be a

good boy, I turned to face Gertie. "Hey, Gertie. Can you hear me? Did you throw up earlier?"

Gertie didn't respond, her head lolling.

"Gertie!" I shouted, starting to panic. "Wake up, damn it."

I shook her again, more vigorously and then she did throw up.

All over me.

"One less thing to worry about," Logan added helpfully.

MARCY ARRIVED while I was in the shower with the EMT's hot on her heels. Between the shit covered monkey and the vomit, there was no hope of saving my cute little sundress that Logan hated so much. I was both shorter and rounder than Gertie and it took me a while to find clothing that fit. Finally, I settled on a pair of pink sweats that had the word juicy written on the backside and a black tank top with one of those built-in bra things. I couldn't ever remember seeing Gertie wearing such clothes and didn't figure she'd miss 'em.

The EMTs debated the wisdom of sedating Gertie in case she panicked but in the end decided the risk was too great to put anything else in her system.

"Will you guys lock up for me?" Marcy asked as we followed Gertie's gurney out into the yard.

"Of course." I took her keys from her. "Hey Marcy, do you know anyone by the name of Rupert Dunn?"

"What? No, why?" My friend was understandably distracted, her eyes on her sister.

Logan handed her the pill bottle. "We think this is what she took and the prescription belongs to a Rupert Dunn."

Marcy looked at the bottle quickly, then did a double-take. "That's not hers."

Logan took it back from her and then went to show it to the EMT.

"She'll be all right. Call me when you need to be picked up from the hospital." I told my fretting bestie.

She didn't answer, all her focus on her sister.

I watched the ambulance drive off, then looked to Logan. "So how did Gertie get the pills?"

He bounced the bottle in his hand a few times. "Maybe it was an accident at the pharmacy. Marcy might not have noticed when she dropped them off."

I shook my head. "That still doesn't explain why Gertie took them all. And don't say suicide, she was fine when I dropped Abu off here yesterday morning. Well, fine for Gertie." I turned back toward the house.

"Can't argue with that," Logan slapped my backside, making me jump.

"What the hell?" I yelped.

"You are juicy. Juicy and sweet like a ripe peach."

I stared at him. "Are you high?" Had he not been present for the last days' worth of drama?

His wicked smile sobered a little. "I'm happy, okay? Sue me."

He was too, I realized with a start. Logan Parker was happy, happier than I'd seen him in ten years.

And I'd made him that way.

I had to brace myself on the porch steps. "Being with me really makes you happy, doesn't it?"

"You're just figuring this out?" Logan asked with a raised eyebrow.

I shook my head, unable to put my feelings into words.

His incandescence faded a bit. "I really don't like the look on your face. Talk to me, Jackie. Please."

I looked up at him, right into his eyes and admitted the honest truth. "You terrify me."

He didn't seem shocked, just asked. "And why is that?"

I almost said something snotty, asked if he was a psychiatrist now in addition to being a medic. But we were past those sorts of veiled quips, weren't we? He'd asked for honesty, so honesty he would get.

"Seeing this sudden transformation in you, I'm not used to it. I mean, I'm glad you're happy but…. It feels major. Like I'm the key to your happiness."

He didn't say anything and I shifted nervously.

"That's not true, is it? You've been happy before this, just not around me, right? Because I always thought I made you miserable."

That seemed fairer somehow as being around him had always made me miserable. Of course, most of that was my guilt over harboring feelings for him like a fugitive from justice right under Luke's nose.

He didn't look away, brave man. "And what if I said no, that I haven't been happy without you, that I *can't* be happy without you. What would that change?"

Everything. Nothing. I didn't know, all I did know was it was too much responsibility for me to tackle. "Logan,"

He kissed me then, effectively shutting me up. "Relax and try not to overthink this."

I snorted. "Have you met me? I overthink everything."

He glowered. "Jackie, it's okay, you don't need to do anything. Just be. That's enough for me."

"That makes no sense." I wasn't fishing for a compliment, just truly wanting to know.

He laughed then. "You don't get it, not yet. But you will. Eventually."

"Promises promises," I muttered, turning back to the house. He swatted the other cheek for good measure but I was determined not to react.

Abu was sitting at the kitchen table eating a banana. He

chittered at me in a nasty tone, letting his displeasure over my abandonment be known.

"Yes, I know and I'm sorry," I spoke in the soothing voice that he responded to the best. "But you still can't go around biting people."

More chittering.

"Nope, not even Uncle Logan." That was my job. "Now say you're sorry."

Abu turned to face Logan. Truthfully, I had no idea if the monkey actually understood me or not, but I kept talking to him like he did out of habit. He made a small mewling noise and held out one hand.

"Don't do it again." Logan admonished, playing the game alongside me. "You do and you're history, pal."

Abu shook his head forcefully then climbed up Logan's shoulder.

"So now what?" Logan asked me, staring around Gertie's kitchen.

"I'm really not sure." I sat down at the battered farm table. "You probably want to go see your dad, huh?"

And Corrine. I tagged on silently. He still had to break up with his flipping fiancée.

Logan sat across from me, rolling the empty pill bottle between his palms. "Honestly? I'd rather find out who Rupert Dunn is and how Gertie got a hold of his medication."

I had my phone out and was scrolling through the contacts for our favorite detective's number when Logan took it from me.

"Hey," I said, reaching to snatch it back. "Use your own phone."

"I went over my data again this month." His eyes were locked on the screen.

"So did I," I complained taking another swipe at it. Stupid cell phone plans. "Give that back."

I was about thirty seconds from launching myself across the table at him when he spun the phone around so I could see the screen.

It was a local news website and the headline read, pharmacy break-in. The date was from yesterday morning.

I took the phone, skimming the article. "Where did you find this?"

"I googled the pharmacy on the prescription bottle."

"So you think the break-in has to do with Gertie's screw up?"

"Look at what else was listed as taken."

I went back over the list. It was long and I didn't know what half the medications were for. Glancing up I shook my head. "I don't get it."

He pointed at the screen. "Right there. Those are some heavy-duty pain killers. Possibly enough to perform illegal surgery."

My head snapped up. "You think whoever knocked over the pharmacy is linked to the organ pirates?"

"It's a possibility, isn't it? One worth mentioning to Sargent Vasquez."

I handed the phone back to him. "You call him."

"Why me?" Logan asked.

I made a sound. "Because he doesn't take me seriously anymore. He thinks I'm a crackpot."

Logan grinned. "If it walks like a duck and quacks like a duck."

"Oh yeah, and what does it say about you, that you want to be with me even though you think I'm damaged goods?"

He sobered. "You aren't damaged, Jackie."

I didn't want to have this conversation with him, not now, hopefully not ever. "Make the call, I'm going to clean up a bit."

He caught my arm. "Listen to me, I'm not just blowing

smoke here. I know I've given you a hard time in the past, but I'm being straight when I tell you that you are one of the bravest, most resourceful people I've ever met. I admire the hell out of you and I do not, for one second, think you are broken."

"Just cracked?"

He shrugged. "Show me someone who isn't. Now, give this monkey a bath, he smells like rotting ass."

"Charming." I took Abu and left the room with a smile on my face.

Twenty minutes later, he opened the bathroom door and beheld chaos.

"He doesn't like baths?" Logan guessed as Abu made yet another bid for freedom.

"How could you tell?" I snagged him by the tail, a maneuver I never did unless I was desperate. "Well, this is what we have to do when you have poo fights with yourself. Looks like you lost that one by the way."

Abu splashed in protest, screeching and trying to free himself.

"Find me something to dry him with will you? He peed on all the towels."

"Of course he did," Logan slipped out and came back with a roll of paper towels.

"So, what did Vasquez say?"

"Not much, other than he would mention it to the detective in charge of the organ pirate case. Without knowing who knocked over the pharmacy, there isn't jack to go on."

Dry and thoroughly irate, Abu scampered down the hall while Logan and I tackled clean up. We set the house to rights and then loaded into the Big Black Truck with a pissed off monkey in the back.

"You know Gertie pretty well, right?" I asked Logan as he headed for home.

"Well enough. Why?"

"I was just wondering, do you think she'd take medicine from someone she didn't know?"

Logan considered the question for a minute. "No," he said after a time. "I really don't think so."

"Right, and we know it's not Marcy or either of us. Hell, I can barely get an invitation past the threshold and I've known her for years. So the question is, who does she trust enough to ask inside, take medicine from and follow his or her advice to down the bottle?"

"Is Marcy dating anyone?" Logan asked. "Most of her goodwill toward me was because she trusted Marcy's judgment."

"From what Marcy told me the other day, no one she'd bring home to meet her shut-in sister."

"You can always call Marcy and ask?" Logan took a turn a little fast and Abu slid across the seat, screaming in outrage.

"That's why you need to wear your seatbelt, little turd." I chastised my monkey and then turned back to Logan. "No, Marcy's got enough on her plate at the moment. I'll ask when she calls and asks for a ride home."

"Let me know if you want me to come with you," Logan said, taking my hand in his and lacing his fingers through mine.

Warmth rushed through me and at that moment I knew everything would be all right.

That feeling lasted until I slid out of the truck and a bullet whizzed past my head.

8

I stood there for a minute, stunned stupid, sure my fatigued mind was playing tricks on me.

"Jackie!" Logan bellowed, from the far side of the truck. "Get down!"

I did without question and went flat, just as another bullet pinged off the rear quarter panel inches from where I'd been standing.

Terror coursed through me. I screeched when something gripped my arm, but it was only Logan. He'd slithered under the truck and was attempting to drag me beneath it as well.

"Move, damn you!" he shouted, his eyes wild.

Startled out of my shock, I did as he told me, elbow crawling until my juicy backside was beneath the vehicle.

"Abu?" I asked.

"Still in the truck." Logan glanced out from our hiding spot. "Any idea where it was coming from?"

I was still getting my head around the fact that those were bullets being aimed at me. On purpose. Again.

There was a muttered oath, the slam of a car door and the squeal of tires as someone sped off.

"Stay here," Logan barked.

"Wait, where the hell do you think you're going?" I clutched his arm in a desperate attempt to keep him beside me.

He shook me off. "To see who it is. Get the plate number, if I can."

"Don't go!" I yelled, terrified for him. "What if the shooter is still out there?"

"Then he could be creeping up on us." Logan belly crawled out from beneath the driver's side.

"Last time I go out without my piece," I heard him mutter.

I squeezed my eyes shut and listened, my heartbeat so loud it drowned out all the noise around me. Still, the sound of a gunshot would pierce through even that erratic thudding.

There was a noise, that of a car door being opened, followed by the anxious chirping of a monkey. A moment later, Abu was thrust unceremoniously beneath the vehicle alongside me.

"Logan?" I asked cautiously.

"I'm getting the body armor, hang on a sec."

I hung, clutching the small furry body curled tightly into mine.

Seconds stretched into years, long ugly fretful years but an eon later, Logan made his way back under the vehicle, thrusting body armor at me.

"Are they gone?" I whispered.

"I think so but I'm not betting your life on it. Put this on."

"Did you get the plate number?" I asked.

He shook his head. "It was an old Dodge Charger from the seventies in an ugly green color. At least that's the car that went up on two wheels around the corner so I'm guessing that's our shooter."

"Should I call 911?" I asked, feeling stupid for not thinking of it sooner.

"No need, you hear that?" Logan jerked his head and I did hear the faint echo of sirens. "That was the craziest thing I ever saw. They were lying in wait and just opened fire. It's a damn good thing they have such shitty aim. Put that vest on, I didn't wrestle it out of there to use as a body pillow."

"But if they're gone," I began.

"I said *I think* they're gone," The Dark Prince corrected. "We have no idea who this shooter is or if there's more than one of them. They could be trying to lure you out."

Getting into body armor was challenging when a body was standing upright. Getting into body armor while lying flat on your stomach requires a contortionist act. I didn't complain, it gave me something to do other than dwell on the fact that someone had tried to kill me.

Logan had just finished strapping my vest in place when wheels appeared in front of us.

We exchanged glances. Tires wouldn't tell us if the vehicle belonged to the cops or the nutcase in the metallic green Charger. Doors opened and several sets of black shiny shoes appeared, surrounding the Big Black Truck.

"This is the police," an official-sounding voice called. "Come out with your hands above your heads."

"That's just what the bad guys would say," I hissed at Logan.

"The people in the car knew where we went," Logan muttered. "And they wouldn't come back with the police closing in."

His argument made sense and I nodded.

"We're unarmed!" Logan shouted.

"And we have a monkey!" I added

When Logan scowled at me I just shrugged. "I don't want them to think he's a rabid squirrel or anything."

Side by side, we inched our way out from under the vehicle.

I was about a third of the way out, hands first when someone gripped a hold of me, dragging me roughly forward. "Hey," I muttered, indignant at the rough treatment.

"Hands up!" the cop— and it was a cop, I recognized the patrol uniform— spun me around and pushed me against the truck.

"Jackie, don't struggle," Logan shouted.

I looked over my shoulder to see him spread legged, hands against the vehicle in a similar position beside me.

"I.D.?" The cop searching Logan asked.

"My wallet's in the truck. Jackie, where's your license?"

"In the house," I said pointing at my bungalow.

"Hands on the vehicle," my searcher snapped.

Another set of tires screeched to a halt and I heard Luke's voice. "What the hell is going on here? Hey, that's my wife!"

An officer moved to intercept him even as I was patted down on my juicy backside. "Technically his ex-wife, but yes, I live here."

The good thing about Logan having gone out unarmed, there were no weapons for the police to find and eventually they let us move away from the truck. Logan was still giving a point by point description of events when Luke made his way to my side.

"Ma'am, did you see the gunman?" The officer asked me.

Not one to hold grudges, I dusted off my borrowed sweats and muttered, "No. I didn't see anything other than my driveway, up close and personal like."

Luke's jaw dropped. "Someone shot at you guys? Here?"

I made a face. "Yeah, it's been a fairly eventful day." I'd have to bring him up to speed on the whole Gertie mess later. One crisis at a time.

"Any idea who would come after you?"

"I could give you a list," I said dryly. "But it might take a while."

"We're eviction specialists. In fact, there was a guy this morning…." He trailed off, frowning.

"I doubt Marv is up and moving around, let alone shooting at people." I jumped in. "He's probably whacked out on prescription pain medication in some hospital."

"I'm going to need a full name and address if you have one," the officer said. "Along with those of any other potential suspects."

"Like I said, it could take a while. Could I maybe drop it off at the station, later on?" I wanted to check in with Luke and Logan before I committed to a final list. Some of the tenants we dealt with were wacky, but having the police go door to door and rattle cages wouldn't endear us to anyone I named. The last thing I wanted to do was make our jobs any more difficult.

"Logan!" A woman's voice cried.

I frowned as Corinne ran up to Logan's side and wrapped her arms around him. "What happened? Was it—?"

She didn't have a chance to finish because Logan scooped her up in his arms and kissed the daylights out of her.

Logically I knew that Logan couldn't just kick Corinne to the curb. He wasn't the sort of boyfriend a woman loathed post-break-up, well discounting me at any rate. No, he was the one that got away, and when he broke a woman's heart, he at least left her with her dignity intact.

But he was with me now, damn it. We'd been there, on the verge of our something epic. I'd agreed and he'd agreed and we'd been on the edge, ready to leap. He wasn't supposed to kiss anyone else, even the fiancée who wasn't really his fiancée that he hadn't had a chance to dump.

And he really wasn't supposed to kiss her that way. Freaking endlessly.

One of the cops wolf-whistled and they finally broke apart. Corinne's big blue eyes were fastened on the Dark Prince as she struggled for composure. Logan didn't even look in my direction, was actually doing his level best to *avoid* my hawk-like stare. Something in my chest withered and died, something that had barely taken a breath, too precious and fragile to name but felt a hell of a lot like hope.

And I knew. Someone had just shot at me or at Logan or both of us. And Logan, being the big fool hero he was, was giving me space in case he was the target. Whatever his ruse was with Corrine, he obviously believed he needed to keep it up, for my sake and maybe for hers as well.

"Jackie?" Luke's hand was on my arm. "Are you all right?"

"No," I whispered. But what if he wasn't the target, what if I was? Being near him or Luke or anyone else I loved meant their lives were in danger. I needed to run, to hide somewhere where the Parker brothers wouldn't find me.

"Logan!" Luke hollered before I could stop him. "Come here! Jackie looks like she's going to keel over any second."

"I just need to lie down," I told him, pulling my arm free of his grip. Luke had already taken a bullet to protect me and married or not, I knew he'd do it again. My mind whirled too fast to make any concrete plans but some inner voice screamed at me that I needed to run, now before anyone got hurt.

"Wait," Logan called but I could feel him coming closer, could sense his presence the way I always could, like a prickle on the edge of awareness. I wanted to lean on him, to soak up his presence and just breathe him in now that I was free to do so, but I couldn't, not really.

I couldn't go in the house, they'd trap me in there and force me to talk, probably talk me out of leaving. I knew myself well enough to know I couldn't fight them both.

Bessie Mae pulled up to the curb in front of Logan's

bungalow and I could see Celeste behind the wheel. The passenger's side door opened and Marge emerged.

Luke was right beside me, Logan closing in fast. I bolted for Bessie Mae. I ignored the sounds of everyone calling my name and sprinted past Marge, shrieking at Celeste to go.

"What?" Celeste looked at me with wide eyes. "Jackie? What's going on?"

I slammed the door and locked it. "I have to get away. Drive, now."

She drove.

———

"Do you want to tell me what the hell is going on?" Celeste asked as we turned into a gas station.

"No." I checked the fuel gauge. It was still reading half a tank. "Keep going."

She pulled up to the pump and turned to face me. "Not until you tell me why we just fled from your house like it was a damn crime scene, complete with police."

I flinched. "Mom,"

"Don't you mom me, Jacqueline Louise Parker," she snapped, yanking the keys from the ignition.

"What are you doing?" I stared at the keys in her hand.

"Going to tinkle. And the keys are coming with me in case you have the bright idea to try and drive off without me. Now, do you have to go?"

"I'm not five years old," I complained. Bad enough she'd three named me. I couldn't remember the last time she'd done that but now she was inquiring into my bathroom habits?

"Fine, then you can just wait here and think about what story you're going to tell me next."

I glowered after her as she headed into the convenience

store, then knocked my head against the seat. So much for my great escape. We were only a few miles from the house and if any of the cops had it in their heads to chase us down, they'd be here at any moment.

Though I wasn't proud of it, the thought had occurred to me that I should ditch Celeste at a rest stop on my way out of town. I wasn't completely heartless, I'd leave her my cell phone so she could call Big John to pick her up. Plus, Logan probably had the stupid thing bugged anyway, meaning he'd find me if I kept it. I could pick up a disposable one at some point. And I should probably get my hands on some serious cash. I had no idea how long I would have to hide out, but using my credit cards would definitely get me caught.

How would I get the keys away from my mother? If she insisted on taking them with her every time she left me in the car, there wasn't much I could do. And if I told her the truth, she'd get stubborn and insist on hiding out with me. I huffed out a breath. Alone time with Celeste, that sounded like the fifth circle of hell.

Okay, so she knew I was running but didn't know from what or whom. And she had to sleep sometime. If she thought I was trusting her, maybe she'd let her guard down and I could sneak away in the dead of night.

I could see Celeste through the skanky windows of the convenience store. She was buying something. Cigarettes, tabloids, a fifth of vodka maybe. Encouraging her drinking wasn't something I wanted to do, but if she did decide to knock a few back, I'd have an easier time escaping. As plans went, it was particularly half-assed, but it was the best I had. Now, to convince her.

She came back to the car, handed me a diet ice tea and a package of cupcakes. When I frowned at her she shrugged. "You look pale. When was the last time you ate anything?"

"I have no clue," I admitted. "But I'm not hungry."

There, that was petulant enough. And it was true, my stomach twisted in knots.

"Eat it anyway," she snapped.

"Only if you agree to keep driving."

"To where, Jackie?"

"The nearest ATM. I need cash."

"Fine." She turned the engine over.

"Fine." I narrowed my eyes even as I ripped open the cellophane and picked up a cupcake. "You want one?"

"No, I went to lunch with Marge."

I blinked at her in surprise. "You got Marge to leave the hospital?"

"A diner across the street. She had the meatloaf special and I had a Cobb salad. The lettuce was wilted but it was still better than the hospital cafeteria."

I ate one cupcake and then opened the bottle of iced tea and took a swig. It was sweetened enough that it stood up to the snack and hit my bloodstream with an almost dizzying rush. "Logan's engaged."

Celeste glanced at me. "I don't think it's serious."

Neither did I, but I frowned at her anyway. "Why do you say that?"

She shrugged until her shoulders hit her pink plastic hoop earrings. "Just a hunch. Now, is that why you ran, because you found out Logan's supposedly engaged."

She'd never buy that, she knew me too well. So I had to stick as close to the truth as possible until she did buy into my B.S.

"He...kissed me," I admitted.

Celeste pulled up to a light and looked over at me. I didn't dare meet her scrutinizing gaze. "And now you're running from him."

"He's engaged!" I burst out, surprising myself with the vehemence that was so close to the surface. "I mean, he basically sticks me with an ultimatum, now or never and when I try to explain that I can't give him everything he wants the second he wants it he vanishes for months without a word and then gets himself a fiancée! Am I supposed to be *okay* with that?"

Celeste said nothing, though her lips compressed.

"He's been my dirty secret for the entirety of my marriage. And now, he intends for me to be his. All that crap about how all I have to do was be, he's got to be full of it, right? I mean, I thought we hadn't talked because everything happened so quickly, or maybe because we were savoring the moment and didn't want to dwell on the hard parts, like him breaking it off with Corinne and me telling Luke. I'm an idiot—there aren't going to *be* any hard parts, are there. He wants a secret affair, nothing more." The verbal diarrhea just kept rolling, I was really committed to this fib.

"Maybe you should talk—"

I waved my hand in a slicing motion. "Do not tell me to talk to him. Talking to him never helps because he omits things. Important things."

"Like what?" Celeste pulled into a bank parking lot. The ATM vestibule

was empty.

I should've gone and grabbed my cash. Instead, I turned to face her.

"What he's left out was that he has no intention of breaking off his engagement just because I've finally come to my supposed senses. Where does that leave me?" I thought back to that moment we'd shared at Christmas, the last moment I'd seen him face to face before yesterday.

I can't keep it up, Jackie. I'm not waiting anymore.

To my horror, tears pricked behind my eyes. "He'd meant it when he said he wasn't going to wait anymore. He's truly moved on from his feelings for me."

"No, he hasn't." My mother gripped my hand and squeezed. "Jackie, you're scared. It's all right. Really. Everything will work out if you just have a little bit of faith."

When I committed to a role, I went all in. I had to wipe very real tears from my lashes. "How can you even say that? Here I thought we'd gotten a second chance. Well, more like an eighty-seventh chance. He knows I still want him and he'll use me and discard me the same way he thought I did to him all those years ago. Revenge must be a dish best served a decade past its expiration date."

"Okay," My mother pulled me into a tight hug. "Here's what we'll do. You go in and get your money. We'll go stay someplace, a hotel maybe. And you can have a little downtime to think before you deal with him. Does that sound good, sweetheart?"

I sniffled and nodded. "It does."

"Good. Now hurry up before the bank closes."

I popped the car door and climbed out. "Thanks, Mom."

She grinned up at me. "Anytime. You're my girl."

I only felt like a little bit of a heel as I headed into the ATM vestibule. In the time it took me to work myself up to Celeste worthy drama two patrons had approached the machine an elderly woman and a short heavyset man who was sweating profusely. I turned and waved at Celeste, who waved back. The guilt grew and I turned away fast.

Okay so a plan, I needed a plan of what to do after I abandoned my mother. No, I couldn't think about that. It was for her own good because if I was a target, she would be too.

The sweaty guy was finished with his transaction and pushed his way through the glass doors and back out to the parking lot. The elderly woman leaned heavily on her walker as she approached the machine.

I pulled out my phone and checked the time. Ten to five. My sugar rush was wearing down and I was on the edge of crashing hardcore. I felt as though I'd been awake for a million years. And what the heck was taking the woman so long?

I glanced back to give Celeste another reassuring wave then did a double-take.

Bessie Mae was gone.

9

I forgot all about my pressing need for cash as I sprinted for the parking lot, dialing my mother's cell phone number as I ran.

"Please pick up," I begged as the phone rang in my ear. "Please, please be okay and answer the freaking phone."

"Hello?" Celeste chirped.

I didn't know if I was more relieved or murderous. "What the hell, Mom! Where are you?"

"Driving."

"Um, I think you forgot something. Like your only daughter!"

She laughed. She actually laughed. "I didn't forget you, baby, I left you there."

My jaw dropped open. "What?"

"Don't worry, the guys are on their way. I called Luke from the gas station and he filled me in."

As if on cue a truck turned into the bank parking lot.

A Big Black Truck.

"I can't believe you, you Judas!"

Celeste made a derisive noise. "Like you weren't looking

for some way to do the same exact thing to me. You're just riled that I beat you to it."

She had me there.

I wasn't startled when the doors popped open, nor at the two figures who approached me from either side. Of course, they were both here. Had I really expected they wouldn't be?

"Guys, I can't—" I began to back away.

"Shut up and get in the truck," Logan snarled.

"Bite me," I snapped back, in no mood for his shit.

"Jackie," Luke began, his voice more reasonable, less aggressive, as always.

"No, okay? Just no. I cannot deal with either one of you right now."

I started to laugh. It was far from an amused sound, tinged as it was with

notes of wild hysteria. They had me surrounded, in every sense of the word.

"Glad you find something funny about being on the run for your life," Logan glowered at me.

"Guys, it's not smart to stand out here in the open." Ever the marine, Luke scanned the area for potential threats. "Logan, get her to the truck and take her to the safe house."

I looked over at him and frowned. "Safehouse?"

He nodded. "You're right about one thing, you'll be safer out of town."

"We can't just all leave Marge and Gerald and Corrine."

"And maybe if you stuck around long enough, you could have heard the plan out. We don't have time now. You're coming with me." Logan stabbed a finger in my direction.

I told him exactly where he could go and what he could do with himself when he got there. I saw his eyes narrow, watched as he made the decision. I took off running.

Logically, I knew I didn't have a chance of outrunning him. Logan could still PT with men half his age and my idea of cardio was hot-footing it through the outlet mall. My only hope now was that someone would see him chasing me and call the police. I'd rather spend the night in jail than go anywhere with him. Hell, I'd rather tango with the gunman at this point.

I didn't even make it half a block before he scooped me up and threw me, none too gently, over his shoulder. I kicked and scratched, trying to force him to let go of me. He gave me a hearty swat on my juicy butt, and I screeched in outrage.

"Put me down Logan Parker or I swear—,"

He did put me down, but only to open the backdoor of the truck. "You'll what? Take off again for no good reason, put your life in danger and scare the hell out of me. Because you've already played that card today, babe. What else you got?"

"I'll scream," I threatened.

"And upset the kids?"

There was a small inquisitive sound and I looked into the truck to see Abu and Sasquatch settled in the backseat. My monkey was looking at me with large, frightened eyes that reflected my own feelings far too well.

"Damn it," I muttered, then climbed into the back of the truck. "For the record, holding my pets hostage is just low."

"No, I'm taking your pets to safety because your house is no longer secure. So, you still gonna act like a lunatic and run from me?"

"I don't want to go anywhere with you," I bitched.

"Tough. Fasten your seatbelt." Logan answered.

Grumbling, I did as he asked, then squawked as he grabbed my wrists. "What do you think you're doing?"

He didn't answer, but then again, it was obvious when he pulled the cable tie out and bound my wrists. I struggled but all I managed was to half choke myself with the seatbelt.

Sasquatch groaned at the upheaval and laid her head on my right leg.

After a satisfied nod, Logan shut us in and climbed into the front, inserted the key and turned the engine over.

Full dark was on final approach. My wrists chafed and I wished I'd used the bathroom at the gas station. Maybe then I could have stopped Celeste from betraying me as well as eased the pressure on my bladder. Hindsight really was 20/20. I glared at the back of Logan's head for a few miles, then sighed and asked, "Where are you taking me?"

He didn't answer.

"Logan?"

He turned on the radio, still ignoring me.

"I deserve to know where I'm being taken," I said.

His eyes met mine in the rearview mirror briefly before he refocused on the road. "Why, so you can make an escape attempt and keep trying to get yourself killed?"

"I wasn't—" I began but he turned up the radio louder, effectively drowning me out.

I shifted, trying to get comfortable, but given my position, secured by the lap and shoulder belt with my wrists tethered together, it was impossible. Within five miles, the leg with Sasquatch's giant head on it was fast asleep. Abu scrambled into the front to ride shotgun with my kidnapper. Logan reached out a hand and I saw Abu tap the Dark Prince's fist with his own, another traitor.

I stared out the window, watching the streetlights fly by. After a few more miles, he got onto U.S. Highway 1 and headed south. The Keys then, that was our destination. It was sad how easily he'd literally grabbed me off the street.

What if he'd been the organ pirate? Would the guy who'd carved that woman's kidney out and left her for dead had any more of a challenge than Logan had picking me up and spiriting me away?

A part of me whispered I should be grateful that it was the Parker brothers who'd found me first. That Celeste had done the smart thing and that it was probably better that Logan had bound me in the back of my own truck because now I couldn't make a wrong move.

I firmly told that part to shut its stupid mouth.

"WE'RE HERE," A male voice stroked my cheek in a soft lover-like way.

Still groggy from sleep, I smiled and then realized, to my horror that I'd been drooling. Mortified, I jerked awake with a start, only to be held captive by various restraints and the screaming protest of stiff muscles.

"Hold still," Logan grumbled, his tone so different than the sweet caress that I decided I must have dreamed it. He was turned around in the driver's seat, facing me, his eyes luminous in the dashboard light.

He gripped my wrists and there was a soft snick as he opened his pocket knife to saw through the tie. I hissed like a vampire blinded by the sun and moved my newly freed hands up to block the light. The motion made my arms ache and dislodged Sasquatch from her nap. "Damn it, give a girl a warning."

Again I was ignored as the Dark Prince turned back around and then popped the driver's side door. "Come on, Abu."

The monkey scrambled out and, not one to ever be left behind, Sasquatch rose upright and vaulted over the seat to get out.

Stiff and pissed off, I was tempted to lock myself in the truck out of spite. Two things stopped me. One, Logan had the keys and could let himself back in any old time he pleased and two, my bladder was about to burst.

Having my sleeping leg come back online was the worst, but I managed to pry my worn-out carcass out of the truck.

A crunch sounded as my feet hit a shell gravel drive and the ocean breeze lifted the hair off the back of my neck. The roaring of the Atlantic came from in front of me and I made out the outline of a tiny seaside modular house to my right, nestled in thick palm fronds and other foliage.

Taking a minute to stretch, I peered down at the beach, wondering where exactly we were and how long the Dark Prince was planning to keep me here. Luke had said he would be by later, but at the time, I'd thought Logan meant to take me to some sleazy motel to hide out. But the Keys…. It would take us hours to get back to Miami from here and I didn't even know which island in the archipelago we were on. If we were on Key West, well, no wonder the Dark Prince had left me alone.

There was a *woof* from somewhere down the beach and I squinted to make out the shape of a man and a large dog in the moonlight. Praying the house was unlocked, I moved stiffly towards it.

The steps were old and rickety and I tread carefully around the peeling paint. A lizard scudded by, making me jump and nearly wet myself. The screen door was unlocked and I let myself in with a creak of tired hinges.

The door opened into what I judged to be a kitchen. I slapped at the wall until my hand located an overhead light and I flipped it on, wincing at the fluorescent glow. The place was old, and not in a cute, restored to its original charm kinda old. No, it was a dilapidated structure with cracked linoleum and battered metal chairs topped with ripped and duct-taped vinyl cushions parked around a dented Formica table. The cabinets were that weird Mediterranean blue that screamed Florida even if most Floridians wouldn't have been caught dead with it in their own homes.

First things first. I ranged ahead and scouted the bathroom. It was also a little dingy around the edges, but clean enough for my purposes. When I went to wash my hands I noticed rust in the sink, but at least we had running water. The entire room was done in a coral pink, probably meant to look like the inside of a seashell, but in reality, turned out more like stomach lining. What the hell was it with Logan and pink anyhow? Did he work for Mary Kay on the side?

Catching sight of my reflection was one of the worst shocks of my life. Not only was I sore from head to toe, but I also looked like I'd been ridden hard and put up wet. My hair was in an impossible snarl that I had no way to fix and the borrowed tank was stained with mud from when I'd belly crawled beneath the truck. The sweats hadn't held up much better, covered as they were in grass stains and dog hair. Plus it was May in Florida and I didn't exactly smell like a bed of roses either.

I was sore and messy and pissed off at my abductor who had apparently abandoned his doting fiancée for the duration of my incarceration. Considering my reflection, I wondered why he would even bother. The screen door groaned again and I let out a slow breath, trying to decide whether to read him the riot act now or take a shower first.

Vanity won out and I stripped, then ripped the shower curtain back. A roach skittered out of whatever crevice he'd been moldering in. I shrieked.

The bathroom door burst open. "What's wrong?"

"Roach!" I hollered, slamming back into the vanity, pointing at the ugly pink tub.

"What? Where?" Logan scanned the bathroom.

"There!" I climbed up onto the sink and gestured frantically.

"That? Chrissakes, Jackie. From the way you screamed, I thought you were being attacked by mutant roach from Planet X and his adaptable laser cannon. You nearly gave me heart failure."

"Just kill it!" I pointed back at the tub where our uninvited houseguest skittered around, having himself a grand old time.

Logan's gaze didn't follow however, instead taking its time perusing my naked form. I did my best to preserve my modesty, covering all the private bits as best I could with my bare hands. They didn't do much good and all the towels were stacked on a shelf behind his cursed head.

Our gazes locked and he grinned. "What will you give me for it?"

My jaw dropped. "What?"

He shrugged. The bastard actually shrugged like my terror was no BFD. "I want to know what you'll give me for killing this roach. Otherwise, I figure I'll just let him be."

"Are you cracked, Logan Parker?" I did not like the way he was looking at me, craning his neck to see what parts were visible in the small mirror behind me.

He lifted one booted foot over the lip of the tub and waggled his eyebrows. "Your call, hotshot."

I was a Floridian by birth, bugs were part of the program. It was just one little roach. My sandals were over by the door, I could just slip them on and kill it myself.

But that would require me walking past Logan in the raw, bending down...

I could ask him to leave. But the jut to his chin confirmed the suspicion that he wasn't going anywhere. At least not until he got what he wanted.

But what *did* he want? Sexual favors were out, but what did men want other than sex and sole possession of the remote control? "I'll cook for you."

Blue eyes twinkled and his lips twitched. "Trying to kill me now, huh? Think I'll pass."

"Well, what the hell do you want? I'm not about to whore myself for a bug."

He set his foot down, a good seven inches from the roach. "I want to know why you took off like an idiot. I want to know why you put yourself in danger after someone shot at you and I want to know how the hell, after pulling all that, you get off being angry with me!"

That last rattled the horizontal windows in their aluminum frames.

I inhaled and closed my eyes. "That's worth more than one roach."

"Don't you think I have enough going on?" Logan asked quietly. "With my dad and this threat against your life. You've been jerking me around since the day we met Jackie so just do me a favor and cut the crap already. I thought we were getting somewhere and then you rabbited on me. Was it Luke? Were you feeling guilty again?"

Wordlessly, I shook my head.

"Then why? Why would you do something so stupid? If Celeste hadn't called us, we might not have found you in time. Did you even stop to think what that would do to me or to Luke, to find you gutted in a bathtub?"

"Luke and I aren't married anymore." It was the only thing I could think to say and I could tell the moment the words passed my lips it was the wrong thing.

Logan stared at me for a beat, unwavering. Then his eyes narrowed to blue slits. "Do you think that means he doesn't give a shit what happens to you? Wake the hell up, Jackie. He's still in love with you. I should know the signs, having been afflicted with the same disease all my life."

I forgot about the roach, my nudity, everything but the words still lingering off the pink tiled walls. "You're calling me a disease, really? You and Luke both caught me like I'm the freaking flu? Guess what pal, I never *asked* for this, never wanted it. Luke was my frigging hero, he believed in me, offered me a better way to live. And in case you've forgotten, I had no idea he was your brother when I agreed to marry him!"

With each sentiment, I'd stepped closer to him until I could've poked him in the chest. He bent down, lowering his thunderous face to mine, filling my vision, drowning everything else out.

"So you're the victim here? Don't pretend that you didn't know before you married him. I was there when you made your announcement."

"He was deploying the next day! What should I have done, said, oh, by the way, I had a one-night-stand with your brother so my bad, I can't marry you? Should I have sent him off to war with a broken heart after he'd been nothing but good to me?"

"Stop using Luke as an excuse," he thundered. "You ran from me and have been hiding behind him ever since."

"No, I've been living my life and you're just bitter because you didn't have the guts to do the same. So don't you stand there and tell me that I don't know what I've done to Luke when what you're really crucifying me for is what I've done to you!"

He was breathing hard, we both were. After a moment he turned his head toward the bathtub he half stood in. He shifted and there was a crunch as the roach was squashed beneath his boot.

"No Jackie," he said, all the anger gone from his voice, his posture defeated. "I'm crucifying you for what you've done to us. And my heart is right there on the cross next to you."

He turned and left the bathroom without another word.

10

After my shower, I wrapped myself in a pink towel and used another to turban my wet hair. The towels were thin and scratchy but they were better than climbing back into the grubby sweats. There hadn't been any toiletries beyond a bar of generic soap in the bathroom, but at least I was cleaner than I had been.

On the outside at least.

Picking up my discarded clothes, I opened the bathroom door and poked my head out. Logan's voice came from the kitchen. He must be on the phone. I headed down the other direction, toward the bedrooms.

There were only two of them, one with a king-sized bed, the other with two twins. This place must be a rental, though as far as rentals went, I'd stayed in better. I went into the one with the king and spotted Abu sleeping curled up on the pillow. Poor guy was worn out.

There was a black duffle bag resting on top of the wicker hamper. I moved to it and started going through its contents. The clothes were obviously Logan's, but I was surprised by the amount of them. It looked like he had two weeks' worth of duds at least. Was he really planning to keep me here that long?

Figuring he could stand to spare a shirt, I extracted a t-shirt and pulled it over my head. It was a mistake, the cotton had absorbed his scent that ranged somewhere between new leather and fresh air and I leaned against the wall as all the memories from our earlier kisses assaulted me.

The scratchiness of his stubble, the softness of his lips. The way his hair slipped through my fingers, the hot hardness of his body pressing into mine. The way he whispered my name.

Damn it, what the hell was wrong with me for still wanting him? Not just because of the way he talked to me earlier, though that should have been reason enough. No, because of the promises he'd made and then dashed.

Fiancée, he had a flipping fiancée. I needed to keep that thought forefront in my brain. He claimed he had no intention of marrying Corrine but he had yet to explain why he wanted everyone to think they were engaged? What possible purpose could it serve? There was no way I would ever be okay with being the other woman, not to Logan or any man. I was enraged that he acted like the wronged party when he was planning to double-dip at the earliest opportunity. *Dark Prince, evil, don't go there, Jackie.*

Snatching a pair of boxers out of the bag, I stabbed my legs into them. Then I lifted his bag and set it out in the hall. That way he couldn't accuse me of sending mixed messages. I shut and locked the door and climbed into bed.

The sheets weren't much better than the towel and it took all my efforts not to think of roaches and other bugs scrambling about the place. Where in the sweet by and by had Logan taken me and how long was he planning to keep me here? And more importantly, could I expect more emotional evisceration with every encounter? He knew just how to wound me, what words to hurl at me so that I'd sit and stew for days, feeling like the most awful person ever to draw breath.

The sound of footsteps drawing closer pulled me back to my current situation. Logan paused outside the door and I wondered if he was coming to apologize or was ready for round two. I just wasn't up to his full fighting weight tonight so I said nothing.

After a long pause, he tapped on the door. "Jackie?"

"Go away," I mumbled.

"I just thought you'd like to know, Dad's doing all right. They've moved him out of ICU. He will be able to go home in a couple of days."

"I'm glad," I said because I was, for Gerald, Marge and Luke. And even Logan. I had no idea who my father was but I knew how close the Parker men were and I'd seen his reaction in the hospital. The thought of losing his father terrified him. He should be there with all of them though, not farting around in the Keys with me.

Another pause. "Are you hungry? There's sandwich stuff and eggs. I could make us an omelet or—"

"I'm fine," I called loud enough to be sure he heard me through the door. The last thing I wanted to do was sit down and share a meal with him.

"Can we just talk?" he asked.

I rolled onto my back. "There's not much left to be said."

He tried the door, I could hear the knob rattling. "Damn it, that's my room. Let me in."

"Why? So we can name call and hurl accusations at each other some more?" I was pretty sure we'd been punted off at the last stop of the No Hope Express. "Not interested."

"No, that's not—," he broke off and took an audible breath "I just…."

I waited for him to finish the statement, but he never did.

Instead, his footsteps headed back down the hall, leaving me to brood.

Celeste had pulled some doozies on me over the years but handing me over to Logan like a piece of freight topped the charts. She, of all people, knew how I felt about him. Okay, so maybe I'd gone a little overboard on the drama, but like mother like daughter, right?

Wide awake now, I stared at the cracked tile ceiling, my heart racing for no good reason as I wondered what he'd wanted. Earlier he'd said he'd wanted answers, but I knew there was more to it. Logan Parker wanted acceptance, the same acceptance I'd been giving Luke unconditionally since the day we met.

But it was easy for me to accept Luke. He was a simple guy and he didn't make me feel as though someone had stuffed a hot poker down my throat and stirred my innards the way Logan did. Luke had been my easy answer, the one that made sense.

But had it?

My marriage was over, my fairy tale ending nowhere in sight. I had loved Luke but it hadn't been enough. As much affection and caring as we shared, we'd been like two puzzle pieces that someone—namely me—kept forcing together. And what Logan wanted from me….

He wanted it all. Maybe more than I had to give.

I frowned. Although when had he ever asked me for much of anything? He'd worn me down about telling Luke the truth, had even threatened to do it himself. But that had been the right thing to do, hadn't it? He'd watched over me for years without my knowing, had told me a truth I hadn't been ready to face.

Luke thought I walked on water, believed I was good at everything and looked to me to fix everything. I liked the Jackie he saw when he looked at me.

But Logan saw me as I was— scared, vulnerable, messed-up, damaged Jackie. The girl from the trailer park who'd been forced to grow up much too soon, who made colossal mistakes.

And he still wanted me.

But not for everything, I remembered viciously. I wasn't going to be enough for him, that's why he'd gone off and gotten himself a freaking fiancée.

Who he'd abandoned tonight to come after me.

The room was stifling and I kicked off the covers. Abu snored. I rolled onto my side and caught a whiff of Logan.

Logan, who should be with his family tonight, celebrating the fact that his father had pulled through major surgery. Damn it, I refused to feel guilty. I hadn't asked to be freaking abducted and driven to the ass-end of nowhere. I was going to do that all by myself. But the heat wasn't coming from anger anymore. No, now it felt more like shame.

It had been stupid to just take off the way I had. I'd still been in a state of shock when I'd left. Someone had just shot at us but I didn't stop long enough to consider the consequences of my actions. Or who would have been hurt if I'd died.

So he had a point. Well, technically more than one. But was it right or fair of him to ask me to be his mistress?

Although, I guess he hadn't. I jumped to the conclusion but the truth was I didn't know a damn thing about his relationship with Corinne. And the only way I was going to find out was to ask him.

But not tonight. No, tonight I needed to do something else.

Rising from the bed, I tiptoed to the door. Leaving it open a crack in case Abu woke up—though I doubted very much that he could make the dump look much worse than it already did—I didn't want him fretting that he'd been locked in again.

The light was still on in the kitchen but there was no sign of the Dark Prince. I poked my head into the living room that sported an honest-to-God rabbit-eared television, a couple of wicker chairs with faded blue cushions and not much else. The bathroom door stood ajar and there was no one in the second bedroom. For a moment I wondered if he'd gone for another walk on the beach but then I heard the click of dog nails on the small front porch.

Logan was sitting on the steps, a beer in one hand and the other on Sasquatch's head. She was circling him in that persistent way of hers, stick dangling from her mouth, doggy language for *get up and play with me, idiot*.

"She's restless," I told Logan. "Too much time cooped up. She needs to burn some energy."

He glanced at me over his shoulder, taking in my outfit from mussed hair to bare feet but didn't comment.

I hadn't thought I'd need shoes when I started my search and I didn't want to leave the relative safety of the porch. Instead, I sat down beside Logan and took the stick from my dog and gave it a toss.

"You throw like a girl," the Dark Prince said and took a swig from his beer and extended it to me.

"I am a girl." I took the bottle and drained it.

Sasquatch came back and dropped her stick on Logan's lap. He chucked it much further than I had and she loped after it with joy.

"Showoff," I handed him back the empty bottle.

He took it, peered inside, then set it down without comment.

I lifted my hand, paused, set it back on my thigh. Sasquatch brought her prize back and I threw it again. This time she laid down to chew it, probably sick of our half-assed efforts. I lifted my hand again and did the hardest thing I'd ever done.

I laced my fingers through Logan's. "I'm sorry I ran. And I'm glad your Dad's going to be okay."

He didn't squeeze my hand reassuringly but neither did he try to pull away. That was better than I'd expected at least. Probably better than I deserved.

"I think about that night all the time," he whispered after a while. "I wonder what I could have done differently, what I could have said so that you wouldn't have run."

"Stop," I whispered. "Please. Let's sit here and not fight, just for tonight. Okay?"

I could sense him turning to look at me but I stared straight ahead. At last, he murmured, "Okay."

I put my head on his shoulder and closed my eyes. "Okay."

THE WALK OF SHAME, it's called. That trek home the morning after you've spent the night with someone and need to sneak back to your life, hoping the whole world doesn't know what you're up to but fearing they do. What in the misty moonlight seemed beautiful or even fated looks like hell in the harsh glare of the bright morning sun.

I'd seen the after-effects of the walk of shame all my life. Celeste stumbling in wearing last night's makeup, sporting a brand spanking new hangover, exhausted and emotionally wrecked. When I woke up in a strange bed, my first thought was that Celeste would be waiting for me, ready to point at me and laugh, possibly saying something about how the mighty had fallen. Which proved how disoriented I was, because my mother didn't talk like that.

Gradually I became aware that I wasn't hungover, not the way I'd deserved to be after countless vodka cranberries. No, my fogginess came from the fact that I was in an unfamiliar bed with an unfamiliar man sleeping next to me.

Man. Holy green guacamole, I was in bed with a man. Odds were that it was his bed. As far as beds went it was pretty nice, with mocha and blue striped sheets and a comfortable duvet, which up until five minutes ago I'd been hogging. My bunkmate, whose name kept darting away like fish underwater, rolled over.

Nature was calling and my mouth felt like the inside of an open sewer. Squinting into the unfamiliar space I spied a door at the far end of the room which I hoped to God was a bathroom. If not, I'd be relieving myself in a stranger's closet.

Luck was on my side, it was a bathroom. With my basic needs seen to, I turned on the hot water in the sink and washed my hands. It was obvious from the lack of cosmetics on the counter that the bathroom's owner was a single man. Nothing but a still wrapped cake of soap and a roll of paper towels on the toilet tank. Nothing frilly or lacey or even very useful. I unwrapped the soap and then lathered my face, washing away all traces of makeup.

Even clean, I wasn't quite ready to look myself in the eye yet. I dodged my reflection in the mirror by opening up the medicine cabinet. Toothbrush, toothpaste, mouthwash. No antibiotics or any prescription medications and an unopened box of condoms. I picked the box up and frowned. Unopened wasn't a good sign. I wasn't on birth control. Either my bunkmate in there had another box of condoms stashed in the bedroom or the anonymous sex I couldn't remember was even more disastrous than I'd believed.

The odd thing was though, nothing felt any different down there. And I was still dressed. Well, mostly dressed. My bra was MIA, but I had panties on. So what did that mean? I mulled it over as I used his toothbrush—I was pretty sure we'd done a little kissing at least—and gargled with mouthwash.

Out of hygienic tasks, I stowed the mouthwash, took a deep breath and closed the cabinet, lifting my gaze to the mirror. I tilted my head, turned it to the left, then to the right. It was still me. And oddly, I didn't feel any shame. Nothing made sense, though a few images were coming back to me from the night before. Dancing, I remember dancing in some of the clubs, and had there been a moonlit stroll in there? I needed a better look at the man with the nice duvet.

I padded back into the bedroom and stared down at the guy. "At least you're hot," I muttered, taking in the thick jet eyebrows, and long dark lashes, the perfect cheekbones that could have been carved from granite. "It'd be terrible if my first walk of shame was on account of some troll."

Lids lifted and blue eyes flashed open and he grinned. Hot may have been an understatement. When this guy smiled angels wept. "Thanks."

"You're awake," I stated flatly, feeling like an idiot.

"I am." He made no move to get up for which I was both grateful and dismayed. Had I really been blackout drunk the night before? That had been my intention when I'd left but seemed stupid now that I couldn't remember his name, where we were or what we'd done in that bed that left the pretty duvet in such a state.

Oh God, had we done it? Had I really carried my V card all these years just to get it punched by some—albeit hot— random guy whose name I couldn't remember?

Said guy cleared his throat. "How are you feeling?"

"Ridiculous," I mumbled before I thought better of it. Heat crept up my face. Stupid pre-coffee brain.

That grin flashed again. "I meant your hangover."

"I don't think I have one." Condoms, had we used condoms the night before? I surreptitiously looked around for the telltale discarded wrappers. Nada. Either he was a neat freak and had had a 3 AM cleaning spree or we hadn't used anything. Damn it, when I made mistakes, I went for broke.

"What…?" I cleared my throat and tried again. "Did we….um…you know?"

He sat up and I got a little lost staring at his perfect upper body. Smooth tan skin, shoulders that looked like they could take on the weight of the world. The perfect amount of chest hair to prove he was a full-grown man but not enough that you started to think of the missing link. "I'm not sure that I do."

He was going to make me ask, I could tell from the wicked glint in his eyes that he knew exactly what I wanted to know but wasn't about to make it easy on me.

I lowered myself to the edge of the bed, wishing I could pull the covers over my flaming cheeks. "I'm a little foggy on the details," Understatement of the decade. "Did we do …it?"

One dark eyebrow rose. "It?"

I made an exasperated noise. "Sex, did we have sex?"

"So, so much sex," he deadpanned.

I stared at him, at his carefully neutral expression and watched as it crumbled into laughter. "You're messing with me."

"You should see your face," he wheezed and then collapsed flat on his back, the bed shaking in time to his amusement. "Oh shit, Jackie, I can't breathe."

I don't know where the impulse came from, but I gripped the pillow that still had a dent from my head and swung. Even I couldn't miss at that distance and I'd put some force behind it. It smacked him square across his perfect face.

His laughter cut off abruptly. "You did not just do that."

Part of me, the part that was horrified that I didn't know this man and had spent the night in his bed wanted to apologize. But instead, my chin jutted up and I smirked at him. "And just what are you gonna do about it?"

He launched himself at me. I didn't have time to brace as he grabbed a hold of me and his momentum rolled us off the bed and onto the floor. He landed on the bottom and his legs, clad in some of the ugliest pajama pants I had ever seen, wrapped around my waist. I was still dressed in my mother's trashy club clothes and the tank top had come untucked. Strong fingers tickled up along my ribs making me squirm and howl.

"Ask me for mercy," he paused, catching both of my flailing arms so I couldn't slug him the way I'd been trying to do. "Or I won't show you any."

"Never." I was breathing hard, and so was he. We were flush up against each other, pressed as close as two people could be who still wore clothes and as the spasms of laughter receded, new sensations swarmed up to take over.

"God, you're pretty," he breathed in such a way that I knew it wasn't a line. I heard the hot thing before, typically when guys, and a few girls, were focused on my chest. And even though said chest was only a glance away, he was looking into my eyes when he said it, his expression a little lost.

"So are you," I murmured.

"I'm going to kiss you now," he said and before I could make a quip about men who talked too much, he lowered his mouth to mine.

It started softly, sweetly, just a brush of lips, but I could tell he was holding back. The almost shy caress stole my breath and before I knew what I was doing, I'd opened my mouth inviting him in.

With a groan he accepted, the kiss turning from sweet to sinful, searing us together. His hold on my wrists relaxed. The hand that had been tickling my sides now wrapped around my back and calloused hands skimmed over bared flesh—a warm, reassuring hold. It was a slow, unhurried kiss, a patient building of heat and pressure. I may have been a virgin but I wasn't totally inexperienced and I knew what was happening between us was different than anything I'd ever felt before. And I wanted more.

My own greedy hands roved over his broad back, pulling him closer, needing to feel him with every cell I possessed. He tried to stop me, more than once and finally tore his mouth from mine. His breathing was heavy, ragged as though I'd been stealing all his oxygen. My own chest felt a little tight.

"You said you were a virgin."

Figures I would have burped up that little nugget of information. "I am." I was too busy trying to peel his god awful Florida Gators sleep pants off him to notice he'd stopped.

He sat up, caught my hands and kissed me. "There's no rush. We can wait."

"Speak for yourself," I grumbled and he laughed again, a pure, honest sound that filled all the cold places inside me.

He cupped my face in both of his big hands, his eyes hot and intense. "Promise me you aren't going to regret this later."

Growing up the way I did, a person develops certain skills early. Like lying. "I promise."

I snuck out while he was in the shower, though I paused by the front door long enough to pick up an unopened envelope. It was addressed to Logan Parker. The name made me shiver and I set the mail down and quickly hurried out. My one and only walk of shame, down to the bus stop and back to my trailer. I threw the clothes in the trash, took a shower and told myself that it didn't matter. He was just some guy. He'd move on and so would I. It's not like we were ever going to see each other again, not like I could bring him home to meet Celeste. Hell, she'd probably try to steal him like she had Greg Finn in high school.

The thing about lying though—it only works when you believe the lie to be the truth.

I could fool plenty of people, just not myself.

11

"So, what's on the agenda today?" I sipped my coffee and did my level best not to stare at Logan's butt.

"Agenda?" He expertly flipped a pancake.

I rested my chin on my hand and sighed, quietly so he wouldn't hear me. The man had mad culinary skills, among his arsenal of other talents. It really wasn't fair to set a newly single woman in his path and expect her not to ogle. Our tentative truce from the night before still held and by mutual agreement, neither of us had brought up the incident in the bathroom, the kisses or my disappearing act.

"Yeah, like what are we supposed to do here?"

He stacked the pancakes and added them to a plate, before turning and setting it in front of me. "We're not supposed to do anything except keep you hidden."

I was starving and the pancakes smelled amazing. "I know, but there has to be something to do here. I don't handle confinement well. It gives me too much time to think." Using the side of my fork, I cut my stack of pancakes into neat little triangles before dumping syrup over the top.

"You don't say," Logan's tone was dry as he turned back to the stove.

I took my first bite of pancakes and almost had an orgasm. "I mean it. I'm going to drive you insane if you don't give me something to do. Dear sweet baby Jesus and a bag of chips this is good."

He glanced at me over his shoulder. "Is that a threat?"

I stabbed another forkful of ambrosia. "It's a promise. And trust me, I don't want to do it, you are my cook after all. Without you, Abu and I will starve."

"Good to know I have some leverage." Logan set his own plate on the table and glanced at the empty plate beside me. "Speaking of Abu, where is he?"

"In the living room, trying to get Curious George on T.V."

"I'm pretty sure that T.V. doesn't work." Logan dug into his own pancakes.

"Doesn't matter, it'll keep him busy." My plate cleaned, I sat back in my chair and studied my surroundings. "Whose place is this anyway?"

"My friend."

"Anyone I know?" I probed.

Logan thought about it for a beat and then shook his head. "I doubt it."

"So how come he's willing to let us stay here?" Even as rundown as the joint was, Logan's pal could have made a mint renting it.

"I've been coming here every few weeks to do a little work for him. In exchange he lets me stay here."

Huh, so this was where Logan had been taking off to whenever he disappeared. "What kind of work?"

He sighed and set his fork down. "Did anyone ever tell you that you ask a lot of questions?"

"Yes. So, is this where you met Corrine? And can we

expect her to show up anytime soon?" It might be a little awkward if I answered the door wearing Logan's underwear.

"No and no. Corrine is staying at my place in Miami."

"Uh, hu." I rose and maneuvered to the coffeepot. I wanted to ask more questions about Corrine, but I was actually more curious about the work Logan had mentioned. "So, this is where you've been hiding out when you disappear from Miami?"

"I haven't been hiding out."

I set the coffee pot down and turned to face him, hands on my hips. "What would you call it?"

He drummed his fingers on the tabletop. "Exploring alternative career options."

I didn't point out the lunacy of his doing that when he had one-third share in Damaged Goods Property Management. Luke had cut him a check faithfully every month, even when Logan took off for parts unknown.

Correction, when he took off for some fixer-upper in the Keys.

"So, how are those other options working out for you?" It wasn't meant to be a quip, though it did sound sort of sarcastic when I spoke the words out loud.

"Some better than others." Logan pushed his chair back and carried his plate to the sink. "If the Inquisition is over for now, I'd like to take a shower."

"I'll get the dishes."

One sardonic eyebrow lifted. "I won't come out here to find you impaled on a spatula, will I?"

I made a face at him then turned toward the sink, no dishwasher, the horror— and made a big to-do about running hot water and sudsing up my sponge.

After a moment I heard his footsteps retreat down the hall and then the bathroom door closed. I counted while washing the dishes and when I reached fifty, I tiptoed to the bathroom door. I could hear the shower running. Perfect.

First, I snagged his cell phone and dialed a familiar number. The call was picked up on the first ring. "Sargent Vasquez."

"It's Jackie."

"Jesus H. Christ, where are you? I heard that someone shot at you and Logan yesterday and then you took off like a bat outta hell. And whose phone is this?"

I debated which question to answer first. "I'm in the Keys. Logan kidnapped me."

A deliberate pause, then "Is this some fantasy role-playing thing?"

"I wish." The words slipped out. "Scratch that, I don't wish. He and Luke and my mom all decided I should fall off the map until you catch whoever the hell was shooting at us. And how's that going by the way?"

"Jackie, it's not my case—"

"Like you guys don't all gossip around the water cooler. Come on, Sargent, I need to know what's happening."

He sighed. "We don't have much yet. Ballistics are back but big surprise, the firearm it came from isn't in the database. We know it's a .45 but that doesn't narrow it down much considering the number of handguns in Miami. Now if you had someone we could question and see if he has a registered weapon that can fire a .45, that would help. Do you?"

"I piss people off on a daily basis, Sargent. They don't usually shoot at me though. Did you find out who the woman in the bathtub was yet?"

"Not my case." He said the words in a perfunctory matter, as if he knew saying so wouldn't make much difference.

"Come on, what are the odds that I find a woman who had her kidney's carved out and the next day someone shoots at me?"

"Not good," he admitted on a long-suffering sigh. "All right. We don't know who she is, but we have reason to believe she was an illegal immigrant and that perhaps she was there willingly."

"What?" I whispered.

He sighed. "I spoke with someone in vice who picked up a prostitute and she had a very interesting story to tell. Some guy offered her five thousand dollars for one of her kidneys. She turned him down because, and this is a direct quote, she thought he looked like a cop."

Chills ran up and down my spine. "Did she give you a description?"

"No. She clammed up and won't say another word until the D.A. agrees to

drop the solicitation charges. But she's the best lead we have for now."

"What else can I do to help?" I had an image of the man I'd spoken to in my head, maybe I could work with a police sketch artist. I'd always wanted to do that.

He grumbled something in Spanish too quickly for me to pick up then reverted back to English. "Exactly what you're doing, keep your head down and call me if you think of anything else. I have to go, Jackie."

"Wait!" but it was too late, the line went dead.

Blowing out a frustrated breath, I set the phone down and shivered. So, some guy who looked like a cop was offering hard-luck cases money for their organs. I drummed my fingers on the countertop. And how easy would it be for the aforementioned guy to decide that hey, he didn't actually need to pay the money and while they had the person help-less and vulnerable, why not take both kidneys, or heart or lungs like some sick all you can hoard buffet.

The room spun and I braced both arms on the countertop and took big gasping breaths. I had to find something to take my mind off the organ pirate, quickly. What though? I glanced around the unfamiliar surroundings. I'd been too emotionally drained the night before to think clearly. Or to do my characteristic snooping through Logan's bag. After he'd shut himself in the room with the twin beds I realized what an opportunity I'd missed in not going through his duffel when I'd had the chance. A situation I could totally remedy.

Abu was still futzing with the T.V. and Sasquatch had sprawled herself in front of the kitchen door, soaking up the early morning sunshine. Even if Logan was the fastest shower-taker on this side of the Mississippi, I had enough time for a quick peek.

With anyone else I might have felt a smidge guilty about invading their privacy, but Logan Parker routinely planted bugs in my bags, my clothes, my cars and if I wasn't extra careful, he'd probably sneak one where the sun didn't shine. Never mind he had abducted my sorry carcass. No, I had no regrets about snooping, none whatsoever.

Unless he caught me.

Creeping into his room, I left the door open so I could hear the sounds of the shower running. I started with the outside pouches, the perfect place to slip receipts, photographs, love letters, the token lock of hair. All I found was his iPod and a spare set of keys for the truck.

Moving on to the inner pouch, I shifted through t-shirts, jeans and cargo pants, underwear and socks, all folded with neat precision. No toiletry kit, but he'd probably taken that with him into the bathroom. So what had I learned? Logan wasn't an unpacker. I was, I unpacked even if I would only be at a place for five hours. Of course, this unplanned trip had left me with nothing *to* unpack. If I had more time I'd scroll through the iPod, just to see what sort of music he favored, but that would have to come later. The bag itself could have belonged to any large man who favored blue jeans and black t-shirts, not even a book or an e-reader to tell me what he was reading.

Perhaps the bag was new. He'd obviously been staying here and if not for my snagging the master bedroom, he might have kept some stuff in there. I zipped it and was about to tiptoe back to my room when I noticed his wallet on the nightstand. It wasn't the wallet that drew my attention though, only the corner of white poking out of the dark leather trifold.

Something that looked a lot like a letter.

Heart pounding, I was about to reach for it when I heard the water shut off in the bathroom. Crap, I didn't know if he planned to come out in a towel or if he'd dress in there, but I couldn't risk getting caught.

I crept like a supervillain back to my room and pressed the door shut, turning the lock for good measure. At least I could go through one room undisturbed.

A second glance told me there wasn't much to unearth. The closet held two extra pillows and a spare blanket and nothing else. The nightstand was an open table with a coral and blue alarm clock and a lamp. No drawers to stow personal stuff, no convenient hiding places anywhere.

Damn, I should have snagged the letter when I'd had the chance. I wondered who it was from. Corrine? Or maybe one of his other admirers. Hell, for all I knew it wasn't a letter at all. It could have been an invoice or a shopping list or any one of a million other things.

Logan rapped smartly on the door to my room, causing me to jump. "What?" I snapped.

"Can I come in?"

I gave the room one more cursory once over. My snooping had turned up diddly freaking squat. I shuffled toward the door and unlocked it.

He studied my face for a long moment and I shifted, uncomfortable. "What?"

He shook his head. "Nothing."

Well, that was a flat out lie. Of course there was something behind the look. I knew better than to dig for it. "What's up?"

"I thought since you're so desperate to do something, we could maybe track down the jenkem tenant. You know, the one who lived in the apartment before the organ pirates snuck in?"

I stared at him, surprised. "But won't that be, you know, a little counterproductive to the whole hiding out thing?"

"We're not going to leave, just to track him down. If we find him, we'll turn him over to the police."

I raised an eyebrow. "If the police haven't found him yet, what makes you think we can?"

He gave me a sardonic look. "Do you have a better idea?"

I really didn't. "Okay then, I'm going to need a laptop and a phone to use as a hotspot. Unless this dump has wifi?" I looked at him hopefully.

"No wifi," he sighed and scrubbed a hand over his face. "My phone bill is going up faster than the national debt."

"Maybe I could sell part of my liver." I grimaced, the joke in poor taste even if we weren't hunting organ pirates.

Logan peeked at me over his hand. "Really? You think someone would actually *want* your liver?"

"You have a point. It's borderline pickled." I followed him down the hall to the living room where he'd stowed his laptop. He set it on the coffee table and then punched in his password too quickly for me to see. One of the generic background screens came up, just yellow stripes on a darker yellow background.

"It'll take me a little while to access our files. You don't remember the guy's name offhand, do you?"

"His name wasn't the most memorable thing about him," Logan muttered.

He was right there. While the details of the former tenant were blurry, I could still envision his pathetic dive for a fermenting bucket of his own waste. "If memory serves, he was Latino."

Logan made a rude noise. "This is south Florida, that doesn't exactly narrow it down."

After hooking the laptop to the wifi from Logan's phone, I accessed the cloud hooked in with my Damaged Goods account. "Okay, that would have been one of the first files... here it is, Estaban Martinez."

"Okay, we have his name. Did you have anything about what happened to him after the paramedics took him away?"

I scrolled down the page. "His lease was enforced and he was evicted. Never showed up to contest in court."

Logan nodded thoughtfully. "So I'm guessing that meant he still had his set of keys."

I made a face. "The property owner should have changed the locks after the eviction but I know he didn't, cheapass so-and-so. Do you remember what he was like, the tenant, I mean."

He nodded. "Strung out, broke and covered in his own filth. Combine that with an eviction and no one else would rent to him, at least no one who had a place worth renting. So if you were suddenly homeless, where would you go?"

"Personally, I'd live on the streets but anyone less stubborn would probably stay with family." I turned back to the computer and pulled up the rental agreement Martinez had signed. "Here, he has a mother in Marathon."

Logan made a face. "No, absolutely not, Jackie."

I huffed out a breath. "What else do we have to do? You know Vasquez isn't going to be able to drive to Marathon for a chat, even if this were his case. We take a little road trip, see if Estaban is there, ask if he still has his keys and then come right back."

"You could just call to ask that." he pointed out.

"But if he knows something, we'll have a better chance of pinning him down and getting a description if we're looking him in the eye."

"Have you forgotten that someone shot at us yesterday?"

"As if you'd let me," I grumbled. It wasn't the organ pirate who looked like a cop, I was sure of that much. That guy looked like he hit his target every time.

"Jackie." Logan had that note in his voice, the one that denoted extreme exasperation.

"Logan," I said in the exact same tone. "You might be okay with falling off the face of the earth for months at a time, but I'm not. If we can dig up a lead then maybe the police can catch the organ pirates and we can go back home."

He said nothing for a minute, just stared at me, his expression inscrutable.

"Please," I asked, teeth sinking into my lower lip.

He breathed out a sigh. "Fine, but one stop, there and back."

I clapped my hands and then hopped up. "Abu, Sasquatch, we're going for a ride!"

"And we're taking this sideshow on the road," the Dark Prince grumbled.

THE DRIVE to Marathon from Key West took a little under an hour and Logan barely said a word. Dressed as I was in his boxers and a t-shirt, I was feeling highly self-conscious and though I didn't want to admit it to him, nerves got the best of me. I shifted in my seat as we grew closer to our destination, and I scratched my scalp in irritation.

Logan glanced over at me. "Everything okay?"

"No," I scratched a little more vigorously. "What if he's not there?"

"Then we keep looking." He was glaring at me. "You sure that dog doesn't have fleas?"

Sasquatch lifted her head and whined. I sucked in an outraged breath. "Of course she doesn't. I took her to the groomer when we first adopted her and they gave her a flea bath and we've kept up with her treatment ever since. You owe her an apology."

Logan's lips twitched. "I'm sorry, Sasquatch. It's just your mistress is twitchier than usual."

I scratched again. "I have sand in my hair or something. That crappy shampoo at the house isn't effective. Next time you abduct a woman, be sure to bring her toiletries."

"Noted. Is this the place?"

I looked up at the sign. "Breezy Shores, yup, this is it. Oh hell, look. It's a fifty-five and up community."

Logan frowned. "What does that mean?"

"Basically, our chances of finding Estaban here just went into one of his fermenting pails. Even if his mother wanted to let him stay here indefinitely, she couldn't without risking a breach of her own lease."

"Still, she might know how to contact him." Logan pointed out. "It can't hurt to ask."

The community was basically a cluster of mobile homes fanning out from around a community house that boasted a private pool and a boardwalk leading down to a well-maintained strip of beach. There was a shuffleboard court on one end of the expansive deck and a juice bar on the other. A group of elderly people doing sun salutations were visible down by the water.

"Cripes," Logan said. "It's like Club Fogey up in here. Mom and dad would plotz."

"Celeste and John, too. Although no porkin' way would you catch him on a yoga mat." I intentionally lowered my voice to Big John's southern drawl.

Logan groaned. "I think that image has been permanently burned into my brain, so thanks for that."

"Anytime," I clipped leashes on my furry friends.

"You're not taking them with us?" Logan frowned.

"The hell I'm not. People who leave their animals in the car in hot weather ought to be drug out to the street and shot." I popped the door to the truck and led them out into the sea breeze.

Mrs. Martinez's trailer was the third from the end, painted a sherbet orange with a blue and white striped canopy extending over a whitewashed deck. The typical Keys greenery encroached on either side of the home, giving the place an enclosed feel.

A large woman wearing an oversized sunhat and floral print muumuu sprawled on a plastic lounger beneath the awning. She had a mystery novel open across her massive chest and a string of drool dribbled down the side of her gaping mouth.

Logan looked from her to me and then back. "Do you want to approach or should I?"

I tilted my head and studied the woman. "If I were her, I'd be more cooperative waking up to your face than I would to mine."

He grinned and then handed me Sasquatch's leash. "Keep a hold of the critters. We don't want them to startle her."

I did as he said, circling the front of the deck and put down Sasquatches' travel bowl of water. Abu drank straight from the bottle, so I took a few gulps and then handed it to him to finish while I watched Logan approach.

"Mrs. Martinez," he said in a low, soothing voice.

She grunted but her eyes didn't open.

"Be more forceful," I called helpfully and was rewarded with a dirty look.

He leaned closer and raised his voice a bit. "Excuse me, Mrs. Martinez!"

She sat bolt upright, startled awake and bashed him in the nose with her forehead. The Dark Prince staggered back, blood streaming down his face. Abu screeched, Sasquatch barked and Mrs. Martinez let out a stream of rapid-fire Spanish, bolted into her creamsicle-esq trailer and slammed the door.

Logan left a trail of blood on the deck as he stumbled down the steps. "Can't hurt, is that what you said?"

I led him over to the Big Black Truck, told the dog and monkey to stay and rummaged for the first aid kit. "Actually that's what *you* said and I believe your exact words were, it can't hurt to ask. And since you didn't ask her anything except her name, this doesn't count. Here, sit down so I can fix your ugly mug."

Logan sat on the floor of the car, his legs long enough to touch the ground. He tilted his head forward so I could examine the mess. I opened the first aid kit on the seat beside him, pulled out a wad of gauze and wetted it with a fresh-water bottle to wipe away the blood. Gradually, the bleeding slowed.

Tentatively, I touched the bump at the bridge of his nose. "Do you think it's broken?"

He shook his head, then groaned. "It's not gonna look pretty for a while though."

"Women the world over will go into mourning. Stay still, you'll splatter blood everywhere." I complained. Other than stuffing half a dozen cotton balls up his nose, there wasn't much I could do.

"Sorry," he said, not sounding sorry in the least.

I tipped his chin up, to make sure I'd gotten him clean. He

was right, the area around his nose was swelling and I thought he'd probably end up with a black eye as well.

I don't know where the impulse came from, but I obeyed it without thought. Leaning in, I laid a quick kiss on him, just a brief brushing of my lips across his. When I pulled back his eyes were huge and staring.

But not at me, *past* me.

Then I heard the racking of a shotgun.

"Just who the hell do you people think you are?" A thickly accented voice asked us.

"Follow my lead," Logan had his hands in the air and spoke softly out of the side of his mouth.

I risked a peek over my shoulder. The woman holding us at gunpoint was a younger, slimmer version of the one Logan had startled from her nap. Her salt and pepper hair was pulled back in a severe bun and she wore tangerine leggings and an aqua tank top, which looked even more bizarre accessorized as it was with a double-barrel shotgun.

"Are you Mrs. Martinez?" Logan asked.

"And just who the devil are you?"

The itch on my scalp that had been driving me nuts all the way from Key West suddenly flared to life. I made a sound of discomfort and eased my hands up, hoping I could work in a scratch on the down-low.

"Hold right where you are," the shotgun was pressed into my back.

"I'm sorry," I said. "But I'm crazy itchy."

"Jackie," Logan warned.

I ignored him, instead focusing on the woman in the yoga duds, pivoting just my torso so I could make eye contact. "Seriously, you know that feeling when you really have to pee, or like when you really need Chapstick and you can't focus on anything else? It's like that times a gazillion."

"Sounds like lice to me." She pointed the barrel up and gestured for me to come forward.

"*Lice?*" I yelped, skeeved out to my itchy core. No way. No *freaking* way did I have lice. I *refused* to have lice.

"My daughter's twin boys had them, every kid in the class got infected. With boys it's easy, you just shave their heads so the nits got nothing to cling to." She was made of sterner stuff than me because she grabbed a hank of my hair and pulled to get a close look at my scalp, gesturing The Dark Prince forward to complete my humiliation. "You see right here? That's the nits. Looks like you have a full hatching going on here."

It took every ounce of energy for me to hold the tears back when Logan muttered, "Huh, I guess it wasn't the dog after all. Unless dogs can give people lice? Or maybe monkeys?"

Mrs. Martinez released me and shouted something in Spanish. A moment later the woman who'd been napping on the porch appeared, shuffling her flowered slippers steadily toward us. She took her turn poking through my hair and made a pronouncement, before waving the group of yoga seniors over for their turn inspecting me.

Mrs. Martinez released me. "Mama says that only people can get people lice. They can't get it from or give it to animals. She used to be a nurse so she would know. You better check your kids though. And your husband."

"I'm not—" Logan began, but I cut him off with a sharp gesture. We had a job to do and lice to get rid of and didn't have time to screw around making sure everyone understood our relationship status was complicated.

"Mrs. Martinez. We wanted to ask after your son, Estaban? Have you seen him lately?"

She blinked, clearly taken off guard. "Estaban? No, I haven't spoken to him in five years. *Por que?*"

My heart sank. It had been a slim hope to begin with but still. "Do you have any idea where he could be? Or maybe your mother does?"

There was a brief exchange of Spanish and a great deal of hand gestures, followed by head shaking.

Logan handed over a business card with his cell phone number. "Do me a favor and call me if he shows up. We want to talk to him about his former apartment."

She took the card, then lifted her chin at me. "Do you have a nit comb? Because you need a nit comb to—"

"I'll take care of it." Logan shoved me unceremoniously toward the truck. "Thanks."

Balling my hands into fists so I wouldn't scratch bloody divots in my scalp, I waited while he loaded Abu and Sasquatch, then climbed behind the wheel.

"I don't…," I began then ran out of things to say.

He blew out a breath, then slung an arm over the back of my seat and turned to back out of the trailer park.

He drove past two drug stores before he found one he liked. He didn't say a word, didn't ask if I wanted to go in and buy my own lice treatment, which I didn't because oh my god, then the clerk would know I had flipping lice. He left the truck running and sprinted into the pharmacy. He was back in under a minute, thrusting a white paper bag in my direction.

I opened it up cautiously, as if he'd stuffed a live snake inside instead of a box of chemicals and a nit comb. "You know if this were a rom-com that would be a pregnancy test, not lice treatment."

"Nothing romantic about head lice," he deadpanned.

Our eyes met. His lips twitched. And we both burst out laughing.

All the humor was gone an hour later when I stood in the tub, naked except for a threadbare towel that didn't quite wrap all the way around. I shivered as he worked the treatment into my hair.

"Can't I at least put on a shirt?" I griped. "I'm freezing to death and being eaten alive at the same time."

"You'll just get it wet and have to change. And clean laundry is at a premium. Hold still. You don't want to get this crap in your eyes."

Since there was nothing to stare at but the crappy tub insert, I closed my eyes. "I still can't figure out how the hell I could have caught lice."

"It only takes one female to start an infestation." His plastic gloves crinkled as he reached for the bucket of clean rinse water

"You talking from personal experience?" It might make this entire process an iota less humiliating if I knew he'd gone through the same thing.

"Nope, no lice for me. A couple of the guys I was stationed with though, they went to this...," he cleared his throat and then muttered, "Never mind."

"To this brothel," I finished for him. His hands paused and I knew I'd been right. Because really, what else would have made him stop talking? "Come on, distract me, the itching is driving me batty."

The hands got busy again, parting my hair into sections. "Brothel is too classy a word for it. But yeah. And they brought back some creepy crawly souvenirs, not just head lice either."

"You mean, crabs?" I shivered from more than the cold. "Ick, ick, ick."

I heard the grin in his voice. "You see, it could always be worse."

"I bet their wives and girlfriends back home were not happy about it either."

"About the prostitutes or the crabs?" His hands were sure and steady as he tugged the comb through the first section of my hair.

"Take your pick," I grumbled, clutching the towel with one hand and bracing the other against the shower for balance. "Either is a hanging offense in my book."

"Mine too. Those guys were idiots."

"You never talk about your time in the Navy. I forget sometimes that you served."

He finished with one section of hair without comment and moved on to the next one.

"Logan?"

"I'm trying to concentrate, here, Jackie. I can't see very well in this crappy light. Maybe we should do this outside."

I made a scoffing sound. "With me in a towel? Never gonna happen."

"Come on. The porch is private," he cajoled. "Who's gonna see you here except me? Besides, this is going to take a while and you'll be warmer in the sun."

"Always with the temptation," I grumbled under my breath. What else was I to expect from the Dark Prince though, really?

"What was that?"

"Nothing."

"So, can we?" He sounded like a little kid angling for ice cream money.

Heaving a sigh, I turned and stepped out of the tub. Logan held my arm, helping guide me out and if he snuck a glance at the gap in my covering, he did so discreetly.

I waited just inside the porch door, while he laid a towel on the second step. He stood up, lice comb in one hand, box of tissues and plastic bag to suffocate any stragglers he found on the step above me. The man could even make nitpicking look good.

I pushed open the screen door a crack and peeked out. He was right, the large dinner-plate-sized greenery provided ample coverage from the beach so that anyone walking by wouldn't be able to see what we were up to and the crunching shell drive would warn us of any cars well in advance. I slid my feet into flip flops and then took a deep breath and stepped out into the daylight.

I lowered myself in as close to a dignified position as possible considering I wore a too-small beige towel, but eventually I was in place. Logan wasted no time setting himself up on the step behind me and re-parting my hair. "I need to start over in case they've moved. The chemicals made them logy, but I don't want to miss any."

"Do what you gotta do." I sighed and stared out at the stretch of beach just visible through the foliage. It looked like a postcard, but even the image couldn't relate the way the sun heated my chilled skin or the warm breeze rich with the scents of sand and surf. The whole scenario seemed just a touch hedonistic, what with me mostly naked and the sexy man tending to me. Just another day of social grooming in paradise. I was pretty sure he wasn't eating the bugs though.

Logan combed thoroughly. "Did you ever worry about that with Luke?"

"Worry about what?" He'd been right about the sun, I was warming up with each passing minute, and oddly relaxed under his gentle ministrations.

He paused. "The whole hanging offenses bit."

I stiffened, my relaxation a thing of the past. "That he'd cheat on me, you mean?"

He made a weird coughing kind of sound. "Yeah,"

I looked at him over my shoulder and spoke the words I could barely admit to myself. "All the time."

The comb stopped. "I don't think that he did."

I smiled, though there was no humor in it. "No, in fact, I'm pretty sure he didn't. Then anyway. But it wasn't just that he'd hook up with someone else. I spent half my time alone convinced that he would ask for a divorce when he got back."

"Why?" The word sounded sort of raw.

"Celeste." It was all I needed to say.

"You never told him...?"

Silently I shook my head. After a minute he picked up the comb and began again.

He didn't speak. I didn't blame him. She was kind of a show stopper like that, my mother.

It had rained that morning, nothing unusual for Florida in May but my soon-to-be mother-in-law had boasted that meant good luck. She'd come with me to the beauty parlor where the two of us stood waiting for Celeste to show up and offer us her employee discount extended to friends and family on special occasions.

"I'm sure she's just running late." Marge had patted my arm in a sweet gesture. "She is the mother of the bride after all. She was probably held up by some errand or another."

"Mmmhhhmmm," I forced a smile even though all I wanted to do was snarl. Celeste had insisted, *freaking pleaded,* with me to come to her workplace so she could pamper me on my big day. I'd fought her at first, said no until I was practically blue in the face. That ugly little scene that had gone down in her trailer a few months back had still been fresh in my mind and if I had my druthers she wouldn't have been involved at all. The only thing she would have been caught up in was the liquor-soaked bedsheets from the night before. And possibly her own underwear, if she chose to wear them.

A car door slammed and a familiar figure had appeared. Not Celeste—she better be dead or I was going to strangle her—but the absolute last person I wanted to see.

"You hoo!" Marge had waved ecstatically, oblivious to my growing unease. "Over here, Logan!"

"What's he doing here?" I asked through tightly gritted teeth that may have resembled a smile from a few hundred feet away. Though I had resigned myself to the awkwardness of having my first lover as my brother-in-law, I was hoping to give the shocking wound time to heal. According to Luke, his brother had been lurking around Miami for the wedding but he'd had some plans to move north right after.

I couldn't flipping wait. Every time those blue eyes lit on me I felt as though I would spontaneously combust under the burning hatred focused my way.

What the hell was I supposed to say to him anyway? My bad that I intended to never see you again after bumping uglies, even though you were so unbelievably sweet to me?

Logan bent and kissed his mother on the cheek. He wore dark sunglasses to combat the relentless Miami sunshine and I could see myself in them as he looked my way.

"Did you get the flower arrangements straightened out?" Marge's hands fluttered like nervous birds.

"Flowers?" I'd asked stupidly. I really was the crappiest bride on the face of the planet. I didn't give a fig about flowers or my hair or my dress or the guest list. I'd pretty much handed over the running of the entire thing to Marge. All my energy went into successfully keeping my mother from humiliating both of us. "What's wrong with them?"

"The ones for the reception hall were delivered to the church and the ones for the church went to the hall. And of course, I had to see to arranging for Ursula's transport so poor Logan had to go take care of it. You did handle it, right?"

"I lost about a gallon of testosterone doing it, but yeah, the flowers are squared away." Logan's tone was flat and unyielding.

"Oh, thank heavens. What a nightmare that would have been. Ursula never would have let me hear the end of it. What about your father's tux?"

Logan chucked a thumb at the garment bag laid out in the back of his car. "Anything else, *Mein Führer*?

Marge glanced around. "Jackie, dear, maybe you should call your mother again, just to make sure she's left."

"She doesn't have a cell phone," I said. Or a license, not since her last DUI.

"Hmmm," Marge scowled and it was adorable, like watching a gnome stamp its foot. "Dear me, I wonder if we should just go on in without her? I have a coloring appointment and it takes at least an hour and there's still so much to do...."

"You know what?" I put both hands on her shoulders, rudely cutting her off. "You should go on in and get started. I'm going to go—" pull her out of whatever mess she passed out in— "and get her."

"But your hair?" Marge fretted, patting at my unruly brown curls.

"My mom's a hairdresser, remember? She'll get me all spiffed up in no time." If she could pass a breathalyzer of course.

"What if she shows up right after you leave?"

"You have my cell number. I'll hop the next bus and be right back here."

"Bus? Oh no, Logan will take you."

"But—" both Logan and I said at once.

"No buts," Marge barked, her titanium will strong in her voice. "It's easier for everyone. Oh shoot, that's my stylist waving at me. I'll see you at the church." And with one final cheery gesture, she disappeared into the salon.

Logan and I must have stood there for a full minute in silence.

"You don't have to—"

"Get in the car," he snarled.

I was half tempted to take the bus anyway, just to avoid spending time with this ghost from sexcapades past. So what if letting him drive was faster? So what if I was late to my own wedding? It wasn't like they could start without me. I'd simply call Luke and tell him...what? That I had inconvenienced everyone because I couldn't endure a car ride with his brother? How the hell would I make it through Thanksgiving and Christmas if I couldn't stand Logan's presence for less than an hour?

I got in the car.

13

"Where am I heading?" Logan flipped the radio to a classic rock station. Blue Oyster Cult's *Burnin' For You* filled the awkward silence.

I told him to head west from downtown and he did. I stared out the window as the song played on, one of my all-time favorites, and the dark presence of menace drove. I really had to make more of an effort with Logan, for Luke's sake. The brothers were close and I didn't want all this tension between the two of us to make Luke feel as though he had to choose sides.

"Did you ever make mixed tapes as a teenager?"

"What?" We were stopped at a light and Logan turned to stare at me.

"You know, like record songs off the radio that you liked."

He grunted, which I guess was an acknowledgment of sorts.

"Yeah I always wanted to get this song but it seemed as though every time I heard it I tuned in at the middle. One time a DJ announced it was coming up and I remember being so excited but then I couldn't find a blank tape in time and ended up only catching it from the second verse. I missed all the stuff about home." I sang a bit of the song, the same lines blaring from his speakers.

Logan said nothing.

"I guess that's a Gen-Xer type problem though. Now there's iTunes and MP3's all sorts of stuff and anyone with a dollar can buy whatever song they want." Not that I'd had many spare dollars growing up to spend on music.

"Why are you telling me this?" Logan's voice was soft. The light changed and we started off again, his foot heavy on the gas.

"Just making conversation."

"Well don't," he snapped. "I don't have anything to say to you, not anymore."

But once I set my mind on a task, I saw it through, no matter what. "Listen, this is going to be as awkward as we let it. Can't we just, I don't know, leave the past behind us and start fresh?"

He hit the brakes then, and if not for my seatbelt I would have gone through the windshield. Behind us, car horns blared but he slammed on his hazard lights and then rounded on me in a black fury.

"Start *fresh*? You mean the part where you went home with a complete stranger or the part where you seduced his brother after you found out our family has money?"

I flinched. "It's not...it wasn't like that!"

"No? You're telling me that if you knew I came from money that you wouldn't have snuck out while I was in the shower. That you would have glommed onto me instead of my brother?"

I reared back, stunned. "Screw you."

"We already tried that, baby." His hand went to my knee, the thumb rubbing suggestively. "Call off the wedding and I take you to bed right now."

I slapped him. It wasn't planned or particularly well-executed and my hand stung as my mind reeled. "What gives you the right to speak to me that way? Huh? I'm not some whore you picked up on the side of the road."

"No, you're some whore that I picked up in a damn techno club!"

I slapped him again, other hand to other cheek so we each had a matching set, just as someone knocked on the car window.

Logan glanced over at the pissed-off middle-aged Hispanic man waving his arms and shouting, then pressed down on the gas pedal and I was thrown back in my seat.

"How much?" he ground out. "What'll it take for you to walk away from him and not ruin his life?"

"I don't want money," I gritted through clenched teeth.

"Luke doesn't have access to his trust. It gets paid out a little at a time. And he's a simple guy. If you're picturing a life of luxury with him or a huge divorce settlement, you're in for a rude awakening."

"I don't want money. God, how many times do I have to say it before you get it through your thick skull?"

"Then what the hell *do* you want?" He asked, just as we crested the rise to my mother's trailer park.

There are some nice mobile home communities in Florida with window boxes full of herbs or flowers and friendly people who baked and baby-sat their grandkids. Celeste's current abode was about as far from that picturesque scene as possible.

I studied the rusted-out junkers that only a truly desperate sort of person would live in. Garbage bins overflowed and trash was strewn across the hard-packed dirt. Buckets of paint sat by one, a bunch of broken bottles next to another. Weeds poked up around Celeste's trailer.

"Jesus, Mary and a bag of chips," Logan breathed. "So your mom…lives here?"

"Third one from the end on the left." I wouldn't cry. It was my freaking wedding day. I. Refused. To. Cry.

The place probably confirmed all the shitty things Logan thought about me. After all, this particular mobile home park had spawned plenty of strippers, professional gamblers, crack whores, meth fiends, and druggies in every color of the rainbow so why not a gold digger or two to class the joint up? Thankfully though, he didn't say anything more as he parked the car.

I had my door open before he pulled to a stop and marched across what passed for Celeste's front yard and scrambled up the steps and pulled back the screen to pound on the door. "Mom?"

Nothing. A dog barked in the distance. The couple in the trailer next door had left their window open and I could hear their T.V. blaring. I tried the door handle only to find it locked. I slapped on the thing with a flat palm. "Celeste! Open up."

"Hey there, Sugar Tits."

I turned and saw Willie Franks from down the way standing at the foot of the steps. "Have you seen my mom around?"

Willie gave me a slow up and down that made my skin crawl. It was different from the way Logan had been coming on to me in the car. I knew Luke's brother was bluffing, but Slick Willie, as he was known around the 'hood, was a suspected rapist who lived with his senile mother. The victim had fingered him in a line-up but had later recanted her statement. No DNA evidence, since the victim had waited three weeks to report the crime. I'd seen her when she came in, a mousy little thing with dark bruises under her eyes. Buzz around the sheriff's office was that Willie had threatened to pay her younger sister a visit, but with no proof, there wasn't much law enforcement could do. I'd always been careful to steer clear of him and ordered Celeste to do the same. The fact that he was lurking around her trailer was not a good sign.

"Aren't you a sight for sore eyes?" he drawled as he moved in closer. His proximity pinned me at the top of the steps with my back against the trailer door. I'd have to leap over the rusty metal railing to avoid brushing by him.

"Gotta go," I offered a tight smile and chucked a thumb at the car where the Dark Prince still waited.

"Aw, stay and play with Willie awhile, Sugar Tits." His beady little rat eyes were locked on my chest.

"Back off." My tone was sharp, almost shrill. I wasn't afraid of him, not really. It was broad daylight and Willie was the kind of scum that liked to slither around in the dark. Besides, Logan was only a few feet away and regardless of all the awful crap he'd said to me on the ride over, I was pretty sure he wouldn't just drive off if some skeevy bastard got it in his head to assault me.

Willie glared up at me. "You're an uptight bitch, ain't you? You and your mama, just a couple of sluts that don't know a woman's place."

My pulse spiked when he brought Celeste into it. "Did you do something to her?"

The sound of a car door slamming diverted my attention and I looked over to see Logan striding around the car. "Jackie?"

I was about to tell him everything was fine when Willie grabbed me by the tank top and yanked me down the steps. He got one arm around my neck. Reflexively, I reached up to pry his arm off my windpipe when I felt the sharp point of a blade press against my skin.

Willie was small for a guy, only about an inch taller than

my own five-foot-five, but his wiry form was all muscle. He stank of cigarettes, stale beer and B.O. and if not for the knife, I would have gagged.

"Let her go," Logan moved into my line of sight. He must have sprinted to get over here so fast but he now moved slowly and carefully with his hands palms up and facing Willie. "If you don't this isn't gonna end well."

"Tell your boyfriend there to take a hike while we get to know one another," Willie whispered, drawing the blade to trace a faint line above his own arm. "Or I'll cut you a pretty new smile starting right here…."

"I can handle this," I managed to wheeze, even though my air was slowly being cut off. Another minute like this and I would pass out. My heart hammered against my ribs and my mind was dulled by panic. "Go home, Logan."

He gave me a look that I could only interpret as *in your freaking dreams* and kept up his slow and steady approach. "You don't want to do this."

"Stop or I swear I'll cut her." Alcohol bled from Willie's every pore.

"You won't." Logan's tone was low and dark and offered an almost sensual promise.

"I fucking will!" The arm on my throat tightened. I made a hissing noise as the blade pressed hard enough to nick the skin.

My gaze locked with Logan's across the few feet still separating us. I couldn't get enough air to speak, but pleaded with my eyes, begging him not to do anything that would get me killed. The look he gave me was one I'd never forget and his gaze flicked down to the arm around my throat for just an instant. I dug my nails into Willie's arm and maybe it was my imagination, but I thought I saw a small nod.

"I ain't playing," Willie snarled.

"Fine," Logan said and took a step backward in a show of good faith. "If that's what you want, Jackie, I'll go."

Willie laughed and the pressure on my throat eased a bit, the knife drawing away. I sunk my fingers in deeper and sucked oxygen, though it didn't keep my head from spinning. Really? Logan was just leaving me?

Some freaking hero.

I watched him pivot on his heel and saw the muscles of his shoulders tighten so I was ready when the command rang out. "Down!"

I dropped like a stone, wrenching Willie's arm hard so he was forced to let go. Willie, whose reaction time had been limited by the copious amount of booze in his system, staggered back. Logan's own knife nailed him in the right shoulder blade, about an inch and a half away from where my head had been two seconds before.

I lay on the wet ground panting as Willie shrieked and swore. His own blade had dropped into a muddy puddle beside my face. In another heartbeat, Logan had tackled the other man and had his arms pinned behind him, the knife still lodged in his shoulder.

"Get it out, get it out," the bastard cried.

"You've got two choices," Logan spoke in a mild tone as if discussing spring training with a buddy at a bar. "Either I call the police and tell them what you just tried to do and we ruin everybody's day. That's not my preferred option, trust me I'm in a shitty enough mood as it is. Or, you can promise me you will never touch another woman like that again and take your sorry self to the nearest hospital and get your shoulder stitched up. I'd offer to do it myself, but I don't like you very much."

Willie was spitting and drooling on himself and blood oozed out onto his wife beater. "Please."

"Door number one or door number two? Or, I could just

castrate you here. You might not bleed out before the paramedics arrive." Logan grip shifted on his knife.

Another whimpering cry and I sat up just in time to see Willie wet himself.

I stared at Logan. The man who'd not only just saved my life but had done so in a stunning burst of violence that had vanished almost as soon as it began. Was he out of his mind?

"I…I promise."

Logan looked at me. "You all right?"

I touched the scratch on my neck but it was clotting already. "Yeah."

Logan sank his fingers into Willie's hair. "Apologize to the lady."

"I'm sorry, it won't never happen again." Willie squeezed his eyes shut.

"Did you hurt my mother?" I asked and Logan shook his captive roughly.

"No, I swear. I haven't even seen her."

"That all?" Logan asked me.

I nodded and he got up, dragging Willie up by the scruff of his neck. The man tried to pull out the knife but Logan held up a hand. "Let the doctors do that in case you nicked something vital. And if I hear you so much as breathe around Jackie or her mother or any other woman, next time we won't be able to have a pleasant conversation after I stab you."

Willie scampered off leaving a trail of blood and urine.

"You're crazy," I whispered to Logan. "You would have done it too, wouldn't you?"

"I've seen plenty of guys like that. Bullies tend to respond better to violence and threats than reason."

I noticed he hadn't commented on whether or not he would have actually unmanned Willie, but figured I didn't want to know. "You could have hit me."

He turned his attention from the small nick to my face. "Only if you hadn't trusted me."

We stared at each other for a beat.

"Thank you." I staggered and he reached out to steady me.

"Sit down before you faint." He led me to the steps but instead of sitting I scrambled back up them and began to pound on Celeste's door. "Mom!"

Logan moved up beside me and extracted something from his pocket. "I'll get us in. Just give me a minute."

I moved down a step, trying not to panic for the thirty seconds it took Logan to unlock the door.

The smell of vomit hit me first and I turned to him. "You might want to wait—"

He didn't even let me finish before he pushed past me. We found Celeste curled around her toilet wearing nothing but a pair of black stilettos and silver hoop earrings that a small car could have driven through.

It probably was a good thing Logan was there, he kept me from bursting into tears. I could have had my throat slit in the parking lot, but that idea wasn't nearly as upsetting as the fact that my mother had taken a real stab at ruining my wedding day.

My hands shook as I reached for her but Logan took both my quivering hands in his.

"Let me."

I turned on the shower and watched Logan pull my mother's deadweight up and support her into it.

"How often does this happen?" he grunted as her head lolled to one side, whacking him in the chin.

"Only on days ending in y." I slipped out to retrieve the mop and bucket from the hall closet.

Celeste roused herself halfway through and tried to grope Logan, but then threw up again. He held her so she didn't crack her fool head on the tub. I finished cleaning up her latest mess and then retrieved a towel for her.

He wrapped her in it and then picked her up and carried her down the hall to the bedroom and lay her on her stomach so she wouldn't choke on her own vomit.

"Thanks," I said and again it wasn't nearly enough.

"She needs help, Jackie. You can't keep covering for her."

"She's been to rehab before, a couple of times." Once or twice court ordered, but I kept that little nugget to myself. "It doesn't stick."

"So you keep coming back to this?" His tone was quiet but I could hear the condemnation and worse, the pity.

"You want to know why I ran out on you that morning? It was because of this." I waved my hands around, encompassing the mess. "Because I liked you and I didn't want you to see this and think I was trailer trash. No one sees where she lives, how I used to live, back when I thought I didn't deserve any better than this. It's the only way I can ever look people in the eye."

"Why do you keep coming back?"

I looked down on her pathetic form. "She's my mother and she doesn't have anybody else. Neither do I."

He was silent for a long time. "Does Luke know?"

"About the state of things here? No. I told you, I don't tell anyone." Not even the man I planned to marry. "The only reason I let you come today is because there's no way you could actually think any less of me."

I wondered if Logan would take the ammunition and destroy the little bit of happiness I had managed to scrape together.

More silence. I risked a glance up at him. "What are you going to do?"

He turned away. "Nothing."

"Nothing?" I repeated stupidly. Was this the same guy

who'd tried to seduce me, to pay me to stay away from his brother not even an hour ago? "But you have what you were after, don't you? You can out me to Luke and he'll call off the wedding. You can get what you want. You can win."

Logan turned back and studied me. "No Jackie," he said quietly. "This is a no-win situation."

"I don't get you." I shook my head. "First you say all that horrible crap to me, then you save my life and now you're keeping not one but two of my secrets? Why would you do that, to hold it over my head?"

He came back into the trailer and stood there, staring down at me.

I waited, chin lifted, hands balled into fists but his words made me lean back against the wall for support. "You could have told me."

I looked away but he caught my chin in his hand and turned my face back up to his. "You have nothing to be ashamed of here. Your mother's choices are her choices and you didn't ask to be born into this. So it's not your fault. Got it?"

His eyes mesmerized me. He was so gruff, but at times so incredibly sweet and at that moment, something amazing happened.

I believed him.

"I'm sorry," I whispered, meaning it. And I was sorry, sorry that I hadn't felt safe enough with him to trust him to deal with my reality. He was more than capable, as he'd demonstrated. But I knew firsthand that just because you could handle some things, didn't mean you should have to.

He just turned back toward the door.

"Come on. Mom will be wondering what's keeping you."

"I have to stay here with Celeste." I pointed to the closed bedroom door. "Make her some coffee and get her on her feet."

Without a word, Logan did a 180 and moved into the small galley kitchen.

"You don't have to," I began but he held up a hand. Clearly, he wasn't going anywhere until both Celeste and I were ready.

I walked into my mother's room and sat on the bed, listening to her snore.

"You've ruined my wedding day," I said to her back. "Did you do it on purpose?"

She didn't answer. She never did when she was like this. And really, even if she had replied, what words would have made me less angry? There was no diffusing me like a bomb.

Since I didn't have a dad, Celeste was supposed to give me away. Maybe the strain of that thought had been too much for her. Frankly, I didn't care what excuse she'd throw down when she was coherent enough to pick up a bottle. I rose and reached into her closet, past the shimmering dress with the cap sleeves I'd bought her for the wedding. I'd maxed out my credit card to get it but didn't even consider trying to return it.

I packed a small bag, yoga pants and tank tops and then carried it out into the living room.

"Coffee's ready." Logan offered me the mug, but I just shook my head, reaching instead for a pen.

In tidy block letters, I wrote. *Go to rehab. Tell them how you ruined your daughter's wedding. And find a better place to live. I won't take your calls until you do.*

"Let's go," I said to Logan and headed out without a backward glance.

14

"I'm still itchy." I complained once Logan was done with my grooming. "And I smell funny."

"Oh, the fun's just getting started. Says here, you need to wash all your bedding and clothing in scalding hot water." He read from the directions that came with the treatment. "Bag up anything that can't be washed in plastic bags for four to six weeks and—"

I snatched the paper from him, read and then swore. "God, this sucks. I feel dirty. Like not just my usual sort of property management slash spawn of the trailer park dirty. Like soul-deep filth."

Logan frowned. "It's got nothing to do with dirt. They're parasites, anyone can get them."

I gave him a yeah, right look. "Like your Navy buddies who went to the whorehouse? You're going to stand there and tell me that's not seedy, especially when they came back crawling with vermin?"

He strode past me to the hall. "Come on, go put a shirt on and I'll help you strip the bed."

I did as he said, pulling a long-sleeved black t-shirt on.

First problem, no washing machine in the place. We decided to boil the linens in a large pot Logan had found on a shelf in the pantry.

"Double double toil and trouble," I croaked in my best crone's voice as I stirred the giant pot of sheets with a large wooden spoon. "Eye of newt and tongue of frog, wing of bat and hair of dog." Then in my normal voice, I asked, "fo I sound like Ursula? No, really."

Logan grinned and shook his head. "If I didn't know better, I'd say you were cooking."

"Sssh!" I hissed, glancing at the ceiling. "The kitchen Gods might hear you and decide to smite me."

One jet eyebrow lifted. "You don't really believe you're cursed, do you? You've never seemed particularly superstitious to me."

"I think this load's done." Setting my spoon aside I reached for the tongs. "To answer your question, no, not really. But enough bad shit has gone down with the women in my family in the kitchen that it became a thing. Celeste believes it wholeheartedly, but I'm in the *don't tempt fate* camp. Crap, this is heavy."

Logan hurried over and snagged my tongs. "You have to let it cool so you can wring some of the water out."

I shot him a dirty look. "Who died and made you Laura Ingles Wilder?" The suggestion did make sense, but we still had a long way to go. "I still don't understand why we can't just load all this stuff in the truck and hit up a laundromat."

He frowned down at me. "Someone shot at us yesterday, after climbing out of that truck. The more times we take it out on errands, the more likely we'll be spotted. Now come on, get the rest of the pillows bagged."

"Hold up," I went to the freezer and pulled out a bag of corn niblets and handed it to him. He'd been so busy seeing to me and my parasites he'd never treated his nose. "Better put that on your face for a few or you'll look like you went three rounds with the Tasmanian Devil by tomorrow."

He grimaced but took the corn. "That bad, huh?"

It was a good thing he couldn't see my face when he laid the frozen pack over his own because I was sure mine telegraphed everything I was feeling. Abu made a small sound from the living room and I made my way in there to see what he and Sasquatch were up to and to take away the temptation of saying—or worse, doing—something I'd regret.

Maybe the chemicals from the lice treatment had seeped into my brain. I was having all those stupid squishy tender feelings for Logan Parker again. The man had abducted me, for crying out loud. Like less than a day ago. So how the heck had I managed to forget it so fast?

Sasquatch groaned and rolled onto her back, all four paws in the air. I crouched down and rubbed her belly while I admitted the truth. It was inevitable, what with our close quarters and mutual attraction, that we'd be drawn to each other. It was still wrong, like it had been that first morning and like it would be tomorrow, but I wanted him. Badly.

"Jackie?" the Dark Prince asked from the doorway. "Are you ready to get back to work?"

No, I thought. "Yes," I said. I could pretend to be smart for a little while longer.

The sun was going down by the time I took the last load of laundry out to hang on the line and the first load was still dripping. Logan, who'd been spritzing out the Big Black Truck with yet another pesticide, slammed the door and then approached.

I heaved a sigh and stretched my aching muscles. "So that's all my pillows bagged, and sheets and the mattress cover washed along with half of your laundry and almost all the towels. What do we have left?"

"Not much," he admitted. "I talked to Luke earlier, told him what was going on."

I groaned. "He didn't find any on him, did he? He slept in my bed the other morning, after the hospital. I wouldn't worry otherwise, we've barely seen each other."

I wasn't sure why I felt the need to babble up all that information and blamed it on the fatigue.

Logan didn't comment on my verbal upchucking. "Not that I know of. He was going to bring a bag of your stuff but since we don't know what's been contaminated, all of that needs to be treated as well, so there's no point."

"Damn." I heaved a disgusted sigh. What a nightmare. It was as if the universe didn't have much going on this week and had decided to pick on me from every angle. I closed my eyes and leaned back against the railing. "I should be there to handle all this. It's not fair that he has to do it all by himself."

Logan cast me a sidelong look. "He isn't. Corrine and Mom are pitching in."

I wanted to make a snide comment about Corrine being Little Miss Helpful, but couldn't muster the energy. Instead, I tipped my head back and stared up at the stars. "We need to figure out what's going on. Find out who the shooter was and if it was related to the organ pirate case."

He didn't argue with me, but he didn't agree with me either. Instead, he headed for the steps. "Come on, let's see what we can scrounge up for dinner."

There weren't too many options. "Condensed soup or peanut butter sandwiches?" Logan asked.

"Soup, if you don't mind. I don't have the strength for chewing. There's a reason why that kind of work is called backbreaking."

He put the soup and some filtered water in a small pot on the stove, turned the heat on and then came around the table and put his hands on the back of my neck, digging into the knot there with his thumbs. I let out an involuntary groan at the unexpected contact, but couldn't keep from sagging back against into his touch.

"Better?" he murmured after a few moments of rubbing.

"Don't stop," I moaned.

His laugh was low and deep. "You always keep life interesting, you know that Jackie?"

"Does Corrine?" I asked, the stupid question popping out before I even knew it was there.

The magic touch fell away and he moved back toward the stove. "I don't want to talk about Corrine." His tone had that hard edge that I'd come to know so well over the last few months. Subject closed.

It pissed me off, my ire giving me a burst of energy. "You don't want to talk about your time in the Navy, you don't want to talk about the organ pirate or the shooting, you don't want to talk about your Dad or Estaban Martinez or where the hell you've been for the last few months. So what exactly do you want to talk about?"

He didn't turn to look at me. His shoulder muscles bunched tighter and tighter as my rant went on and on. "With you? Nothing. There's nothing left to say."

I sucked in a sharp breath, feeling as if he'd just driven a knife into my chest. My tender feelings withered and died. I was so sick of feeling like the villainess. "Damn it, Logan. I refuse to do this anymore."

"Do what exactly?" He turned and the bruises combined with his tone put out a menacing vibe.

"This hot and cold treatment from you is giving me whiplash. Either be sweet to me or be an ass, but make up your mind and stick to one path, okay? Because every time you shut me down like that you gut me and I just can't take it anymore."

I didn't wait for his reply, one wasn't needed. Instead, I

stormed past Abu and Sasquatch and into the bare bedroom, slammed the door and flung myself down on the bare mattress.

He didn't follow me, for which I was grateful. He was right, there wasn't much we could talk about without fighting and we were both exhausted from the day's labors. Regret filled me, I hated that we were like this, taking big bloody chunks out of each other and using them to chum the waters. I heard him moving around in the kitchen and thought about going back out there, offering an insincere sounding apology, sitting down and eating the soup he'd thoughtfully prepared while giving me a shoulder massage. He wasn't a bad guy and I wasn't a mean girl so why did we do this to each other?

Who'd thrown the first punch? I know he thought it was me for sneaking out on him after that one-night-stand. But what I thought he understood was that I didn't have a choice. What I had was Celeste and her trailer park of baggage and an endless sea of shame and unanswered questions. I thought Logan accepted that. But the way he'd reacted when I'd bolted after the shooting made me think that maybe he never had accepted my reality, that he didn't understand that I'd wanted nothing more that first morning than to keep him.

I was surprised to find tears tracking down my cheeks and pulled down the sleeves of the t-shirt I wore to wipe them away. Of course, he didn't know how much I wanted him because I'd never told him. He'd seen my shame and I thought he got me but one thing I kept underestimating was that, in his own way, Logan Parker was just as insecure as me. He hid it better, but those flashes of vulnerability, when-ever I said or did something that crept under his defenses, were real.

I'd been hurting him for years. He'd done the same to me. And yet when I thought about the way he'd combed my hair, the hours he'd spent helping me decontaminate the house, the jolt of tenderness I had whenever I saw his bruises, felt the shoulder rub, witnessed the cooking all of that other stuff just...went away.

Though it always came back.

Out in the living room, his phone rang. I sat up and listened. His voice was muffled by the closed door and he spoke too quickly for me to hear the exact words but it was less than a minute later when his footsteps echoed down the hall.

I was waiting for him at the door. "What? Is it your dad?"

He shook his head. "No, it's Estaban Martinez. We might have found him."

"ARE you sure you know what you're doing?" I called to Logan a few hours later as we sped through the night in our rented boat. I was perched on the seat beside him as he drove the boat out into the dark sea at a much faster clip than I was comfortable with considering we couldn't see a damn thing.

Logan gave me that sardonic half-grin but otherwise didn't answer. He seemed confident enough, so I tried to distract myself by recalling the information Mrs. Martinez had related.

"He's been working on a shrimp boat." Logan had told me as we drove to the marina. "Apparently he'd talked to his grandmother a few weeks ago and told her that much, but asked her to keep it from his mother in case it didn't work out. After our visit yesterday, she decided to spill the beans to her daughter."

"Where is this boat docked?" I'd asked, hoping the answer was close by.

"Right here in Key West. It's out right now, but that's the

best possible place to locate him. We could rent a boat and catch up with him tonight."

The idea of being out on the open ocean at night terrified me. "Can't we just wait until it comes back into port? Do we really have to go out after him?"

"They're not coming back to South Florida for a few months. The owner is from South Carolina. Do you really want to wait a few months?"

I didn't and he knew it.

"But won't it be like looking for a needle in a haystack? Especially at night?" I gave it one last go.

"I have the transponder frequency for the boat. It'll act like a beacon, bring us right to him." He didn't volunteer how he'd gotten that information and I decided not to ask.

So there I sat, getting battered by the rush of sea wind as the boat sliced through the dark waves, praying that Estaban hadn't gone back to his old ways because I really didn't want to set foot aboard the S.S. Shrimp-N-Shit.

Logan slowed and cut the engine. Without the roar of wind and power, the night grew still. We bobbed about, the waves coming at us from the left side and dipping us to the right. Or was that port to starboard? Starboard to port? Stem to stern? Eh, I was a landlubber, I'd check with the former Navy man later. I tugged at my life preserver which had a stranglehold on me and craned to see into the night.

Logan spoke into the radio, tersely identifying ourselves and asking the shrimping vessel to reply. There was static for a few moments and he tried again. Still no answer.

"They should be right here." He said. "According to the signal, we're right on top of her. But I don't see any lights, do you?"

I scanned the horizon but the only lights came from our own craft and illuminated a small diameter surrounding our vessel. "No, and I don't hear anything either."

Logan shook his head, then rose and climbed up onto his seat.

"What are you doing?" I asked, panicked at the thought of him falling overboard.

"There's a couple of spotlights up here," he muttered, fumbling with the lights. "I'm checking to see if we can maybe detach them and use them to search."

"Search? What are you thinking?"

"Nothing good," he muttered. "Here, take this."

It took me a minute to stand with confidence and another to stagger across the way to him. He handed me one of the spotlights and then detached the other for himself.

"Don't fall," I warned him.

With the light in his hand, I couldn't see his face but his tone sounded odd. "Why are you so paranoid? You used to love being out on the water."

"The last boat I was on blew up," I reminded him.

"That wasn't the last boat you were on." He scanned to the left with his spotlight.

I scanned right. "Think I'd remember."

"No, because we took the coast guard boat back. Besides, it doesn't count if you're the one to blow the boat up intentionally. Bring your light to the bow, I think I see something."

I did as instructed, grateful I at least knew that the bow was the front part. There was a small v cut out with a few padded benches and a metal railing, which I gripped with my right hand. He was right, as he so often was, the actual last boat I was on was the rescue vessel after Logan had pulled me to safety.

Had I ever thanked him for that? I couldn't remember. Luke had been so upset because he hadn't gotten to the boat in time to be part of the rescue operation and I'd tried to downplay the whole thing for his benefit.

"Did I ever say thank you?" I asked him, keeping my eyes on the rippling dark water ahead of us.

There was scuffling behind me and I hoped that meant he'd climbed down from his ridiculous perch. "What for?"

"For saving my life. For coming after me the way you did. I can't believe you actually jumped in the water after me."

He moved up on my left and gripped the railing right beside me. "It wasn't something you thought about. And yes, you did say thank you."

"Oh, okay." I felt stupid for bringing it up in the first place.

"You also told me I was your favorite person." He spoke quietly, almost as if he didn't want me to hear what he said.

"At the time, you were." There had been several of those moments over the years.

He glanced down at me. "And a few hours later you called me a lying jackass."

I grimaced at the memory. "You were that, too."

He nudged me with his shoulder, carefully so I wouldn't lose my precarious balance. "I must be pretty talented if I can be both your favorite person and a lying jackass in the same day."

I lowered my light to the padded bench, angling it until it shone out over the dark expanse of the water and didn't blind us. "I'm not sure if that says more about my mental instability or your mad multitasking skills."

He lowered his light too. "Corrine is the sister of one of my Navy buddies. He died a few weeks ago. Cancer."

"Oh, God." I put my free hand on his arm. "Logan, I'm so sorry."

"I was with him when he died. He asked me to help her get away from her ex-husband. The guy was abusive and Chris made me promise to help Corrine hide from him. Start her life over."

Between the rocking of the boat and his surprising admission, I needed to sit down. "Didn't she have any other family?"

He shook his head. "No, their parents died in a car accident when they were teenagers. She wanted to leave and I think Chris's death was the catalyst she needed to get out of a bad situation. She didn't want to go to a women's shelter. I think she was embarrassed about the abuse. So we decided it would be better if she pretended to be my fiancée, at least until she figured out where she wanted to go and what to do next."

I blew out a breath. "And your family knew all this?"

He lowered himself to the seat next to me. "I didn't want word to spread. So I only told Luke because I knew he could keep the secret."

And there went another chunk of my heart. "You mean from me? Didn't you trust me to keep her secret?"

He didn't say anything for a minute.

I slid my hand down along his arm until I could feel skin. "It's okay, I get it. After the way we left things at Christmas, I'm not even surprised."

He pulled away, knocking his light onto the deck. It hit his profile and made him look eerie. "I wanted to make you jealous, okay? I'm not proud of it, using my dead friend's sister, who'd already been through so much, as a fucking prop. But she asked how she could help me, wanted to do something to thank me for helping her. I've been eaten up with envy over my own damn brother for *years* and I just wanted you to feel a little bit of that agony."

He was breathing heavily, had risen and backed out of reach.

This time it wasn't a chunk he tore off me, it was a clean slice right through the middle of my still-beating heart. I stood, carefully, cautiously as though approaching a wounded animal. "And it worked. I was jealous, crazy jealous."

"I hate myself for it." Logan turned to lean on the railing, presenting me with his back. "For lying to Mom and Dad, especially after what happened to him. I hate what I've become...."

He trailed off and I sank back onto the seat and finished the thought for him. "Because of me. You hate what I've made you."

"Jackie—," he began but I barreled over the top of whatever he was about to say, not wanting to hear anymore.

"It's okay," I said. "I get it. Hell, I probably deserve your hatred. I'm so sorry, Logan." I stared at the light on the ground, telling myself it was the high wattage that made tears gather in my eyes, that they had nothing to do with the yawning chasm of grief or wishing I could just crawl off and die.

Logan gripped my arm, hauled me to my feet and pointed. "No, Jackie. Look. It's the shrimp boat."

15

It was indeed a shrimp boat, I could tell by the two outriggers that stuck out on either side of the mast like reaching arms. The name on the stern read *Sweet Release*, which sounded both ironic, since it was a commercial fishing vessel, and raunchy. "Why are there no lights on the deck? Do they scare away the shrimp or something?"

Logan looked at me and I shrugged. "Yeah yeah, it's a stupid question, but what I know about shrimp fits in a cocktail glass and comes with horseradish and chili sauce."

The Dark Prince fixed his gaze back on the trawler. "It's dangerous that they don't have lights on. Even if the boat was anchored and everyone aboard was sleeping they should still have running lights at the very least. Either something happened that shorted out their power, or they're doing something they aren't supposed to be doing. As in, something illegal."

"Which would explain why they'd hire someone like Estaban in the first place." I blew out a breath then asked, "What do we do?"

Logan shook his head. "Well, they aren't shooting at us, so

I guess that's something. They have to have caught sight of us by now. I don't hear any voices, do you?"

I listened, but all was quiet. "Maybe we're too far away?"

Logan shook his head. "Sound travels over open water. We should be able to hear them talking."

"Should we radio for help? The Coast Guard or something?"

"And say what? We came across a dark shrimp boat?" Logan stared at the boat and then nodded. "Right. I'm going over there."

He turned back toward the wheelhouse and I grabbed his arm. "What? You just said you think they're up to something shady and now you want to just pop over for a chat?"

He shook me off and reached into a compartment withdrawing his sidearm, a Smith & Wesson .38 and handed it to me. "You know how to shoot, right?"

I did, though I didn't have the best aim. I tried to give it back. "You keep it."

"If I go over there armed and they are up to something illegal, I'll be in bigger trouble than if I'm unarmed. This way if anything happens to me, you have a way to protect yourself."

Panic clawed at me at the thought of being left alone on the boat while he risked his stupid heroic neck. I checked the weapon, made sure the revolver was loaded and that the safety was on before setting it on the nearest seat. "Let me go instead."

"Jackie," he began, but I held up a hand.

"Logan, I can't drive the boat and I don't have your aim. If something happens to you I'll probably die of dehydration or be captured and killed."

His jaw clenched. "I'm not letting you go over there by yourself. Besides, if it is some sort of equipment malfunction people could be hurt. They might need medical assistance."

I lifted my chin, squared my shoulders and murmured, "Then it looks like we're going together."

He opened his mouth as though he was tempted to keep arguing, but then closed it again. Instead, he picked up the handgun and tucked it into the waistband of his cargo pants. Since I was once again sporting his boxers, that hadn't been an option for me.

"I've got a bad feeling about this," he grumbled.

He wasn't the only one. My teeth sank into my lower lip and I took a seat while Logan climbed back to the wheelhouse to move our boat closer to the trawler. I wanted to tell him that we should turn around and head back to our little hideout, that I'd behave and quit complaining about having nothing to do if he turned the boat around right now and left the *Sweet Release* to be discovered by someone in a better position to do something about it. What the hell did it even matter if Estaban Martinez still had the key to his old apartment? I kept my mouth shut though while he hung out the bumpers and wrapped some line around the little metal thingies in preparation for tying off.

The wind picked up and we drifted closer to the other boat. Logan occasionally did something that made the engine hum and the propellers churn up some water, though he didn't turn it on full power. Afraid to distract him, I stayed quiet until we were practically on top of the trawler. The biggest problem I could see was the size difference between the two vessels since the deck of the *Sweet Release* was a good ten feet above our little rental. "How are we going to get on board?"

"There." Logan pointed to something that looked to me like a few ropes dangling down the side. Beneath them several old tires hung, presumably to act as bumpers. Logan threaded the line through the tires, tethering our boat to the larger vessel.

"Oh no, I never made it up the rope in gym class." And that was almost twenty years ago. Too top weak and bottom heavy.

He reached over and pulled on it so I could see a sort of makeshift ladder. "It's a cargo net. You can climb up."

If I hadn't been pants pissing terrified, I would have said something about how if he wanted a climbing buddy he should have brought Abu. Instead, I stared up the "ladder" that I could barely see and then contemplated the watery grave waiting below.

He looked over at me, his expression inscrutable in the dim lighting. "You can still stay—"

I held up a hand and grabbed the horizontal rope above my head. The nylon was thick and scratchy under my palm. After sucking in a deep breath, I put my left foot on the thing and hauled myself upward, grabbing the rung above with my other hand.

My right foot scrabbled for purchase, but I couldn't find the next foothold. The boats rolled as the wind and waves picked up. This wasn't going to work, it'd be dawn by the time I made it up to the deck, and that was if I didn't plunge to my death first.

Warm fingers wrapped around my right ankle and Logan guided my foot into place. "Stay there a minute."

I might stay there for the rest of my natural life. My palms were sweaty and, precarious as my perch was, I couldn't risk taking even one off to wipe it on my shorts. What in the sweet by and by did I think I was doing?

The cargo net shifted as Logan climbed up behind me. Like right freaking behind me. His thighs pressed into mine, his front into my back, his arms and legs shadowing my own trembling limbs. Since he was almost half a foot taller, his grips were both higher and lower than my own but it felt as though I were perched in his lap.

"I've got you," he breathed into my hair. "We'll go up together, just like this. Okay? You know I won't let you fall."

"What if *you* fall?" It wasn't out of the realm of possibility that my bigger than was socially acceptable backside could knock him over like a bowling pin.

"Trust me, Jackie. We've got this. Push up with your legs. You want to let them do all the work. That's where most of your strength is based. If your arms get tired, wrap them through the loops of the net and hold on. Got it?"

"Yeah," I croaked.

He didn't wait to see if my fit of nerves got the better of me. Instead, his left knee lifted, pushing at the back of my leg, guiding me up to the next perch. He found his easily and to my astonishment, mine fell into place as well. It felt almost natural for my hand to follow his, then the other arm and the last leg.

With his heat at my back, the wind didn't bother me as much and before I knew it we'd ascended half the net.

"Do I know how to show a girl a good time or what?" Logan grunted as he pushed my leg up for the next step.

A laugh escaped. It had a hysterical edge.

He paused. "Are you having fun or something?"

"I always have fun when I'm with you," I admitted.

"You're just saying that because you think we're going to die," he bitched and reached for the next handhold.

I followed suit. "No, actually I really mean it. I never thought that would be the case when we started Damaged Goods, but it's true."

"Rest here." He assisted me in looping my arms through the netting. His body pressed into mine in a way that just felt right. I told my libido to take a hike, this was neither the time nor the place to notice how delicious he smelled, how warm and solid he was or how much I was relishing his proximity.

He was noticing the same sort of things. Given our close

quarters, there was no hiding the fact that his body responded to the nearness of mine. Or maybe it was the adrenaline. Luke had said something about inappropriate reactions after combat.

Note to self: Leave Luke out of this.

"I have something I need to tell you." The Dark Prince grumbled.

"*Now?*" I wheezed. "Can't it wait until I can put my feet up and have a few cosmos?"

"No," his tone brooked no argument.

I sighed and leaned my head back against his pec so I could sort of see his face. He was looking off to the side, his expression stormy.

"Okay," I said. "What is it?"

He turned so he could look me in the eye as he spoke. "Do you remember that day I helped you clean out your mother's trailer? That story you told me?"

I did. The conversation he was referring to was when I'd told him about one of my more horrific childhood memories. Celeste had gone out and a drunk had stumbled into our trailer and tried to have his way with me. It wasn't the only event like that in my messed up childhood, but it had been by far the most terrifying. I still didn't know why I'd told Logan about it but I murmured one word. "Vividly."

"I looked for him," Logan confessed. "The man who came after you."

I didn't say anything, though my grip on the rope tightened so that the rough texture chafed my already stinging palms.

"After you told me what he'd done, I had this urge to track him down and beat the shit out of him. Or at the very least, have his ass tossed in prison for child abuse. Unfortunately, I didn't know where to start."

"And you didn't tell me because you knew I'd object," I guessed. "Better to ask forgiveness than seek permission?"

He made a disgusted sound and shifted his grip. "What was I supposed to do, let it go? You wouldn't have told me unless you wanted me to fix it."

Spoken like a big, strong, testosterone riddled dumbass. "Maybe I just needed to tell someone and you happened to be there."

He blew out a sigh. "If that's what you want to believe, Jackie. Anyhow, after you told me about it, I went to Celeste and asked for his name. She told me the son of a bitch was already dead. Liver cancer, according to her."

Maybe I was a bad person, but I was glad for it. Not for cancer or for the fact that the man was dead, but because the thought of Logan going after him, getting himself arrested or worse, hurt over something that had almost happened to me years before chilled me to my marrow.

And maybe, though I would never admit it to him, I was glad that he cared enough to look on my behalf.

He rested his chin on top of my hair. "I just...wanted you to know."

I let out a slow, shaky breath. "Promise me you won't do anything like that again."

Though I couldn't see him, I felt his head shaking back and forth even before he said, "I can't."

Now he was just being difficult. "Bull."

"Now's not the time for an argument," he grumbled.

"Well, you started it. I'm serious, Logan. Don't do crap like that for me. I'm—"

A hand clapped over my mouth. "If you tell me you're not worth it, I swear I'll climb up the rest of the way and leave you here."

We both knew it was an empty threat, but I nodded my agreement against the palm of his hand.

He reached up once more and I guessed the break was over. "You are, you know. Worth it."

You're the only man who's ever thought so. I inhaled sharply and focused all my energy on climbing.

"Climbing therapy," the Dark Prince grunted as we ascended. "Wave of the future."

WHAT SEEMED like eons later but was in reality probably less than half an hour from the time we'd started, we reached the deck. Logan told me to wrap my arms through the rope so he could go first and take a look. The speed at which he scrambled up and over the railing made me realize just how much he'd held back for my sake. Under normal circumstances, I would have kvetched and probably resented him for it. But after the climb, I could only feel gratitude he'd been so patient and waited for me.

I counted to ninety-seven before he reappeared just above me and extended a hand. "Just like we thought, no one on deck."

I reached for the hand and he hauled me up without any horrific grunts or groans at my weight. He tugged and I slid up and over the railing, though the dismount needed a little work. He must have lost his footing because he stumbled, dragging me with him. We both went down hard onto the deck, with me on top of him.

"Oh shit, sorry," I babbled at the same time as he wheezed, "Are you all right?"

We were both fine and I smiled down at him. He didn't say a word, though his gaze was locked with mine. My focus went down to his parted lips and I swallowed hard.

"Jackie," he whispered.

Time and place! My inner voice shrieked. I was tempted to

stay exactly where I was but worried I was crushing him to death. I rolled off Logan onto my back and took great gulps of air, filling my lungs as far as I could with the damn life jacket. Logan didn't waste any time getting to his feet then crouching over me. I noticed the revolver had appeared in his hand once more.

I sat up and looked around. We were on what I guessed was the main work deck. Ropes were coiled and stowed, life preservers hung in neat rows. Giant ice chests were pushed back against the base of the superstructure. It smelled fishy, but not unclean. "You don't suppose this is like a plague ship or something?"

"No. they were just docked in the Keys twelve hours ago. Even the fastest moving virus in the world couldn't wipe out the whole crew so fast and we would have heard about an epidemic." He pulled me up with his free hand and murmured. "Stay behind me, okay?"

For once, I didn't argue.

With no lights to go by, we picked our way carefully around the deck, checking for any signs of life.

"Where to?" I asked Logan when we'd made a complete circuit. "We can split up if you want. Cover more ground."

"No. There's only one weapon between the two of us. We need to stick together," he breathed, much to my relief. It had been an entirely insincere offer and I was glad he hadn't decided to take me up on it.

"Right then. Maybe something's wrong with the boat and that's why the lights aren't working. Maybe they all had to abandon ship." It seemed plausible.

But Logan shook his head. "We would have heard a distress call. We should check the wheelhouse first and see if we can restore power."

He led me toward it, pointing out the main winch drums, the try net winch cathead and a bunch of other crap I wouldn't recognize if my life depended on it. I really hope that wouldn't be the case.

It took me a while to figure out why he was telling me all this, relating information as though we were cramming for a trawler quiz. I gripped his hand and pulled him to a stop. "You're rambling because you're worried, aren't you?"

He didn't deny it. Stoic, terse, never say a sentence when a single syllable will get the point across Logan Parker was suffering from word vomit.

"Sorry," he muttered. "This is really freaking unsettling."

"Tell me about it." I held up a hand. "On second thought..."

"Smartass," he muttered but didn't let go of my hand and I didn't try to get away.

"Well, I'm glad I came along so you don't totally lose your shit."

He didn't say anything, just squeezed my hand as he headed up to the wheelhouse.

The wheelhouse was clearly dated, the technology several decades behind our rented cruiser. And empty. Logan scanned the controls and flipped a few switches. Lights came on in the small space as well as all over the ship.

I blinked in the harsh fluorescent light. After so much time in darkness, it seemed brighter than the noonday sun.

"Everything seems to be working fine. Radar, sonar, trawl sensors, GPS, maritime distress system." Logan muttered and gave me a significant look.

"Meaning someone had to shut it all down intentionally," I concluded. The question remained, why?

Logan flipped a switch. "I'm activating the Emergency position-indicating radio beacon station. I'd rather have to answer some uncomfortable questions with the Coast Guard and be safe rather than sorry I didn't later. Let's check out the crew quarters. See if we can unearth anything about our boy, Estaban."

With the lights turned back on, the vessel should have seemed less unnervingly eerie. It didn't. There were signs of life everywhere and no life to be seen. The trawler was quite literally, a ghost ship.

The crew quarters were not much more than rows of bunks with cot sides, which I presumed were to keep the sleeping fishermen from rolling out of bed, and lockers. I counted six in the first room and eight in the second. The lockers held changes of clothing, rubber boots and a few personal items like bombs, razors and the occasional photograph.

"Nothing," I told Logan as I slammed the last locker. "I couldn't even begin to guess which one belonged to Estaban. It's not like they write their names in their underwear."

We went to the small galley next. It was tidy, the pots and pans clamped to keep them in place while the boat traversed rough seas. It really did look as though the trawler had been abandoned.

"I don't get it." Logan ran his hand over his jaw. He hadn't shaved for a few days and between the red rimming his eyes from lack of sleep and the beard stubble, he looked worn out. "Why would they all abandon the ship in the middle of the night?"

I'd been asking myself the same question since we'd set foot aboard the *Sweet Release*, but nothing made sense. "Do you think they actually were trawling for shrimp? You said they were headed up the coast, right? Maybe they weren't fishing at all. Or weren't *supposed* to be fishing."

He lowered his hand and nodded. "Could be. This boat is big enough for a commercial license which means government regulations on how much they fish. Let's see if they left anything in the hold."

We descended to the lowest deck, past some whirring machinery in the engine room, crates and barrels and other various equipment storage. The fish hold was in the back, the cold storage necessary to preserve the shrimp long enough to get to market. The large metal door had one of those wheel things that you needed to spin to unlock.

Logan handed me the revolver and moved toward it.

"Careful," the word slipped out before I realized it.

He nodded once then set to work. I could see his muscles straining as he fought with the door. Rust was visible around the hinges and I made a mental note to see that he got a tetanus shot as soon as possible after this little adventure.

"Come on you son of a motherless goat," He cursed and with a creak of stubborn gears, the door finally gave over.

The fish hold was frigid and a gust of cool air greeted us along with an awful stench.

"Phew, I think their cargo's gone bad." I stood on my tiptoes to see past Logan. There was no light in the hold, other than what spilled in from the corridor.

Logan didn't move.

"Hey," I moved up beside him, craning my neck to see what he was staring at.

The gun clattered to the deck with a plunk of metal on metal.

We'd found the crew.

16

"Well, the good news is I didn't have to climb back down the cargo net," I gave a wan smile to the humorless police officer who'd been interrogating me for the last several hours.

"Ma'am, do you find this funny?" He was short, bald and apparently had no taste for gallows humor.

"No, I don't," I told him soberly. "I also don't see a point in going over the same information multiple times for no good reason. What do you think I'm not telling you?"

He gave me the squinty-eyed death glare. "You and your companion were found at the scene of multiple homicides. You had no valid reason to be there." He'd added the word valid, squinting at me with a challenging look in his eye.

"Someone we knew was a member of that crew. He told us where to meet up." I spoke the lie Logan and I had agreed on while we waited for the police.

"Shouldn't we just tell them the truth?" I'd been incredulous that he'd wanted me to lie to the police.

"We'll be in more trouble when they find out we were involved in a drive-by in Miami earlier in the week and then fell off the map only to pop up at the scene of a mass execution."

I'd swayed a little at the word. It had been an execution. Ten people in that hold and every single one had been duct-taped and gagged and had a neat little bullet hole in their forehead, including Estaban Martinez.

Logan had kept one arm around me as the Coast Guard and police swarmed over the trawler. The gesture was partly to hold me up and partly to cement our cover story. "Better they think we're idiot newlyweds honeymooning in the Keys who went out to meet up with an old friend."

I'd shivered and he pulled me in tighter until I whispered in his ear, "Why newlyweds?"

"Because we're too young to be looking to retire here. If we say we're on business, they'll want to know what that business is. Honeymooners aren't expected to have anything better to do than screw like rabid minks. And it helps that our I.D's have the same last name, so they shouldn't ask us to produce a wedding license."

It had made sense, though I didn't appreciate the rabid mink comparison. As soon as we'd been offloaded from the *Sweet Release*, Logan and I had been separated, probably so they could match up our stories.

"I want to see my husband," I told my humorless interrogator.

He narrowed his eyes on me. "Soon. Let's go over it one more time. You and your husband decided to take out your friend's boat at night?"

"We were busy all day you see." I gave him a half-embarrassed, half-rueful look. Up to him to assume the busy meant sex, not lice treatment.

"So you took the boat out and just happened to find the *Sweet Release*?"

I didn't appreciate his tone, he sounded as though he

knew I was lying. Time for a new strategy. I could either pull the huffy indignant female or the empty-headed space cadet. Sadly, my empty-headed routine was often the one that worked best, especially on men who almost seemed to be expecting it.

"I can't wait to tell my friend Marcy about this." I giggled like a total flaming fool. "She won't even believe it. Hell, *I* can barely believe it. Do you mind if I borrow your phone? I want to take a selfie." I made a show of fluffing my heinous windblown nitpicked hair.

The interrogator pinched the bridge of his nose and sighed. Exactly the reaction I was going for.

I thrust out my braless chest, which was much more impressive without the life jacket squishing the girls into funbag jelly. "Do we like, need a lawyer? 'Cause my daddy has a lawyer and we could probably call him."

Someone knocked on the door. The Detective whose name I'd forgotten got up and cracked it open. There was a brief conference with whoever stood on the other side of the door and then he waved me up. "You're free to go."

"Really?" I chirped, hopping to my feet and clapping excitedly like I was about to start a cheerleading chant.

He narrowed his eyes on me and I made a mental note not to overplay my hand. "Where's Logan?"

"Jackie?" I heard him before I saw him, coming out of what I could only assume was another interrogation room.

I rushed down the hall and threw myself into his arms. He played along perfectly, scooping me up, spinning me in a half-circle and then setting me down only to plant a searing kiss on my lips.

Between one shared breath and the next, I forgot that we were playing pretend, forgot that he sort of hated me and that I sort of despised him and that he had been set to possibly kill for me and that we'd just found a bunch of half-frozen dead bodies.

Logan tried to pull away first but I held on tight. Deepening the kiss, moving into him until our bodies were pressed together. I could taste his surprise, but he didn't fight me. I wished I could convince myself that I hung on like a parasite because I wanted to put on a good show for the cops or because I needed the comfort. But no, I just got lost in a moment and wanted to pitch a tent and take up permanent residence in it, with him.

Forever.

A wolf whistle broke into the moment and I finally released him. Claps sounded from all around us, the noble men and women appreciating the show. I ducked my head and didn't have to fake the heat creeping up my cheeks.

"You're free to go." Logan's interrogator seemed a great deal more civil than the misogynistic asshat that had been grilling me. "We have your phone number and the address where you're staying if we need to follow up."

Logan nodded and tucked me into his side. The clapping followed us out of the building and my face flamed brighter. I glanced back over my shoulder. "No, it's not at all weird that a whole building full of people think we're going off to have sex."

"Aren't we?" Logan asked with a raised eyebrow. "'Cause that was a *do me, you great big stud kiss* if I've ever experienced one."

I elbowed him in the ribs. "Jerk. I'm surprised they let us go."

"No evidence to make it seem as if we were lying," Logan grumbled. "There's our ride."

"Where?" I looked around and didn't see any familiar vehicles. Then the door to a rusted out station wagon opened and a large and familiar figure wearing a mammoth tropical print shirt emerged. "Oh no, you didn't call my *mother*, did you?"

"Guess the sexcapades will have to wait, hot stuff." He smacked me on the rump then waved to Big John. "Thanks for coming."

Celeste too emerged from the crappy vehicle. "Jackie!" She wore a large straw hat and hot pink plastic hoop earrings the same exact shade as her halter-style sundress. They looked like a couple of dimwitted tourists.

"Judas," I greeted her.

She ignored my tone and pulled me into a tight hug.

"Careful," I warned her, not hugging back. "I have lice."

She withdrew as if I were covered in head to toe flames, her eyes wide with horror. "Oh no, when did that happen?"

"My best guess is sometime between the shooting and the abduction," I grumbled and climbed into the car. "Are we going now?"

Though Celeste offered to ride in back with me, Logan waved her off. I buckled in and ignored all three of them, too tired to deal with even basic conversation.

Another car was waiting for us in the driveway. It was a nondescript sedan so my guess was another rental. I shuddered to think how much this entire operation of *hide the process server* was going to cost my family and friends.

Then I saw who was waiting on the steps and forgot all about money. "Luke!"

"Hey, Ace." He grinned when he saw me, the same goofy sideways grin filled with open warmth and affection. There he was, my ally. Seeing it, seeing him, I couldn't help but burst into tears.

"Whoa, whoa! Are you okay?" Luke sprinted across the shell drive and took me into his arms.

I shook my head. "No."

"What the hell happened?" Luke asked over my shoulder. "Hey wait a minute. Where are you going? Logan, get back here!"

He let me go and I wiped the moisture out of my eyes long enough to catch the full force of the blistering rage coming off of Logan in waves. His back was to me, but that was almost worse. Luke ran up to his side and there was a furious back and forth. Logan did turn my direction then, eyes like chips of blue ice. He shook his head and continued off down the beach without another word.

"So what exactly happened between you and Logan?" From the other side of the shower curtain, I heard the distinctive sound of the toilet lid being set down. Apparently, Celeste was going to wait out my shower.

I leaned back under the falling spray. "I know you've never been aces with personal space but could I at least have a few minutes to myself?"

"No." Her defiant tone took me by surprise. "I bought you all those brand new clothes and toiletries, the least you can do is tell me what's going on."

The toiletries were nice, the shampoo, all herbs and citrus. The shower gel decadent, even when applied with the rough washcloth. But still, asking for fifteen minutes to lather, rinse and repeat didn't seem like a big selfish gesture. "Celeste, I have maybe three hours of sleep out of the last forty-eight. I'm tired, I'm hungry and I just saw a whole bunch of dead people. Can't we discuss my latest fall out with the Dark Prince later?"

"Stop calling him that." Celeste snapped. "He's no more evil than you are. Jackie, can't you see you hurt him?"

I ripped the shower curtain aside so I could see her. "How? I didn't *do* anything!"

She looked like a white trash queen, perched on the toilet all prim and indignant. "You ran to Luke. Cried in his arms."

I rolled my eyes. "Stop overdramatizing everything. It wasn't like that. I was exhausted and Luke's always been there to comfort me. And can you at least shut the bathroom door?"

She appeared totally baffled by this request. "Why? John's the only one in this house who hasn't seen you naked. And he and Luke went to the store for some supplies."

I might as well try to teach Sasquatch to howl *Stairway to Heaven* as to explain the concept of modesty to Celeste. "Because showering in public wasn't on my bucket list, okay? And just leave it alone. This is just Logan being Logan. He doesn't need you to be his champion."

"Jackie, just admit that you're scared."

"Of course I'm scared. People were shooting at me just the other day!"

"Not about that, about Logan."

"What about Logan?" A deep voice said from the door.

I sighed and shut the shower curtain again before he could see me.

"Mind if I have the floor, Celeste?" Logan asked.

"What?" I squeaked. "No, Celeste don't you dare—"

But she wasn't listening to my threats. "Be my guest."

"Mother!" I called out desperately.

"We'll talk later, after your shower. Toodles." I heard the click of her high heeled sandals as she left me to my doom.

I didn't say anything and neither did he. I knew he was still there though, a big dark shape lurking on the other side of the shower curtain.

The water had cooled from its normal tepid to frigid. I shut it off and stood there, naked and shivering.

"You have to come out sometime," he sneered in a mocking tone. "You can't hide in there forever."

"I'm not hiding," I lied. "Why should I hide from you? You're the one who—"

"Who what?" The shower curtain was violently ripped aside. "How exactly have I fucked up now?"

I yelped and took a step away from him until my back hit the wall. Logan stood there, fuming at me. For once he didn't take advantage of my nakedness, his attention didn't leave my face.

Truth be told I didn't even know what had gone wrong. And that infuriated me. I sure as hell hadn't done anything wrong. "You're the one who's all stomping around and angry."

"Don't I have a reason to be? You ran into his arms, Jackie."

"No, I didn't." Why did everyone think that?

"He's just as guilty of your so-called abduction as I was. So how did I end up being the asshole again after cooking for you, indulging the madcap goose-chase that ends up on the Shrimp boat of horror and *lying to the police* for you? And somehow he's your shining hero? Tell me how this works."

"Can I just get dressed and we can talk about this calmly," I tried.

But he shook his head. "No, I am miles past calm."

The AC had kicked on and was blowing right down on me. Enough, I wasn't going to turn into a human Popsicle because he'd decided to corner me in the bathroom. I reached past him and yanked a towel off the rack. "Your jealousy is your issue, Logan. I didn't do anything wrong."

"Should I just pretend that you weren't married to my brother for the last several years? Act like it never happened?"

"Of course not, but you keep bringing it up like you're

trying to drive a wedge between us with it." I scrubbed furiously at the water droplets on my damp legs.

He laughed and it was a hollow sound. "Babe, if you feel guilty about marrying my brother, that's on you."

"I don't feel guilty," I snapped. "Stop trying to make me feel guilty."

"Stop dodging me," he shouted and ripped the towel from my hands.

"Give me that," I snapped and made to grab it back.

"Just get another one." He held the towel well out of my reach. "There are ten more on the shelf over there."

"I want that one, it was mine first."

He threw the towel down on the floor and leaned down until his nose was an inch from mine. "Now you know how I feel."

With that he stormed out, slamming the bathroom door behind him.

I picked up the towel and wrapped it around myself and sank onto the closed toilet lid.

Stupid Dark Prince and his stupid towel metaphor. So what if he'd had me first and I'd picked Luke, even after I'd known that Logan was his brother. I was with him now, wasn't I?

I thought back to that first day when Luke had brought me home to meet his family. I'd been living with Marcy for the past six months and Luke had shown up at my doorstep.

Of course, since I hadn't known he was coming, I was wearing my ratty gym shorts with a hole in the crotch and a stretched out tank top. Accessorizing my world-class outfit was a pint of Rum Raisin, and the spoon I was using because it was too much like cooking to scoop it into a bowl.

The carton, still half full had hit the floor when I'd seen who was on the other side of the door. "Luke? What are you doing here?" I flung myself at him, wrapping my arms around him and holding on for dear life.

He laughed and whirled me around, kicking the door shut behind him. He was in civilian clothes, jeans and a blue T-shirt and he smelled incredible, like fresh-cut grass and soap. "Did you miss me?"

"Of course." I grinned up at him. "Why didn't you tell me you were coming? My God, I'm such a mess."

"You're beautiful," he'd said and kissed the daylights out of me. "It's just a short stopover, an overnight, but I want you to meet my family. My brother is in town and I figure since we're engaged an all, it's long overdue."

"Your family," I echoed, my enthusiasm at seeing him was waning a bit. Of course, I knew this was coming, eventually. But I hadn't thought this flipping weekend.

Luke noticed my expression and frowned. "You don't have plans, do you?"

I snorted and waved at the T.V. "I think the *Veronica Mars* marathon will be just fine without me."

"Then what's the matter?"

"Honestly? I've never met anyone's family before, not in the official girlfriend capacity. The whole idea freaks me out a bit." Plus he'd be expecting to meet Celeste, who I hadn't spoken to since the day he'd proposed.

Luke pulled me into a tight embrace. "Hey, relax. They're going to love you as much as I do."

He did love me too, this incredible, handsome man actually loved me. At first, I thought maybe it would go away, that his feelings would change. Good things didn't happen for people like me unless they came with a catch. But here was Luke Parker, a big handsome monument to perfection and he wanted me, Jackie Drummond. And not just for a quick nail and bail, which we still hadn't done. No, Luke wanted to keep me forever.

Until he sees where you come from. My snarky inner voice hissed. *And he finds out what trash you are.*

"So what do you say?" Luke's enthusiasm is contagious and I laughed.

"What should I wear?"

An hour later we pulled up in front of an enormous house in Coconut Grove, the ritzy neighborhood on the water in southernmost Miami.

"Your parents live here?" I gaped.

"Part-time only. They have a ranch further north, but my dad has a lot of business connections so they go back and forth. Come on. I'll give you the grand tour."

I checked my chin for drool as Luke came around to open my door for me. The lavender and blue sundress was one of my favorites but seemed like a cheap rag when facing the pristine mansion with two-story Corinthian columns that seemed to take up the entire afternoon sky.

"Oh God, I don't think I can do this."

"They won't bite," Luke took my hand, dragging me forward.

"You didn't tell me you came from such…means." His folks were probably lounging by the pool, sipping their mid-afternoon martinis and laughing over the latest million they made playing the stock market. People like Luke had brunches and watched horse racing wearing big fancy hats. The closest I'd ever been to a horse race was the dog tracks.

Here it was, the big ass catch I knew was lurking. Luke was perfect and he came from money and for some unknown reason, he wanted me. But his parents…. People who lived in houses like this could probably smell the trailer park wafting off of me at ten yards.

"Babe, it's fine." Luke took my hand in his. "Just be yourself."

Well, it was good to know now, anyway. There would be

some terrible awkward meal, where the elusive brother, probably on break from Harvard or Yale, would make some joke and they would all laugh and I wouldn't get it so they would all think I was ignorant as well as trashy.

And then Luke would turn and look at me, without the blinders and politely offer to pay for my cab fare home because clearly, I didn't belong here.

I was not going to hyperventilate or pass out. I wasn't. I would get the hell through this and then move on with my life, letting the scalding humiliation remind me that I shouldn't ever reach for perfection because it wasn't meant for girls like me.

"Luke!" A woman shouted and then Luke was laughing as the small middle-aged woman wearing jeans and a tank top hugged the stuffing out of him.

I stood back, observing them discreetly. The maid maybe. Or the nanny. Although why would the Parkers even have a nanny, when Luke was a grown man. Maybe the brother was younger than I thought? I wracked my brain, trying to remember if Luke had ever mentioned his brother's age, or his name for that matter.

Luke released the welcoming committee with a grin and then reached for my hand again and blew all my silly assumptions to shreds. "Mom, I'd like you to meet Jackie, my fiancée. Jackie, my mom, Marge Parker."

My jaw dropped. This short, round competent looking woman with the bright smile was the owner of this massive house?

Marge seemed just as stunned to meet me. Her eyes grew larger in her round face and she repeated the word? "Fiancée? Are you messing with me?"

My heart sank, she hadn't even really looked at me and already she didn't like me.

She may not have been the whipcord thin WASP sort of

woman I'd been expecting, but clearly she knew trailer trash at first whiff.

Luke laughed and tugged me tighter into his side. "Yup. We're engaged."

Marge's gaze turned from Luke to me. I wanted to look away, to duck my head and hide but forced myself to extend my hand and lie. "It's very nice to meet you."

Then she did the unthinkable. She hugged me. Not a gentle embrace that was mostly arms and air kisses. No, she hugged me the way she'd hugged Luke, the body slam of affection with nothing held back. "Oh, welcome to the family, sweetness. It's so good to meet you."

Luke was laughing, most likely at the look on my face and mouthed *told you so.*

"Oh my dears, I am so happy for the both of you!" Marge pulled away, still grinning broadly and tucked her arm through mine. "Gerald will be thrilled and your brother, oh wait 'til he hears!"

"I didn't see his bike in the drive, he's still coming, right?" Luke asked anxiously. "He'll kick my ass if he's the last to know."

Marge patted him on the arm. "Don't worry, he called to say he'd be a little late and that we shouldn't hold dinner on him. We'll wait to share the good news with Ursula then. She can be the last to know."

"And Ursula is…?" I asked hesitantly.

Marge's expression soured a bit. "She goes by many names, Satan, Beelzebub, but Gerald calls her mother. Don't worry Jackie, we'll have you well prepared before we inflict her on you."

"Like a test?"

"Like a Whiskey Sour, or three. You do drink, don't you dear?"

"Um…?" I'd been sober since the night of my one-night-stand.

"Mom's been taking a mixology class," Luke told me. "We've all been subjected to her potions."

"What's your favorite drink? I'm mostly a rum girl myself. Both spice and white, depending on the drink."

I laughed. I'd been sure I was in for the interrogation of a lifetime and here Luke's mom was offering to make me my favorite cocktail. "I'm up for anything, really."

Marge's eyes lit up and she clapped her hands together. "Wonderful. Come, you simply must meet Gerald, he's out back, tinkering with his new smoker."

Marge led me through the amazing foyer, past the office, the library, and the sunroom and through the gourmet kitchen and out to the back patio. The view stole my breath, with an infinity pool overlooking the ocean. A man stood next to a heaping pile of what looked to my untrained eye to be scrap metal. He looked like Luke if Luke had decided to be an accountant instead of a marine. His complexion was far too pale for someone who had a cattle ranch and he wore horn-rimmed glasses. He looked a little lost in the sea of parts all around him.

"Marge, I'm going to have to call the store. These instructions are in German."

"Oh Gerald, leave that ghastly thing alone and come meet Jackie."

Luke's dad focused bright blue eyes on us. "Oh, hello?" He sounded confused.

"For the love of grief, Gerald this is a momentous occasion and look, you've ruined your shirt."

"What's that?" Gerald looked down at the smear of dirt on his blue polo. To me, he looked more surprised to be wearing clothes than that he'd gotten them dirty.

"I told you to have Heinrich do that." Marge scolded.

"Some things a man's got to do for himself, right dad?" Luke slapped his father on the shoulder.

"Well, nevermind. Gerald, this is Jackie, Luke's fiancée." Marge announced proudly.

Gerald was still frowning down at his scrap heap and his wife elbowed him in the ribs. "Did you hear me? Your son is getting married!"

"What now?" Gerald finally looked at me though I wasn't sure he actually saw me. "Who's married?"

"Honestly, you are hopeless. Leave that thing and put the salmon on the grill. "Come on Jackie dear, let's hook you up with a drink."

I don't remember much about the meal itself, though I'm sure it was wonderful. Other than the perpetual haze, I liked Luke's father as much as his mom and they made a great team, her making sure he didn't accidentally set himself on fire by standing too close to the grill, and him casting her looks filled with affection and appreciation.

Little by little, I relaxed. It wasn't just the pre-dinner cocktail, some scary blue-green concoction Marge had served to me in a hurricane glass. Luke's parents were so, so normal. Exactly what I'd always imagined real parents to be like. Marge made off-color jokes and Luke teased her about her "drinking hobby." Gerald asked Luke about his liberty and where he'd be stationed next. I got the impression he forgot the answer as soon as his son told him but Marge was keeping careful track of every word, probably to remind him later.

They asked about my job, not seeming at all upset that I was a process server, actually making a big deal about my position in the Sheriff's Office. They asked how my wedding plans were going, which I answered that I hadn't made any yet.

"But you'll be staying here, in Miami?" Marge perked up at this.

I nodded. "Since I just started working for the Sheriff's Office I can't take time off. And My mom, well, she's here too."

Marge patted my hand. "What a darling girl you are. Well, I don't want to step on any toes but I'd love to help."

I nodded eagerly. "That would be great."

The sound of a motorcycle carried on the wind and Marge jumped up. "That must be Logan, just in time for dessert. I made a coconut rum gelato. You like coconut, Jackie?"

I was too startled to speak for a minute, so I just bobbed my head. Marge scurried out of the room and I cast a look at Gerald, but he was staring back at the pile of smoker parts so I turned to Luke. "Logan? Your brother's name is Logan Parker?"

He picked up his wine glass. "That's right. Didn't I tell you that?"

"No," I whispered, trying to convince myself that Miami was a huge city and there were probably tons of Logan Parkers milling around. The one I'd run out on couldn't be related to Luke, he just couldn't.

Even if they looked alike. A lot alike. As in the same Parker gene pool alike.

And then I heard Marge's busy chatter and the deeper resonances that had given me shivers.

Shit. Shit. Shit. A thousand times shit.

"You're going to love her," Marge was saying a second before I caught sight of the neon blue gaze that had haunted my dreams.

I sat perfectly still, drinking him in. The same stubble, the same high cheekbones. The same brilliant smile.

Said smile disappeared the second his gaze fell on me.

Recognition flared in those neon blue eyes that I now knew he got from his father. Excitement turned to confusion and then morphed into an unsettling silence.

Logan Parker, Luke's brother.

I picked up my empty cocktail glass and turned to face Marge. "Would it be all right if I had another?"

17

It soon became obvious that the house wasn't big enough for all the people in it. Though I'd been exhausted, the good-natured ribbing between my mother and Big John was loud and distracting. Luke was on the phone. Logan had disappeared after our latest row. I'd gone to look for him once I'd dressed but his room was empty. I snagged his iPod out of his bag and then took Sasquatch for a walk down by the water.

I scrolled through the eclectic song selections as I walked, oddly impressed. I'd never really thought about Logan having any particular taste in music. But if I'd had to pick, I would have pegged him for a classic rock and metal guy. But his tastes ranged from R&B to Pop, to country.

Intrigued, I exited out of the main menu and accessed his playlist, wondering if he bothered to arrange them, and if so, how.

Halfway down I spotted a playlist titled *songs for her*.

Her? Heart pounding, I opened it up and nearly doubled over. Blue Oyster Cult's *Burnin' For You* was the first song listed. Then some techno number I didn't recognize until I popped the earbuds in and hit play. It was a clubbing song. Had it been playing at the club where we first met? Journey's *Separate Ways*, followed by Sinatra's *I've Got You Under My Skin*. Aerosmith, *I Don't Want to Miss A Thing*, Santana's *Black Magic Woman* and Kings of Leon's *Sex on Fire*… on and on it went, with no discernable pattern, no rhyme or reason and only one thing to unite the hodgepodge from different artists, different decades, they were all songs I recognized.

All love songs I recognized.

I was the her. And Logan Parker had made me a freaking playlist.

I had to sit down. So I did, right there in the wet sand.

No, he hadn't made it for me, he'd made it about me. There was a distinct difference. He'd never expected me to see this. So why had he bothered? Maybe as a reminder, to help him keep his distance? Maybe he'd just been bored one day and I was reading way too much into it.

I'd tried so hard with Luke, tried to be what he needed, what I thought his family expected me to be. The dutiful military wife, a working professional. I'd waited and dreamed, thrown my entire self into the relationship, lived in an unfinished house for five years and went to bed alone most nights and it hadn't been enough. Logan had seen all that, had witnessed my epic failure so how could Logan even ask me to…what?

Right the wrong. To pick him. That small voice grew louder, more insistent.

I couldn't though. I didn't even know why my marriage to Luke had failed. He'd wanted it and so had I. We had chemistry and shared interests, devotion, and mutual respect.

"And what do you change," I grumbled at the iPod. "I'll tell you what, absolutely nothing."

Someone tapped me on the shoulder and said, "Talking to yourself, Ace?"

I whirled, yanking the earbuds out as I went. "Luke."

"Hey, I didn't mean to startle you." My ex-husband looked around and frowned. "Where's Logan?"

I frowned back. "I didn't know it was my turn to watch him."

He studied my face. "You okay? Are you and Logan fighting again?"

I let out a breath. "The surprise would be if we were getting along, right?"

Sasquatch, who'd been in the ocean up to her shoulders trying to bite the waves, let out a triumphant bark when she saw Luke and charged. He laughed as she jumped up and toppled him into the sand.

He looked up at me then and his grin faded. "What's gnawing at you, Ace?"

My lower lip started to tremble at his honest, caring question. I was mad at him, I reminded myself. He'd encouraged my kidnapping after all. But after years of turning to him for comfort, both physical and emotional, I couldn't just shut it off. "Everything, I guess. This week has been frigging awful, Luke and your brother...."

"What's he done?" Luke put a hand on my shoulder.

If I told him it would change everything. Hell, everything had already changed so what was I clinging to? "Made me fall in love with him."

The pause that followed was one of the longest of my life and I wished I could call the words back. Would Luke go after Logan, maybe slug him? I'd seen the two of them fighting before.

"Bout time," Luke said.

My head whipped around. "What?" I wasn't sure what I was expecting but it sure as hell wasn't that.

Luke's smile was a little sheepish. "Did you think I didn't know?"

"But, but, but," I stammered not sure which objection to lodge first. They were all crowding in like Black Friday shoppers outside an outlet mall at 11:59 PM on Thanksgiving. "Aren't you upset?"

Sasquatch had retrieved a stick and dropped it at Luke's feet. He picked it up and chucked it for her. "Honestly, I'd be lying if I said I was thrilled about it. But I'm tired of coming in between the two of you."

"You're not," I began but he held up a hand.

He ran a hand through his hair and sighed. "Jackie, it's okay, we can talk about this. I know I went ballistic at Christmas, but you've got to understand, at the time I believed my brother was breaking up my marriage. He was with you all the time while I was gone and then he was so against you joining the team, I don't know. I guess my imagination ran away with me."

I picked up a handful of sand and let it trickle through my fingers. "I told you. Over and over again, I told you nothing was going on. Didn't you trust me?"

Sasquatch returned with the stick and Luke picked it up and hurled it again out into the waves. "You know Logan. From a completely neutral perspective, does he seem like the sort of guy to carry a torch for a woman who's not sleeping with him? And for more than a decade?" He shook his head.

I did know Logan, I realized, better than his own brother apparently. "Yes," I muttered.

He frowned at me.

"But you believe us now?"

Luke nodded slowly. I couldn't see his eyes behind his aviator sunglasses but I knew he was looking directly at me. "I've been talking to him over the past several weeks. And I've been actually listening this time to everything he's said. He knows you Ace, and he wants you, badly. I think, well, don't ever let this get back to him but I think he actually needs you. He's been moving around from place to place, staying in various shitholes like this one," he chucked a thumb at the battered modular house and I grinned.

"But the house next door," I said. "Back in Miami. He bought it. That sends a pretty clear *I want to settle down* message."

"You mean the house you love and went into debt to furnish, that house? Come on Ace, don't be dense. Of course he bought it for you."

I looked out at the churning waves. "I already have a house."

"No, you already have a construction zone covered in monkey piss."

"You have a point," I grumbled.

"So back to Logan who never settles down at one job or with one woman because he's smart enough to know that's what it would be—settling. I doubt he'll ever admit it, but it's the truth. You know how hard that is for me to say."

"I do." I reached out and squeezed his arm, grateful that we could talk like this, openly without worrying about bruising tender feelings or crushing fragile egos. He rose and then helped me to my feet. We really could still be friends.

"All he ever does is protect you," Luke murmured. "If there's one thing you can take to the bank, Ace, it's that Logan has your best interest at heart."

I COULD SEE Logan up on the roof of the rental house as Luke, Sasquatch and I approached. Typical Dark Prince, he was up there with his shirt pulled off, hammering away at something. The rusted out station wagon was gone, meaning either Big John, Celeste or both had gone out.

"Need a hand?" Luke called up to his brother.

Logan didn't even bother to glance our way.

Luke sighed. "Not like we don't have enough to do, he's got to tackle someone else's DIY projects. Stubborn pain in my ass."

"Logan, come down. We need to talk." I called, my heart racing.

He did look then, but not at me. I frowned and turned toward the crunch of seashells under tires. A huge Black Escalade pulled to a stop where Celeste's car had been.

"Are we expecting anyone else?" I asked Luke as I studied the new vehicle.

"Not that I know of," Luke muttered back.

Four men got out of the SUV, all carrying assault rifles.

"What?" Logan rose to his full height on the roof. "Who?"

It happened in less than a heartbeat. One man raised his weapon and fired. I shrieked as I watched Logan stagger back and then pitch off the roof.

A scream tore from my throat and I ran in the direction Logan had fallen. It was only one story. There was a ton of foliage on that side of the house, maybe it had broken his fall.

"Down," the man who'd shot Logan raised his weapon and aimed at me.

Someone pushed me face-first into the sand. I spat, trying to get the grit out of my mouth, cursing at Luke.

He was right next to me saying something I couldn't make out, not over the roaring of my ears. Logan had been shot and fell. I needed to get to him, to see how badly he'd been hurt.

"You can't help him if you're dead," Luke whispered and it was only then that I realized I'd spoken out loud. "Be smart, Ace."

I looked over at him. He had tackled Sasquatch, and she was pinned beneath him. The poor creature was struggling to get out, the look in her eyes murderous. I was with her. I didn't want to be smart. Every single fiber of my admittedly messed up being was dying to run to my Dark Prince's side.

Logan couldn't be dead. He could. Not. Be dead.

Shoes appeared on the sand in front of me. Men's dress shoes. They looked very wrong together, like high couture meets happy hour. He gripped me by my hair and pulled me upright. "This her?"

I stretched on my bare feet, trying to relieve the pressure on my roots. Tears welled at the burning pain and it took me a minute to recognize the man standing in front of me. Chills shot through me as I whispered, "You."

The man from the art gallery. The one with the deep-set blue eyes that held no hint of warmth. The man I suspected was a cop turned organ pirate.

"Hello, Jacqueline." He turned and called over his shoulder. "Check the house. There should be a spider monkey in there, but make sure no one else is around to surprise us."

The remaining two men stormed into the little house and were back in seconds. "Empty."

"Did you find the monkey?"

"No, Sir."

"Where is he?" The one in charge turned to me. "Did you drop him off with anyone?"

"No. He's probably hiding under the house. Loud noises upset him." It was BS, Abu had never been beneath the house to my knowledge, but I had no idea why the man was after him and I wanted to keep Celeste and John out of this if I could.

He studied my face and a small, creepy smile appeared. "You're lying. Kill the one in the bushes."

"No!" I tried to reach for him but the grip on my hair held me in place.

He held up a hand and the two thugs on the porch stopped. "Where's the monkey?"

"I really don't know. He was in the house when I left." I sobbed. "Please, don't kill anyone."

Again he assessed me and then nodded. "All right. We have what we came for."

"What do you want? Why are you doing this?" They were ridiculous questions, cliché even, but I really wanted to know so then maybe I could figure out a way to keep all the people I loved safe.

If it wasn't too late for Logan.

He ignored my questions, instead of looking me over from head to toe. "You proved more difficult to corner than I anticipated. I wonder if I underestimated you."

I had no idea what he was talking about and the question sounded rhetorical, so I kept my trap shut and hoped he'd get to the point before Logan bled out.

He tipped his head to the side. "It's been like watching a television drama unfold, you and your tangled love life. Tell me, is it Luke or Logan this week?"

I swallowed hard, then regretted it. I could have taken a page from the mad spitter's book and hocked a big old lugie at him. The best I managed was "Go to hell."

He actually broke into a grin at that. "Plucky to the last. Load her in the car."

"What about this one?" The man who still held my hair asked the one who seemed to be in charge.

"Depends on which one he is. Remarkable genetics, don't you think Jaqueline? Take his sunglasses off, let me see his eyes."

The man released me and I staggered. He reached towards Luke's aviators but Sasquatch snarled and snapped from beneath him. The weapon came up and I saw in a flash what was going to happen. The guy would hit Luke with the butt of his rifle and then shoot Sasquatch when she broke free from her master's grip.

"That's Luke," I shouted, hoping I hadn't just traded his life for the dog's. "It's him. Logan was on the roof."

The man next to me smirked. "Well, she would know." He turned to Luke. "You're the one who thinks things through, so let me lay it out for you. Your brother was shot in the leg and had a bad fall. He requires medical attention. You're going to take him to NAS Key West and get him help. The medical staff there will save his life. If you try to stop us, all three of you will die and the animal as well. So be the hero instead of the punchline for once, save your brother and say goodbye to her."

"Jackie," Luke had gone pale beneath his tan. I could tell he was thinking furiously, as I was.

"Help him," I begged Luke. "Save him. I'll be all right."

Then I was being dragged toward the vehicle, Luke still calling my name from his position under guard.

I stumbled along, shocked and doing my level best to figure out who the man was and what he wanted with me. He seemed to know me, he knew about Abu, about my complicated relationship with Luke and Logan. It was almost as though he was reading my mind. And that bizarre comment about my life being like a television drama. Where had I heard that before?

Dismay filled me when I saw the station wagon turn off the road and into the crushed shell driveway.

"Well well," The man in charge murmured. "I was hoping to see her again."

I looked him up and down. "You know Celeste?"

"Intimately," Again that snakelike gaze snared mine and held me in thrall until he decided to strike. "Haven't you figured out who I am yet?"

"Brian?" Celeste had climbed from the car, her face a mix of horror and shock.

Unlike me, my mother recognized this man. I looked at him again, and it clicked into place.

"What?" This from John. "Celeste, who the porkin' hell is this joker?"

"Do you want to tell him, Jackie, or should I?"

I was still processing, still trying to deny the odd feeling of familiarity I'd had since I'd first laid eyes on him.

"I'm her father," the man named Brian announced, right before he drew a Glock from his waistband and shot Big John Garrison between the eyes.

18

"Load the women in the vehicle," Brian ordered loud enough to be heard over Celeste's screams.

"You bastard," I shouted and pulled out of his loosened grip. I sprinted for where Big John had gone down, praying for a miracle and knowing deep in my gut that I wasn't going to get one.

John lay flat on his back, his eyes staring sightlessly up at the sky. Execution style, just like Estaban Martinez and the crew of the *Sweet Release*.

Someone approached from behind me.

"Why?" I asked, sensing his presence.

"You needed to know I was serious." Brian—my father, the killer, said. "I figured he was a better choice than one of your precious Parker brothers. He was your competition after all, both professionally and then for your mother's attention. You should thank me."

Thank him? The man was certifiable. And he was also armed and obviously willing to kill.

I rose to my feet and turned to face him, the wind lifting the hair off the back of my neck. Looking into his eyes I saw only death, my death. "I want to see Logan. I want to say goodbye."

Again with that creepy grin. "Is that right? He's your pick then? I thought so. I should have bet more than fifty dollars. All right, I think we all want to see the end of this." He gestured to his goons who had gagged Celeste. From the backseat of the station wagon, I saw a small primate head pop up and then duck back down.

I stepped around him, my hands clenched into fists. "You don't need her."

"Oh, but I think I do. And not just to control you. Celeste owes me. If you want to say goodbye, do it now. We don't have much time."

I walked on wooden legs toward the foliage, Brian right behind me. Logan lay on his side, his right leg covered in blood.

I knelt beside him and checked for a pulse, found it sure and steady. Ran a hand through his hair. "Logan? Can you hear me?"

He mumbled something, might have been my name, and I looked up to see Luke, still holding Sasquatch by the collar, being prodded forward.

"He's alive," I told my ex-husband. "Take off your belt."

Brian laughed. "You're incredible."

"I want to use it as a tourniquet," I said through gritted teeth. "To stop the bleeding."

"If I let her go…." Luke looked down at Sasquatch. I took note of all the short spikey hairs standing on end along her long body. Yeah, letting her go would cause chaos. It was a mark of respect that she wasn't struggling in Luke's grip.

"You'll have to remove it for him." Brian sounded delighted. "Should I wake Logan so he can watch?"

"Asshole," I muttered and then stepped up close to Luke.

"You don't have to go with them." Luke urged me.

All my attention was focused on the task at hand but I whispered. "Abu is in my mother's car. John's beyond help. Please, promise me you'll take care of yourself. And of Logan."

"I will."

With a final tug, the belt came free and I crouched by Logan's side. It was probably a good thing he was unconscious because he would never, not in a million years, let me leave with Brian and his cohorts.

I tightened the belt around his leg and he let out a shuddering groan. Then I bent down and whispered in his ear. "I think I've always wanted to be the woman you see when you look at me. The woman who deserves your playlists and your sacrifices and your faith. I'm sorry I was so scared, sorry I kept running and that we never got our chance. I love you, Logan Parker and I always will."

"Time's up. That was beautiful, Jacqueline. I'm truly moved." The Glock prodded my spine.

Logan's face was pale and he was shivering despite the heat. Was he going into shock? I had no idea what damage had been done in the fall, maybe he'd been paralyzed or had internal injuries. Though I didn't give a damn about Brian's timetable, the sooner I got him and his goons out of here, the sooner Luke could get Logan to the hospital.

I kissed him once and then turned on my heel and headed for the Escalade.

We were on the road in moments, Celeste and I in the second row of seats. Brian sat in the front beside the driver, and the goons with the assault rifles sat behind us.

My mother gripped my hand hard and I stifled the wince. Though I was just as terrified as she was I was more pissed off than anything.

"Why now?" I asked.

"You mean, why did I pop back into your life?" Brian turned in the seat to face me. "I need something from you."

"You think I'll want to help you while you're holding my mother hostage?" I asked him.

He shrugged. "No, you won't want to help me either way. I know that much. But you see, I don't require your cooperation."

"What do you want then?"

He just smiled that unsettling smile and turned to face forward.

Through the windshield, I saw the blue lights of police vehicles. Traffic slowed to a crawl as each car rolled down their window and spoke to an officer at the barricade.

Hope filled me. Was it a DUI checkpoint? Or maybe someone had reported the sounds of shots being fired and the police had closed off the road. Regardless, four armed men and two terrified women were sure to send up red flags.

The driver slowed and I was shocked to see no one made even an attempt to stow their weapons. I sucked in a breath. Were they going to kill the cops?

The face that appeared by the driver's side window was familiar. It was the jackass who'd interrogated me all morning. He smirked at me and then turned to face Brian. "Have everything you need, Sir?"

"Yes, thank you, Sam. Your information paid off handsomely. I'll make sure you're well compensated. "

My mouth fell open. A dirty cop. So much for help from the boys in blue.

"Do you want a police escort to the airport?"

"Unnecessary. But when we've gone, make sure the Parker brothers are silenced for good. No loose ends."

I hissed, "You bastard! You promised to let them go!"

He turned around to face me. "Gag her."

Someone grabbed me from behind and forced a rag into

my mouth. I tried to spit it out but a piece of duct tape was stretched across my lips. I struggled, but between the seatbelt and the grip on my shoulders, it didn't get me anywhere.

Luke, I thought desperately. *Logan. I'm so sorry.*

No one spoke as we drove to a small private airfield. I'd expected to see a plane but it was a helicopter that sat at the ready. Apparently, the black market organ business was booming.

We were loaded unceremoniously from the Escalade and dragged on board the helicopter. The noise from the rotors was too loud for me to hear anything, but at least Celeste and I were together. I had no idea where we were going or what horrible fate Brian had planned for us on the other end. I had no weapons, not even my mouth.

I leaned against my mother and wondered if I had it all to do over again, what I would have done differently and if it would have helped.

THE CONSTANT ROAR of the rotors lulled me into a dazed sort of state. I thought about that night at the Parker's house, back when they'd still lived in the big house in Coral Gables. The night that I'd picked one path and stuck to it.

Logan hadn't taken his eyes off me since he'd arrived at his parent's house. Honestly, I was surprised no one else had noticed his probing stare, but Marge chattered about wedding plans and Gerald had pulled Luke into a discussion about stock prices and cost of feed. I emptied the grapefruit-flavored cocktail in record time, before realizing the error of my ways. Namely, that what went in had to come out.

"So Jackie," Logan said, his first words since he sat across the table from me. "I don't believe I caught your last name."

The double meaning dripped like a melting icicle from

his frosty words. I squirmed, as much because of my full bladder as his chilly tone. "It's…uh…Drummond, actually."

"That right?" Those eyes missed nothing. They were so much colder than I remembered. Subarctic even. Not that I blamed him. I had rabbited while he was in the shower. He leaned back in his chair, ignoring the drink his mother set in front of him.

"Logan, I made this especially for you. It has whiskey in it as I know that's your drug of choice," Marge twittered, clearly oblivious to the tension between me and her older son. "It's called the Seething Jealousy."

Logan's gaze flicked to the drink and then back to me. "Fitting."

The bladder situation was growing dire but I was terrified that the second I excused myself from the table, Logan would have every opportunity to announce what a hobag I was to Luke's entire family.

Of course, there was nothing stopping him from outing my hobagishness while I sat there in a puddle of my own making.

Put that way, I could only hope to minimize the scalding humiliation. "Where's your restroom?" I asked Marge as she set a slice of cake in front of me.

"Down the hall, last door on the left. Do you want me to show you?"

Logan popped up from his chair like he had a spring in his back pocket. "That's okay, Mom. I'll show her. I could use a pitstop myself."

Oh damn. Damn damn damn. I hadn't taken that possibility into consideration. That he'd corner me on his own and…what? What could he do?

Other than ruin the hope for the rest of my life, of course.

My heart thudded in my ribcage as I moved away from the sounds of conversation and in through the kitchen. What would he say? How would I respond? As Logan Parker silently escorted me through the humongous downstairs of his parent's house, a million possibilities of how this would play out flashed through my mind.

He stopped by a door and gestured. "In there."

That was it? "Thanks," I murmured and slipped past him, shutting the door behind myself.

Okay, so maybe he wasn't going to make a big deal out of the fact that he'd once taken me home like a souvenir glass from a bar. Maybe he also really had to pee and was just being gentlemanly in escorting me. Maybe I could answer nature's call and then scuttle back to Luke's side before he finished whatever it was he had to do. I'd remembered him being insanely polite, almost sweet. It was possible that he was too well-bred to make a big deal out of the entire awkward scenario and we could just pretend that night never happened.

After attending to my needs, I washed my hands and fluffed my hair in the mirror, convinced that Logan wasn't going to be an issue.

He lounged against the wall outside the bathroom and I offered him a tight smile as I gestured to the bathroom. "Go for it."

"Go for it?" his tone was mild, but I wasn't fooled. He caught my elbow and dragged me closer. Though he wasn't holding me hard enough to hurt me, his message was crystal clear. I wasn't going anywhere. "That's all you have to say to me? Go for it?"

"What would you like me to say?" The words sounded breathy, like something a not so bright bar bunny would whisper.

His eyes flashed and he tilted his head a little, his expression menacing. "How long have you known my brother?"

"A few months." Again I tried to jerk my arm free but he wasn't having it.

"So he got the benefit of your last name? You told him where you lived, I take it."

"It was a completely different set of circumstances."

Hurt flashed in his face, so quickly that it was gone before I was even sure that's what I'd seen. "You can't marry him," he hissed.

"And why the hell not? Your parents seem to like me just fine."

"They don't know what you're really like though, do they? Not the way I do."

Part of me wanted to ask him what gave him the understanding of my character, but I was still trying to salvage the situation. "They'll get to know me."

Logan was shaking his head, dark hair falling over his eyes, making him look a little sinister. "No, you've got to call it off. You can't just marry my brother, not after what we shared. Call it off or I'll tell him."

My jaw dropped. I couldn't believe he was doing this here, outside of his mother's powder room. So much for class. "Are you threatening me?"

"Call it what you like but he deserves to know," Logan did release me then, but his words had rooted me to the spot. His voice got louder as he said, "Either you tell him or I will."

"Lower your voice," I snapped. My mind was whirling, unable to believe that this was really happening. Of all the rotten, good for nothing luck. Just when I'd started to turn my life around, just when I'd put Celeste in my rearview and had planned to make a real upstanding life for myself, fate dealt me this shitty hand. "It was a mistake that happened years ago. Do you think Luke plans to tell me about all of his lovers?"

"He would if you were going to be *related* to them," Logan

snarled. "You can't keep this from him, not if you really care about him."

"That's exactly why I don't want to say anything. What good will come from telling Luke we had sex before I even met him?"

He leaned in, his expression foreboding. "It was more than sex, at least it would have been if you'd bothered to stick around until I got out of the shower."

I pulled back, his words making me see him in a new light. "So is that what you're upset about? That I chose to stay with Luke when I left you?"

He flinched. It wasn't a huge gesture but I'd been looking for it. He didn't know Luke and I hadn't consummated our relationship physically, and I wasn't about to tell him he was still the only man I'd ever been with. I didn't want to hurt him more but that seemed unavoidable at this point. Besides, he wasn't pulling his punches either.

"So you're jealous, huh? Well, let me tell you something, Buster. It never would have worked out for us in the long run. I can see how you really are now."

"And how am I?" He leaned in again, his features tight.

I looked him over slowly from head to toe. It was an assessing look, but even so, I could still see the tightness of his abs, could appreciate the breadth of his shoulders, the power in his arms. I shrugged. "You're sin incarnate. Not exactly the marrying type though."

There was no mistaking the flinch that time and I pressed my advantage. "Are you really going to be so petty to take away your only brother's shot at happiness? I know how much you mean to him. Do you really want that on your conscience?"

He didn't, I could see that from the rigidness of his posture. "So you won't tell him?"

Holding his gaze, I shook my head slowly from side to

side. "Not now, not ever and I hope I can count on you to do the same, for Luke's sake."

This time he didn't try to stop me as I brushed past him. I was ten feet away when he called, "Jackie, do something for me."

I made the mistake of looking over my shoulder. His expression of anguish stole my breath. He was good at hiding his emotions and it was even more jarring when he didn't. "What is it?"

A muscle jumped in his jaw. "Promise me you won't hurt him."

My lips parted. I blinked at him, unable to believe I had made him look so retched. No, it was just the situation. Logan probably hadn't thought about me in years, would probably never have remembered what I looked like if not for this bizarre scenario. "I promise I won't hurt him. I do love him you know."

He turned away, heading towards the front door. "Tell mom I got a call from work and had to go."

"Alright." I'd won. He wasn't going to tell Luke or ruin my reputation with his family. He'd agreed to keep my secret. So why did watching him walk away make me feel as though I was losing something precious?

I wanted to tell him I was sorry that I hurt him but I didn't want to rub salt in his wound. And he was wounded, the naked pain on his face could be from nothing but a soul-deep injury. Was it possible I'd mattered to him? That he had remembered me with the same sort of longing I'd felt for him?

"Logan," I called before I realized my intention.

He had the front door open and turned to look back at me.

Why was my throat suddenly so dry? I tried to swallow,

but there was something stuck. I couldn't pull a full breath as I stared at his profile backlit by the setting sun.

The words that came out were heartfelt, if not what I'd intended. "Take care of yourself."

He scanned me up and down. "You do the same." Then he slid his sunglasses on and shut the door behind him.

Somehow, I stumbled my way back to the patio. Marge jumped up when she saw me. "Oh Jackie dear, are you all right?"

"Just a little light-headed," I forced a smile. "Those drinks pack a punch. Logan had to leave, by the way."

Marge waved this last bit off. "Did I make your drinks too strong? Would you like ice water?"

"Actually Mom, I should probably take Jackie home." Luke came to the rescue.

Marge fussed over me a bit more but in the end, she wished me well. "I'll contact you next week. We can get together for lunch and start planning."

"Sounds great," I said, meaning it.

Much to my surprise, Gerald gave me a hug. "It was so nice meeting you, Jackie."

Frankly, I was astonished he'd known I was there, more so that he'd remembered my name. "You too."

Luke chatted about nothing in particular on the drive home. I made appropriate sounds whenever there was a lull but I really wasn't paying attention.

He pulled into a visitor spot in my parking lot and shut the engine off before turning to me. "Okay, so what's wrong?"

"Huh?" I blinked. "Why would you ask that?"

He made an exasperated sound. "Come on, Ace. You've been distracted most of the night. And what were you and Logan talking about so long?"

So, our absence had been noticed. Luke was more perceptive than I realized. I decided to stick with the truth, just not the whole truth. "He asked me not to hurt you."

A smile spread across Luke's face and he shook his head. "Always the big brother."

"Yup. I promised I wouldn't, just so you know."

Luke took my hand in his, his eyes searching my face. "You sure that's all?"

I looked him over closely. So like Logan and yet so different. There was a golden aura surrounding Luke where Logan had such an imposing air. At that moment, I was convinced I'd done the right thing. Instead of answering his question, I asked one of my own. "So, how long are you going to be in town again?"

His fingers threaded through mine and he brought my knuckles to his lips. "Got to head out early tomorrow."

"Wanna stay the night?"

He searched my face. "You're sure?"

"Absolutely," I'd lied. I wasn't sure of anything at that point, other than the fact Luke was leaving in a few hours and I wanted to think about something other than the horrible expression on Logan's face when he'd left.

It had sort of worked. What would have happened if I'd been completely honest with Luke that night? What would have happened if I told him his big brother was my first and only lover and his kindness and acceptance had snuck past my thorny defenses and into my soft heart years before Luke and I had met? He would have been upset, sure, but knowing Luke the way I had, he would have forgiven me. Eventually. And Logan and I would have had our chance.

The thump of the helicopter setting down broke me from my recriminations. Celeste had fallen asleep beside me, her head lolling against my chest. I was sweating like crazy beneath the tape, but it still hurt when one of the goons ripped it from my face.

"We're here," Brian said jovially.

My throat was cracked and covered with scales, at least if felt that way but I managed to croak. "Where's here?"

He only smiled and pulled me from the helicopter.

I stumbled after him, squinting against the azure sky. The brightness was blinding after the dim interior of the helicopter. I could see sand and palm trees and water, but had no way of discerning if we were still in Florida, or even in the United States any longer.

Celeste was hauled off in another direction, clawing at her captors and screaming my name. Brian ignored her and after a moment of contemplation, I did as well. It was ridiculous, considering that he was a first-rate bastard, but I wanted to show him that I wasn't just Celeste's daughter, that I wouldn't throw a tantrum every time I was dragged around, that there was more to me than my messed up love life and abandonment issues.

The son of a bitch thought he knew me. And I was determined to prove him wrong.

He strode through the door of a large building. A blast of arctic coolness streamed down on us and if I thought the light outside had been blinding it was nothing compared to the glaring white that surrounded us. People strode past us, no one as much as batting an eye at the blood on my sundress. I guessed from their quick, businesslike movements they were medical professionals. This was a hospital of some sort.

Brian took me down a hallway and made a series of complicated turns. He didn't say anything and neither did I. We strode past doors, both open and closed. The open ones showed empty hospital beds. No one stopped us.

Finally, he paused in front of a closed door. There was no number on it, but a small window cut above it. There were blinds over the window but they were pulled open. He gestured for me to look inside.

After a moment's hesitation I did.

A young woman lay resting in a hospital bed, her brown hair dark against the pillow. Her face was gaunt, her cheekbones jutting out obscenely. Her body looked emaciated to the point that at first, I thought she was a child. A dying child.

"That's your sister. Maryanne. She's twenty."

I put my hand on the door, wishing I could touch her. "What's wrong with her?"

"Cancer," He said simply. "This is her second bout with it."

"I'm sorry," I said and I was. Not for him, he could rot in the fiery depths of hell, but because it was an awful disease.

I stepped back from the door and he looked in. "She's had so much chemo her organs are starting to shut down. We've already replaced her liver and her kidneys but she needs a new heart. Your heart."

"What?" I stepped back, away from him.

"You're her half-sister and the closest biological match we have."

"But," I looked from the room containing the dying girl to him and back. "But, I'm still using my heart."

He smiled as he muttered, "Not for long."

19

I was taken to a small white room by one of Brian's thugs. He pushed me inside and told me to strip to my skin and put on a pair of blue scrubs. I raised my chin and told him where to go and what he could do with himself when he got there. I was smacked for my efforts and told Celeste would lose a digit every time I defied them. I put on the scrubs and he tossed the dress stained with Logan's blood in a pink bag marked biohazard.

Then came the questions. Had I ever taken intravenous drugs? I thought about saying yes on the off chance they'd decide not to use my heart, but then figured they would just shoot me in the head. No. Had I ever been diagnosed with a blood disorder? No. Smoked. No. Contracted a sexually transmitted disease. Not that I was aware of. Next up, the tests. So many tests that I was surprised to have any blood left by the time they were done. Was informed my blood pressure was high. I wanted to hiss *no shit, Sherlock* but didn't for the sake of my mother's digits. Then I was hooked to an I.V. and left alone.

After checking for any sort of surveillance equipment, I

spit out the small metal disk I'd lifted from Logan's pants pocket when I'd tended him and had hidden beneath my tongue after whispering my goodbyes. The red light glowed reassuringly, letting me know the tracking system was working. Thank god I hadn't swallowed the thing. It was a sturdy little bugger but I didn't think it would survive stomach acid.

Whether anyone was alive on the other end to receive its signal was another kettle of fish.

Tears stung my eyes and I let them fall. Defiant was one thing but I was being prepped for open-heart surgery, and I wouldn't have a heart at the end of it. No heart, no life, no more Jackie.

The door opened and Brian came in. I wiped furtively at my face, taking the opportunity to pop the tracker back in my mouth. His expression was neutral as he approached.

"How long have you known about me?" I asked.

"Since you were born. Your mother told me she was pregnant. Of course, I didn't know for a fact that you were mine until I had a paternity test done a year ago when you were hospitalized after a boating accident."

"Boating accident? Is that what they told you?"

He waved it off. "It was easy enough to get a hold of your blood and test it. To make sure you were really mine. When I found out you were, I decided to keep tabs on you."

"In case Maryanne needed any spare parts?" I snapped.

The bastard shrugged. "If that's how you want to look at it. The hardest part was getting you out of Miami. You're almost as plugged in as I ever was. People like Sargent Vasquez or your connections at the Sherriff's Office, who had the resources to protect you. You're very well-liked, Jacqueline. People would notice if you went missing." He sounded almost proud.

Something clicked into place. "Unless I was already on the run for my life. The hunt for whoever shot at me was focused around Miami. Logan said the shooter had crappy aim. And I did exactly what you expected, I ran." If not for Celeste and the Parker brothers, he would have caught me days ago

He made a face. "It was going perfectly, then my men lost you. They were supposed to inject a locator chip in the monkey. You have a bizarre bond with that animal."

"I saved his life. But how could you have gotten a hold of Abu?"

"We knew you dropped him off with your friend's crazy sister, but you showed up before she passed out from the drugs my operative had changed out for hers."

"Jesus," I breathed, almost in awe of how elaborate his plan had been. I remembered Marcy telling me about a date, some guy going through her purse. Was that when they'd swapped out the medication? Poor Gertie. "And the girl in the bathtub? Did you kill the entire crew of the shrimp boat just to get the key for Estaban Martinez's old apartment?"

He snorted. "Of course not. He sold me the key months ago for twenty bucks. You don't want to know what he did with it."

"But then why did you kill the entire crew?"

"Because they were part of my operation. They transported people from all over the world here for harvest. There's no money in commercial shrimping, not with EPA regulations being what they are. But when you disappeared from Miami, I knew you'd hunt for Estaban and I couldn't risk the authorities linking me with the crew of the *Sweet Release*. And I knew you would report your findings to the nearest authorities. As I said before, I'm very well connected."

My father was a crime boss. And a braggart. Not to mention a total fucking psycho who had seemed oddly intrigued by my love life. I didn't want to talk to him, not only because he was a horror of a human being, but because

I'd entertained so many fantasies over the years about my real father and this guy, Brian, was killing those as effectively as he had executed Big John.

I turned my head away so he wouldn't see the fresh wave of tears. Big John, who was a hillbilly pain in the ass, but had called me princess the way a real dad should behave. He'd deserved so much better, especially because for a few short months he'd made my mother happy.

But talking to him might buy me the time I needed to get myself out of this mess.

"Do you have anything you want to ask me?" Brian asked. "Maybe how I met your mother?"

I turned to look at him. "What made you become an organ pirate? You used to be one of the good guys, didn't you?"

He leaned back in his chair. "What did your mother tell you about me?"

"Nothing." It was the truth. Celeste had always been vague when I asked pointed questions about my father.

He didn't look hurt or angry, no normal human emotions for dear old dad. Nope, he was a cold son of a bitch who only nodded as if he hadn't expected anymore. "I'm not surprised. She didn't know all that much, to begin with. I busted her and some of her friends for smoking weed and she offered me a few favors in exchange for not arresting them. I took her up on it. "

I guess I was wrong, he had never been a good guy. "So you've always been a dirty cop?"

That seemed to get under his skin. He shifted and narrowed his eyes, his tone forceful as he said, "I was an entrepreneur. A self-made man. I saw shit on the streets that would turn you green. What the fuck purpose do most people serve? Shooting up, shooting each other, rotting away in a gutter. Better that at least a part of them be useful, don't you think?"

I just looked at him because we both knew he didn't give a rat's ass what I thought.

"Celeste showed up at the stationhouse and told me she was pregnant. Told me her super religious parents had thrown her out on her ass and she had nowhere else to go. I gave her forty bucks and the number of an abortion clinic. You and Maryanne are both lucky she decided to take another path."

I flinched. God, I had been so rotten to Celeste over the years. Was it any wonder she'd hid from her own reality with drugs and liquor? She'd given up everything just to have me. I'd known about her parents kicking her out, how she'd spent a few months on the street before I was born, but hearing how he'd turned her away set it all in a new light for me. If it had been up to him, I'd never have taken my first breath.

Though I loathed the response, his cold dismissal of me stung like frostbite. My father didn't hate me, didn't care about me at all. Would never have come near me if he didn't need something.

"So now I'm to be *useful*?" I asked, repeating the word in the same way he had, with an utter disregard for human life.

He smiled. "You've risen higher than I ever would have believed possible. You're respected, liked. But at the end of the day Jacqueline, women like you and your mother are discards. Is it fair that my daughter, who is a beautiful artist dies while someone who rolls around in shit for a living and sleeps with a pair of brothers, destroys a family, goes on? No. I'm righting a wrong, fixing a cosmic injustice. You want to see me as a villain, fine, but tell me, what parent wouldn't do the same?"

It was odd, hearing him spout the kind of words that had

haunted me my entire life. He'd essentially told me that I was worthless, had dismissed me as easily as he had my mother. All my life I'd longed for a father, had convinced myself I needed one. And yet in a twist of fate, he needed me desperately and I was past the point of letting what he thought about me matter.

"What are you going to do with Celeste after I'm gone?"

"If I told you I was going to let her go, would you believe me?"

"No." Not after he promised to spare Luke and Logan. Emotion welled but I ruthlessly tamped it down, knowing this man would see anything but wry amusement and bitter hatred as weakness.

He watched me closely. "Then I won't bother lying to you. She'll be typed and if she's a match for any of our donors, she'll be harvested."

"I want to see her." It wasn't a request. We both knew I had no power in this game, that I was a pawn, a discard as he'd so succinctly put it. But the man held obvious disdain for emotion and I wanted to keep him off his guard for as long as possible.

Brian tilted his head, his gaze weighing me on an invisible scale. "You're different than I thought you would be. Not like Celeste at all. Maybe you did inherit something from me after all."

"Does that change anything?" I asked flatly, already knowing the answer.

He shook his head, then stood. "I'll see Celeste is brought to you."

I turned away, not wanting to give him the satisfaction of watching him go and wondering just what the hell I was going to do next.

"Jackie," Celeste rushed into the room. She too had changed into scrubs and her face was washed clean of make-up. "Baby, are you all right?"

"I'm fine," I sat up in the hospital bed, knowing they would come for me soon. My visit with Celeste was to be my final request and then...

"We've got to get out of here," Celeste said.

She was right. I had to focus on the now. On staying alive as long as possible and hoping help would come. "Do you have any idea how many people are here?"

"I've seen at least five different guards," She said, surprising me. "Not including the three with Brian."

I considered her carefully. I'd expected a train wreck, a sobbing mess that I would have to console and reassure right up until the minute when they cracked my chest open. But though her eyes were red-rimmed, she was calm, focused. Celeste could actually be a help in our escape. Hadn't she helped the Parker brothers abduct me in the first place?

She must have interpreted the look and gave me a half-smile. "You've always underestimated me. And yourself. I made shitty choices, but I'm a survivor. And so are you, baby-girl."

I took a deep breath. "Okay. We'll have one chance when they come to take me to surgery. Once they have me in there, I'll be outnumbered."

Thankfully she didn't ask for details on the surgery itself or ask what Brian wanted from me.

Keys jangled, indicating one of my captors was coming in. A moment later the door opened and a nurse came in. She wore an old fashioned white uniform and carried a large covered tray. Setting her burden down on the table, she nodded to us and left without saying anything.

Celeste lifted the lid, revealing a large plate with steak, mashed potatoes and green beans and a large slice of chocolate cake along with a pitcher of milk, enough for a last meal for two. That wasn't standard hospital fare, more five-star restaurant quality. The smells alone made me realize I hadn't eaten anything in almost twenty-four hours.

We exchanged a look and I shook my head slowly.

"He must think we're stupid." She covered the food and pushed the tray to the far corner in front of the door.

"Actually he thinks we're useless." Which reminded me...

Celeste gasped as she saw me grip the needle. "What are you doing?"

"There's more than one way to drug a person." My face tightened as I extracted the needle from my arm, then flopped back against the pillows. "How come you never told me about him?"

"And have you go looking for him? I knew he was a son of a bitch, but I never knew what exactly he was up to. Now I'm sorry I didn't take Logan up on his offer."

"What offer?" I struggled to sit up.

"He wanted to go looking for your father. Said you needed closure. I refused though. Told him the only thing that man could give you was heartbreak."

The irony wasn't lost on me. "When was this?"

"Not long after Christmas." She said and I blinked.

"Christmas, when he told me he wasn't going to wait around. How come you never told me?"

She patted my hand. "There are some things a woman has to figure out for herself."

My lip trembled. I'd expended a lot of energy trying not to imagine the worst, that Luke and Logan were dead and Celeste and I were on our own. "I'm sorry about Big John. He was a good guy."

"You hated him," my mother said with a rueful smile

"He wasn't my favorite person, but I didn't hate him. In

fact, I kind of liked him recently because he treated you well. You deserve that."

My mother squeezed my hand tightly and then looked around the room. "So, what's the plan?"

There wasn't much to our advantage. We were on his turf, unarmed and surrounded by men with guns. If we had any chance of making it out we'd have to do so by stealth. And even then I had no idea where in the world we were. Brian might own an entire island. We had no supplies, no fresh water that we could trust, no way to call for help. But first thing's first, we needed out of the medical facility. I looked at my mother's blue scrubs. "I think you need a change of wardrobe."

Slowly, our half-baked plan came together and when the nurse came back for the tray, we were ready.

Celeste moved to the door and poked her head out into the hall. She gave me a thumbs-up, meaning there wasn't a guard in hearing distance. I waited until the nurses' hands were full and then wrapped my IV tubing around her neck.

The tray clattered to the floor. She struggled, but I maintained my grip, desperation making me stronger than I'd ever believed possible.

Slowly, the fight leached out of her. I would have stopped when she lost consciousness, but Celeste ended it by whacking her across the face with the heavy tray.

The woman's eyes rolled back in her head and she went limp.

"Celeste," I panted, releasing my burden. She hit the floor like a bag of potatoes. "I had her."

"I was just trying to help." My mother crouched down on the floor beside the unconscious nurse. "Help me get her undressed."

I did and soon enough we had the woman stripped down

to her undies. "Why'd you take her bra off?" I asked my mother.

"To gag her in case she wakes up. We don't want her calling out for help, do we?"

I stared at her in amazement. "Who are you and what have you done with Celeste

Drummond?"

She actually rolled her eyes at me as she shucked her own clothes. "Quit being a wiseass and help me into this thing."

A few minutes later the unconscious—not to mention topless—nurse was secured to the *oh-shit* handle in the hospital bathroom with my fitted sheet and her bra wrapped around her head. Celeste was decked out in her naughty nurse uniform.

"Your boobs are too big," I told her. "You look like a nurse from a bad porno."

She hastily collected the tray of food and held it up over her cleavage. "Better?"

Not really but I didn't have the heart to tell her so. "Remember, find some sort of sedative, something we can use to subdue the people who come get me. If you get stuck or I'm gone before you get back, run. I'll find my own way out."

"Come with me." She urged again.

"We don't know what's outside this hallway. A nurse with a tray is less suspicious than a nurse with a patient." It was a challenge to hug her around the tray without a nipple slip but I managed, afraid this was goodbye forever. While I was at it, I slipped Logan's tracker into her pocket. His last gift to me. "Go, quickly, before someone checks back in."

She struggled with the set of keys to unlock my door. "I love you, Jackie."

"Love you too, Mama. Go."

She went. I sagged in relief against the door as all the

fight drained out of me. There wouldn't be one last stand, not for me. I'd done the only thing I could do. I didn't hold out hope for my own rescue. But maybe I'd given my mother a fighting chance to escape.

I'd been looking after her too long to let the habit die now.

Taking the towels from the bathroom I mopped up the spilled food from the floor as best I could and stuffed them in the bathroom. Slowly, I moved back toward the bed. Sat down and arranged the top sheet, hoping no one would notice that the bottom one was missing

Minutes passed, and time stretched out. I must have dozed off because the next thing I knew, Brian stood beside my bed.

"What happened to Celeste?" He didn't sound angry, merely curious.

"I asked one of the nurses to take her out. I didn't want her to be here when you took me."

He turned and faced the IV. "And here?"

I shrugged. "It itched and I had to pee."

"What happened to the food?"

"I flushed it." Dear God, Don't let him check the bathroom. There was no clock in the room, so I had no idea how far Celeste could have made it, but I was determined to buy her as much time as possible.

That creepy half-smile had emerged like a snake from under a rock. "You have an answer for everything, don't you?"

"Usually." Though it wasn't the right answer. I almost told him he could ask Logan, but stopped just in time. My heart hurt. Maybe it would be better to pluck the damn thing out. I didn't want to live without my Dark Prince.

He nodded, looking thoughtful. "It's time."

A man with a rifle strapped over his shoulder pushed a wheelchair into the room.

I looked at it, then deliberately turned to Brian and gave him the finger. If I was going to meet my maker, I wanted to walk execution-style, not be wheeled out like a patient.

The goon approached but Brian waved him off. "No, she can walk. It's not far and won't put much strain on her organs."

The floor was like ice on my bare feet and I didn't bother to stifle my shiver. We exited my holding pen and moved down the empty corridor.

"You said organs," I pointed out.

"I did," he confirmed. "Since you're dying anyway, I didn't think you'd object to saving a few other lives."

I didn't answer. Part of me was running around, shrieking at the top of her lungs, wondering how the hell I could be so blasé about this. I told her to STFU. Logan was dead, Luke was too, it was all my fault and how could I possibly bother to care if I lived another five minutes or fifty years because he was gone, gone, *gone*.

I only had one task to accomplish now. Call it making up for lost time, but I wanted to piss my father off as much as humanly possible.

And when I put my mind to something, I gave it my all.

The corridor emptied into another and then down a flight of stairs and into a large hallway. I wondered what they would have done if I had taken the wheelchair. There was probably an elevator around here someplace.

Two armed guards stood outside a room, assault weapons at the ready. They didn't look at me as I strode by, didn't even twitch. If the universe was at all just, they'd end up on that table someday.

Then the doors were opened and I laid eyes on an operating room table. There were three people decked out in surgical gear, two men and a woman. The men had masks covering their mouths but the woman's was down. She blinked at me, then at dear old dad. "She's still awake?"

"She didn't take the drugs." Brian didn't sound the least concerned about it.

"But the heart, the stress—"

I moved past the doctor, closer to the operating table. When I stood directly before the place where I was meant to die I looked down.

Brian moved up beside me. "She's lost the will to live. She knows death will be a release. Don't you, Jackie?"

"Mmmhmm," I mumbled.

The doctors got busy doing whatever organ profiteering doctors did pre-surgery. To the left, there was a bank of windows. I didn't look at it, didn't want to think about who was out there. To the right, lines of hard-sided coolers. Presumably where my organs would go to be transported to the recipients.

I'd thought I'd been prepared to die. Seeing the reality of it though...

"Any final requests?" Brian asked. He sounded so smug, so confident. Thought he had the winning hand of cards.

"Yeah. Die." I said and sliced out at his face with the scalpel I'd palmed.

My father stumbled back, a hand clapped to the bleeding gash in his face. I'd missed his eye, unfortunately, but blood spattered across his white dress shirt and the operating table. His blood. I smiled with grim satisfaction. The medical staff made horrible squawking sounds and huddled in a corner. The men outside the door heard the commotion and barreled into the room. Two rifles were aimed at my head. Brian held up a hand and shouted, "Stop!"

"Makes it kind of tough, that you don't want them to shoot me." I smiled at him and took a step closer. "You see, all of your leverage is gone now. You don't have anyone else to threaten."

"Celeste," he wheezed, looking discomposed for the first time. "I have Celeste."

"Do you?" My grin grew. "I don't think so."

"You're bluffing," he spat. Blood ran over his fingers and dripped down his arm.

"Have them go check." I leaned back against the operating table. "I've no place to be."

Brian stumbled toward the door, but I intercepted him, pressing the sharp edge of the scalpel into his neck. "Not you. You promised me some bonding time."

"Sir?" One of the thugs took a hesitant step forward.

I pressed the blade deep enough into his pulse point to draw a fresh trickle of blood. "Uh oh, I'm not sure where the jugular is. Better hope I don't slip and nick it."

"Go, find Celeste," Brian gasped.

They left.

"You three, out." I indicated the gang in green scrubs.

"Do what she says," Brian added.

They scrambled for the swinging door.

I dragged him back into a corner so no one could sneak up on me. I was weak from hunger and exhaustion and my adrenaline rush wouldn't last forever. Given enough time they'd either find Celeste or think of another way to incapacitate me. Eventually, I'd lose the upper hand.

But not before I got him.

I could do it too, slit my own father's throat. For Celeste, for Logan and Luke and the girl in the bathtub that he'd called a discard. The man had no remorse and if I was about to die, I would damn sure take him out with me.

"Wanna know how you fucked up?" I asked.

He swallowed and the blade went in a little deeper.

I didn't wait for an answer. "You underestimated the discards."

Shouts reverberated from the outer hallway. I didn't pay them much attention, my sole focus was on him, this son of a bitch who'd ruined my life. He was going to die in this room. We both were. I'd made my peace with that.

"You think anyone will want your parts?" I asked him, bile rising in my throat. "Maybe your pickled old liver? Or lungs? You a smoker?"

I was babbling, losing my cool. So why didn't I just do it

already? Draw the blade, slit his throat and then my own? I'd seen enough evil to know that hesitation led to mistakes. I couldn't risk waiting too long. I had to do it.

For Big John. For Celeste. For Luke.

For Logan.

My hand was shaking, just a slight tremor. I licked my lips, the shouts drew closer.

Do it! This time the inner voice was a taskmistress, demanding I see this through.

I'd spent my life serving up justice. There were systems in place that saw to criminals. Systems that he'd abused and manipulated for his own personal gain. I'd seen him kill Big John with no remorse and he was going to sell his own daughter for spare fucking parts so why *the hell* was I hesitating?

"Jackie?"

I looked up, blinked. "You're alive?"

Either they were pumping some hallucinogenic gas into the O.R....or Logan Parker was standing before me.

His leg had been wrapped in a huge bandage, and he was definitely favoring it. He had his own assault rifle strapped across his chest. "What are you doing, babe?"

I swallowed. "He...he needs to die."

"Okay." Just like that. "Let me do it for you."

"This...this is a trick." Tears filled my eyes. "You're not really here. I can't let him go."

"Jackie," his tone was brisk, matter-of-fact. "It's no trick. I'm here. So's Luke, he's with your mom."

"Prove it." Even as I doubted I drank him in with my watering eyes.

"I heard what you said yesterday," he murmured. I noticed he wasn't moving any closer, giving me space. "That you want to be the woman I see when I look at you. That woman isn't a killer."

My eyes filled, overflowed. "I want to believe you."

"Please, Jackie. Please believe that it's all right. We've got our chance now. If you want me to take care of him for you, I will. But don't you do it. It'll destroy you." His lips twitched. "One of us needs to be the hero."

I swallowed past the lump in my throat. "Okay. Um…how do I get out of this?"

He withdrew a handgun from his pants pocket and aimed it at Brian center mass. "Just shove him away from you. No, don't move the scalpel." He cautioned as I started to do exactly that.

"Oh, sorry," My resolve was dissipating and my thoughts were muddled.

"I'll keep him in my sights and you get behind me," Logan said.

I shoved Brian as hard as I could and sprinted for Logan. He caught me on his right side and held me tucked in close. The handgun never wavered.

"I've got you," he said and kissed the top of my head. "Jackie, I've got you."

"I thought you were dead," I sobbed, coming completely unglued.

"No." he squeezed me once then put his other hand over the handgun to steady his aim. "Just hopped up on pain killers."

I looked along the line he was sighting to where Brian was huddled on the floor. His cold façade was completely gone, he looked lost and scared. Vulnerable.

"Sucks to be on that end of things," Logan said, adjusted his aim, then pulled the trigger.

"Tell me again what happened." Sargent Vasquez frowned at me, and then at Logan.

"I told you, the gun went off." Logan did a palms up.

"It went off?" The cop asked me.

"Was the darndest thing," Logan was fighting a grin.

"Jackie, anything to add?"

I was watching my father being wheeled out on a stretcher, his leg bleeding from the bullet Logan had sunk in him. "He killed Big John and was going to have the rest of us dissected. I'd say he got off light."

Vasquez made a disgusted noise. "You two have a lot to answer for and Logan, get off that leg. I knew I was *loco* to let you come along."

"Like you had a choice." Luke approached, shaking his head. "He sat up the second the car turned out of sight and demanded I go get his damn laptop so he could track you on our way to the hospital. I would have had to shoot him again to keep him down. Makes me feel like a wuss."

Acting as Logan's crutch, I helped him over to a large fountain and eased him down. "But I don't understand, I heard Brian give the order to his henchmen to kill you guys."

"We were expecting it." Logan gritted his teeth, his painkillers obviously wearing off. "I called Vasquez here and had him make a few calls. We had half the on-duty personnel from NAS Key West ride to the rescue. A few crooked cops were outmanned and outgunned."

"Sorry I missed it," I breathed.

"But your man here was too damn stubborn to stay in the hospital," Vasquez continued. "I told him I'd get you out but he had to be here himself."

I looked around and frowned. "Where exactly is here?"

Luke looked surprised. "You don't recognize it?"

I looked around again, noticed the sun was low on the eastern horizon, just coming up. "Should I?"

"Jupiter Island," Logan smiled. "Not too far from Mom and Dad's place."

Luke nodded. "Speaking of which. I better call them. Mom was frantic when she heard about what happened to Jackie and Celeste."

"I still don't know why you told her," Logan grumbled.

"Speaking of Celeste," I craned my neck, hoping to catch sight of her. "Are you sure she's all right?"

Vasquez nodded. "Yes. She almost took my head off when I said I didn't know where you were, but otherwise she seemed unharmed. She was hiding in the bushes. Good work, putting the tracker on her. Otherwise, we might never have found her." He gestured one of the EMT's over and waved at us. "These two need to be checked over. Before I can officially release them."

"You don't fool me," I told Vasquez. "You are out of your jurisdiction, so it's not up to you to release us."

"No, but I do have pull with the people who are in charge, so zip it."

"I'm beginning to grow on him," I told Logan.

"Come here," he held me and made small noises of discomfort as the medic examined his leg. "Where should we go after this?"

"Somewhere to rest." The guy examining Logan's stood up. "Preferably a hospital."

Logan shook his head. "No way."

The guy took my blood pressure, which was still high. Checked my eyes and asked if I'd hit my head, then, thankfully, buggered off.

"How about your parents' place in Ft. Lauderdale?" I suggested. "You said it was close."

"And they have a hot tub,"

"No hot tub," The EMT called over his shoulder.

"Damn, he has good ears."

"You weren't exactly being discrete."

He made a small humming sound. "That would work, especially because they're still in Miami."

"I have to warn you," I told him softly. "I'm a terrible nurse. I have no patience and get snappish."

"That's okay. How about I play doctor this time."

"With a bullet in your leg?"

"It went all the way through."

I squeaked and buried my face in his sweat-slicked shirt. Not wanting to think about seeing him get shot. "Joke all you like but we can't just abandon Celeste after...everything that happened."

"We won't." Logan curled his finger under my chin, forcing me to look up and meet his penetrating blue gaze. "Not ever. She's your family."

"I wish I'd gone easier on her. She put up with so much for me. You don't even know."

"But you'll tell me, right?" He raised a brow.

"I'll tell you whatever you want to know."

He studied me, then asked. "Are you sorry I didn't kill him?"

Was I? After a moment I said, "No. You were right, I would have regretted it. Not because he deserves to live or anything. But I wouldn't want to bear the weight of being judge, jury, and executioner. Even if you were the executioner."

He kissed me then, a long, soft lingering kiss that was full of hope and promise. When he pulled away he tucked a strand of hair behind my ear. "I love you, Jackie. I'm sorry I'm not the hero you deserve."

"Silly man." I leaned into him, relieved that we got another shot and determined not to waste it. "Don't you know? I don't need a hero, I need a Dark Prince."

Want to see what happens next with Jackie, Luke and Logan? Snag
Maintenance Is Murder
Damaged Goods Book 4
Available now!

IT'S NOT MY WORDS THAT COUNT…
IT'S YOURS!

Please consider leaving an honest review for this book. Reviews help readers like you find books they enjoy, or warn them off from ones they won't. Reader reviews help the authors you love sell books and help them put money toward the next title. Even a sentence or two can mean the difference between a series that continues and one that flops. I found one of my favorite series from a two star review. So if you want more, tell the world.

Miami's hottest property management team is back in action in an all-new mystery!

Certified Process Server Jackie Parker's life is finally on the right track. Her cozy little bungalow is finished, her business is booming, and her relationship with the Dark Prince is better than she ever could have imagined. So what if she's still living with her ex and her mother who wants them to buy matching tiny homes? Who cares if Logan is sharing his house with a woman on the run from her abusive husband? No big deal if an onsite manager is stealing rent or tenants are turning tricks on her client's property. It's nothing Jackie and the guys haven't dealt with before.

Until Logan is arrested for murder.

Jackie's all set to do what she does best and find the real killer. But

Logan insists she should stay out of the mix and let the professionals handle it. Sure, Logan wouldn't be the Dark Prince if he didn't have some shady dealings. But Jackie knows Logan. He's a tough guy who will do anything to protect the people he loves. He isn't truly capable of cold-blooded murder.

Is he?

Buy Maintenance is Murder *now!*

ABOUT THE AUTHOR

USA Today bestselling author Jennifer L. Hart writes about characters that cuss, get naked, and often make poor but hilarious life choices. A native New Yorker, Jenn now lives in the mountains of North Carolina with her imaginary friends. Her works to date include the Damaged Goods mystery series and the Magical Midlife Misadventures.